ALL IS SWELL

All Is Swell

Trust In Thelma's Way

◆

ROBERT FARRELL SMITH

Deseret Book Company
Salt Lake City, Utah

Library of Congress Cataloging-in-Publication Data
    Smith, Robert F., 1970–
        All is swell : Trust in Thelma's Way / Robert Farrell Smith.
            p.   cm.
        ISBN 1-57345-466-4
        I. Title.   II. Series: Smith, Robert Farrell Smith, 1970–   Trust
    Williams trilogy ; bk.   1.
    PS3569.M53794A45   1999
    813'.54—dc21   99-11472
                                                                                CIP

Printed in the United States of America

10   9   8   7   6   5   4   3   2   1   72082 - 6434

1

ORDER UP

◇

It was here. I stuck my hand in the mailbox and pulled out the letter. Then, with a patience nurtured by TV and the flash of everyday life, I tore it open. My stomach exploded with butterflies.

I couldn't believe this!

I shook the paper, as if jostling it about might rearrange its contents.

The words remained the same. Forget the fact that I had prayed for it every night for the last year. Forget the fact that I had taken language courses in school. God had not seen fit to send me someplace prestigious and foreign. My blue eyes simmered as I stared at the paper. This was not the mission call I had envisioned receiving. The population of Knoxville, Tennessee, was about to increase by one clean-cut, dark-suited, two-year missionary.

God was keeping me stateside.

2

Fared Well

The chapel was packed. People pushed up against each other like putty, making room for more. The place was filled to capacity. I couldn't believe it. Even some of my nonmember friends from work and school had come to say good-bye.

Wendy, our neighbor, was sitting in the front row, obviously unaware that we Mormons discouraged eating in church. She had a bag of chips and a Coke resting on the end of the pew. I guess she thought Church was like a trip to the movies. She was probably hoping for a few good laughs. She'd probably get them.

Showtime.

The chapel organ began to bellow the first notes of the opening song as I reached up to feel my newly shorn brown hair. I stared at the odd-looking wing tips on my feet. I brushed the leg of my dark suit.

Heaven help itself, I was turning into a missionary.

I looked at my hands as I sat there on the stand listening

to Bishop Leen say nice things about me. My fingers seemed . . . longer? Or shorter? Different.

For a moment, I wanted to jump out of who I was becoming and run home barefooted. I wanted to climb one of the big trees out in front of my house and spend the afternoon throwing seed pods down at passing cars. I wanted to work on math homework with my mom, torment my brother, Abel, and sit in wonder over Lucy, my first and only love.

I looked at my family sitting out in the crowd. None of them had wanted to speak today. Dad was a pillar in the community but no more than a flimsy support beam to the Church. He had more money than faith and sort of liked it that way. Mom was the believing one, but despite her Noah-like faith, she still couldn't be talked into taking the stand in front of all those people. My twelve-year-old sister, Margaret, was not about to give a talk, and my eight-year-old brother, Abel, had wanted to speak but had been banned from coming to the microphone ever since the "incident" in fast and testimony meeting last summer. Yes, I would be the only Williams on the program today.

Trust Andrew Williams. I had a name like a political sound bite.

My parents had named me Trust out of fear. I was their firstborn, and I had come out boy when they had specifically asked the heavens for something frilly and pink. It wasn't that they hated boys, it was just that they had heard so many bad things about tiny males from our neighbor Wendy. So they named me Trust, hoping it would help the budding hellion in me surface slowly if at all.

3

I had grown up all right.

Sure, if pressed, my parents could produce a list of trespasses and transgressions, but I had managed for the most part to keep my life on track. Now here I was, about to embark on a two-year mission for The Church of Jesus Christ of Latter-day Saints. Scared. Nervous. But embarking. Mom was thrilled, and Dad, despite his own inactivity, was happy too. He saw the whole mission thing as a big training camp for my future career in business—sort of a divine Book of Mormon salesman internship.

I gazed at the tip of my tie as I sat there on the stand, my childhood suddenly seeming too short. I felt my heart tighten. My nerves were buzzing just below my skin. I wasn't ready for this, was I? I didn't know how to feel.

The call to Tennessee had been a surprise, but I was determined to make the best of it. After all, if I believed anything about this gospel that I was going to be preaching, it was that the Lord was at the head. And while I had sort of imagined myself looking sharp in France or stunning in Greece, I guess He sort of saw me in Tennessee. I'm not saying that didn't concern me, but I would do this favor for God. There had to be *something* worth seeing in Tennessee.

The heavens were consoling me, sending down a calming silence to my troubled soul. I sat in relative peace and quiet—actually a little too quiet.

There was no one at the podium, and everyone was staring at me. I realized it was my turn to speak.

I had daydreamed my way through two talks and an intermediate hymn sung by our home teacher's

teen-year-old daughter. I picked up my scriptures and
se to my feet.

I spotted Lucy Fall in the crowd three rows back and to
he left. Her blonde hair was shining under the bright flu-
orescent lights. She acknowledged me with her blue eyes. I
was going to miss Lucy. She nodded at me as if to say, *Go
on.* Her lips parted a tad, giving the world a rare glimpse of
her perfect white teeth. She sat there looking better than
everyone else and knowing it. Some people thought Lucy
was stuck-up. True or not, I was too stuck on her to care.
All I knew then was that I was going to miss her.

I stood at the pulpit and cleared my throat. There were
so many faces looking up at me. I tried to smile. I made a
lame attempt at a joke. The crowd laughed mercifully.

I was going to miss the Thicktwig First Ward. I didn't
want it to change while I was gone. I wanted to come back
in two years and see each family sitting just where they
were in front of me: the Johnsons three pews back and to
the right; the Lewises strategically sitting on the back row
next to the door—to make it easier for Sister Lewis to haul
out the twins if necessary; the Falls in the middle section,
boxed in by Sister Cravitz and Bishop Leen's wife and family; Brother Vastly in his designated spot, the last padded
bench to the right, in front of the overflow chair sitters.

If there was any rift in our ward, it was between the
bench sitters and the chair sitters. The chair sitters were
always complaining about the awful treatment they
received sitting in the back: cold metal chairs, poor sound,
an uneven ratio of noisy kids to listening Saints, and there

were never enough hymnbooks. Week after week the chair sitters were forced to hum.

The bench sitters had little compassion for the overflow Saints. They figured that if the chair sitters wanted to badly enough, they could show up on time and claim one of the soft benches for themselves. Most of the bench sitters also piously considered themselves worthy of sitting so close to the podium because of their clear consciences, claiming that the chair sitters parked their behinds on the fringes due to some sort of subconscious unworthiness.

There was a true division.

One time when Brother Treat stepped out of the chair section and tried to retrieve a hymnbook for his wife from the back of one of the benches, Sister Cravitz almost drew blood by jabbing him with a small easel she was planning to use later in her Relief Society lesson to prop up a picture of Christ. Three days later Brother Treat accidentally spilled two gallons of bleach across Sister Cravitz's prize-winning azaleas and front lawn. The bishop had to step in to smooth things out. He used part of the Young Women's budget to buy more hymnbooks for the chair sitters.

Of course, Sister Luke, the Young Women's president, was not at all happy about the cut in her budget, and the Young Women were not compassionately giddy over their money providing hymnal text to the subconsciously guilty chair sitters. They were even less thrilled about it later that year at girls' camp when, due to their depleted budget, they went without warm meals and mattress pads.

But things had smoothed out for the time being. The chair sitters sang, and the bench sitters continued to sit, somewhat self-righteously, on their pampered behinds, always looking forward.

But none of that seemed to matter now. I was speaking at my farewell.

I talked a little about my desire to serve a mission. I was hoping the words I was using would help trick my soul into feeling comfortable with the whole idea. I told a story about myself as a child. I bore my testimony. I closed, clutched at my scriptures, and sat down.

At meeting's end, everyone came up to me and wished me well. Every handshake and hug made me more and more frightened to leave it all behind. Sister Johnson kissed me on the cheek. Brother Vastly shook my hand without lecturing me. Lucy was kind enough to hug me. Then she just stood there looking gorgeous. We had grown up together. We had dated a couple of times, but more than that, we had just always been. She liked me like a brother, and I liked her like a love-crazed, emotionally wavering, wishful-thinking third cousin.

"Good luck," Lucy said, her hands clasped together in front of her. She was impeccably dressed, as usual, her cutting-edge fashion sense clashing with the rest of the congregation's outdated wardrobe.

"Thanks," I replied.

Lucy wriggled her nose and bit her top lip, as if on cue.

"I'll write," I offered.

"I can't believe we're this old," she replied, showing a sliver of the soft under-self she usually kept locked up behind her perfect exterior.

"I'm going to—" I started to say, "really miss you," but Lucy sensed my borderline blubbering and interrupted.

"I'll be here when you return," she said almost coldly.

I wanted to fall on my knees, to beg her not to make me go. But I figured that wouldn't really leave a favorable last impression. I would do this. I would turn my fledgling testimony into a true conviction. I would take two years to better the kingdom. I would even try not to be bitter about the whole Tennessee thing. I would do anything if the heavens would only promise me that on my return I would be good enough for Lucy Fall.

Before I could say anything else, Sister Cravitz slipped between me and Lucy and hugged me tightly. She sort of stroked the back of my hair and whispered something about being so very proud. I watched Lucy slip off the stage and out of my life for two years.

Sister Cravitz squeezed me tighter. The big brooch she was wearing on her lapel dug into my chest.

"So, so, very, very proud," she said again.

3

BIG THINGS, SMALL PACKAGES

I spent a couple weeks at the MTC and two nights in the mission home in Knoxville with President and Sister Clasp before my mission really began.

President Clasp was big, loud, and funny—three attributes I would never have envisioned my mission president having. He was also stern, a trait I had expected. He had very little hair, but he insisted he wasn't bald. It was just that he had an extra wide part. The enormous part topped off big eyes and crooked teeth. Before being called as mission president, he had been a safety inspector at a toy company in Wisconsin. Sister Clasp, who was also big, loud, and funny, dispensed hugs like an overzealous mother bear. She always wore a billowy blouse tucked into an elastic-banded skirt.

President Clasp taught us quite a bit in those first three days. At the conclusion he interviewed me and went on and on about how he used to have a dog named Trust. I felt like part of the family.

After those few days in the mission home, I was driven in a big gray van to a small town called Collin's Blight. I had tried to take in the scenery and figure out which direction we were going, but it sped by so fast that my eyes couldn't properly digest it. My poor sense of direction asserted itself.

From Collin's Blight I was transported in a tiny green car to the mid-sized town of Virgil's Find. At Virgil's Find—which, by the way, was no great find—I was met by my companion, Elder Boone, who then escorted me on foot to our destination: Thelma's Way, Tennessee.

To get there, we had to hike along a well-worn footpath that cut through the mountains like a poorly sewn seam. Next to the trail ran a line of weathered utility poles that were heavy with wire. On every other pole was posted an orange piece of paper that read:

COME ONE, COME ALL
Pre-planning meeting
this Saturday at 6:00 A.M. for the Thelma's Way
Sesquicentennial Pageant

Together the posted poles and tiny path provided a lifeline to my new home. After following the trail for about four miles, through thick trees and steep hills, we came to the meadow where Thelma's Way lay. With one glance I could take in everything the town had to offer. The mountains all around it sloped their soft shoulders down to a clearing where a few shacks and dwellings sat huddled together. There were maybe eight poorly built buildings in all, laid out as if they had been thrown down during a spoiled fit. Bushy trees surrounded the meadow, and a smoky gray sky gave the place a closed-in feeling and charged the air with uneasiness. A thick river ran swiftly along the far side of the clearing.

"This is it?" I asked as we stood up on a hill looking down.

"This is it," Elder Boone replied.

"There's nothing here!"

"There's more people hidden in the hills."

I couldn't tell if he was attempting to warn me or comfort me.

What was I doing here? Thelma's Way was a weed patch, a city so hidden that even upon discovery it was nothing. It was a few shacks and a large meadow. It was a bad neighborhood smack-dab in the middle of Mother Nature's lower back. It was remote, regressive, repulsive, and really making me homesick. The moist air gummed up my brain. I swallowed hard, willing myself to do my best regardless of where I was, and blinked a few times, hoping the rapid eye movement would make this green town in front of me appear more like home.

Elder Boone saw my expression and sensed the need to explain a few things. We sat down on a soft patch of grass. Big grasshopper-like bugs the size of Twinkies jumped about, chirping. Elder Boone swatted a black-winged thing away from his face and proceeded.

Thelma's Way was the most remote spot in the entire mission. Remote and difficult. According to Elder Boone, the missionaries in the town of Virgil's Find had it easy compared to us. They had running water and electricity.

"Luckily, the big Girth River runs right next to our place," he consoled.

What luck, I thought.

Thelma's Way had just been opened up in the mission. There had been no missionaries since the early days of the Church, when Parley P. Pratt stopped off and got sick from eating some bad ham. It was a small place with a small number of active members and inactives aplenty.

Two months previous President Clasp had felt impressed to open up Thelma's Way to the good word of the gospel. There had been some big problems with apostasy in the area, and the Church felt that full-time missionaries would be able to help reactivate and reconstruct what Elder Boone referred to as the crumbling Thelma's Way Ward.

Elder Boone had opened this area with Elder Frates, whom I was replacing. Elder Frates had not done very well here in Thelma's Way. He just didn't have the patience to put up with these laid-back country folks, having come directly from a rather affluent "Seven-Habits" family in Orem, Utah. Elder Frates couldn't handle everyone's casualer-than-thou attitude toward life.

During his second week in Thelma's Way, Elder Frates had had his parents Fed-Ex fifty day planners for him to distribute among the locals. Fed-Ex brought them in by motorcycle, and Elder Frates distributed them to the desperately disorganized Saints.

Well, the locals accepted the gift but didn't exactly

understand the application of pen and paper planning. A couple of the women in town propped their floral day planner binders up in the front windows of their homes for decoration, and some of the men found that they came in handy when a body needed something soft to sit on. A boy by the name of Digby Heck had collected a few of the unused ones and incorporated them in the construction of his small rock fort down by the Girth River.

The infraction that got Frates's goat, however, was when far-from-feminine Sybil Porter used her day planner as a place to store her fishing worms. Sybil had emptied the planner's innards and had been storing worms and soil inside the zippered case.

"Dark and moist," she had reasoned.

Elder Frates lost it. He started yelling and called her a heathen gentile. Sybil in turn picked Elder Frates up and threw him into a muddy hole full of stagnant water. Furious, he pulled himself up, got his bearings, and stormed off to Virgil's Find, never to return. Elder Boone waited with the Virgil's Find missionaries until the mission president was able to send me as a replacement.

"The people here didn't exactly like Frates," Elder Boone said, exercising diplomatic restraint.

"Great," I said, pulling at the long grass we were sitting in.

"Life's a little slower in Thelma's Way, and the work's a little different here than in the rest of the mission."

"Any good things?" I asked hopefully.

"Church is only two hours long," he offered. "There

13

aren't enough active members right now to staff Sunday School."

This didn't seem like a perk. The last thing we needed was more free time. I couldn't see clearly how we would be able to fill our days here in Thelma's Way as it was.

"Anything else I should know?" I asked.

"Everyone here mistrusts each other. The local apostate, Paul, has torn the ward apart, leaving everyone bitter and hurt."

And to think I had wanted to go foreign.

"President Clasp didn't say anything about all this," I said, frustrated.

"Maybe he didn't want to ruin the surprise."

I was surprised all right.

"Listen," Elder Boone said, "if you're anything like me, after you got your mission call you probably rushed out to the local bookstore or library and read up on Tennessee."

I nodded.

"Well, forget everything you think you learned," he went on. "Thelma's Way is not your typical Tennessee town. It's a bunch of Mormons who got lost on their way to Utah over a hundred years ago. The rest of Tennessee likes to pretend Thelma's Way doesn't even exist. You see, Tennessee is the buckle of the Bible Belt, and this little community of inactive Mormons is an unsightly smudge. It's an embarrassment to the rest of the state."

I was embarrassed for them.

"But you'll learn to like these people," Elder Boone added. "On the surface they may seem like misfits, but they'll grow on you. This is actually an exciting time for

14

the town. This Saturday they're holding their first pre-planning meeting for the big sesquicentennial celebration."

"I saw the signs," I said. "So when is the actual celebration?"

"Oh, it's not for over a year and a half. They just want to get a real jump on it. They've been waiting a hundred and fifty years for this."

The anticipation was already killing me.

We sat there for a moment shooing bugs in silence.

"Ready?" Elder Boone finally asked.

We stood up, dusted ourselves off, and shuffled slowly into the thriving metropolis of Thelma's Way.

4

LUCY

Lucy was pretty. Pretty spoiled, pretty demanding, and pretty stubborn. She liked herself as much as she enjoyed the company of those who felt likewise. Lucy spent her days thinking about what she should wear the next day, and her nights dreaming of how she would look when she did. Rumor had it that someplace beneath her expensive clothes and hardened exterior, Lucy did possess a soft spot. As it stood, however, no witnesses had yet stepped up to corroborate such an opinion.

Lucy's life was tight, with no give. She had no patience for the unexpected. Surprises to Lucy were like an embarrassing blemish on the glossy lips of life. Today was planned, tomorrow was scheduled, and she already had a pretty good idea of what the next two years of her life would entail.

Piece by piece.

Lucy admired her perfect cheekbones as she walked past the hall mirror and into her bedroom. She closed her door and took a few minutes to write down the day in her diary. Journal keeping was more than a commandment to Lucy, it was an accurate way to chronicle her remarkable existence. She knew she couldn't possibly count on some future historian's doing justice to her story.

After one full page of writing, Lucy closed the diary and changed into her pajamas. She then sat on the edge of her bed and read the letter she had received from Trust. The letter was simple, with three spelling errors and tired penmanship. Trust would have to do better if he had any hopes of her waiting around for him.

Lucy sighed. The moment seemed to call for it, and she liked her moments to be traditional and normal. She folded the letter up and stuck it into her stationery drawer.

Lucy liked Trust. He had been gone for only three weeks, but already she was considering missing him. Trust was tall, blue-eyed, and handsome in a rustically un-oafish way. Trust was also the only Mormon her age that Lucy could even tolerate, and her life plans called for a Mormon. Southdale didn't offer too many great options. Lucy would settle for Trust. Sure, he was a little rough around the edges, but she could mold him into someone truly worthy of her love.

Lucy was confident that Trust liked her. For years he had existed with an eye single to her glory. She could make him blush like a modest Mormon in a nudist camp simply by calling his name slowly. Trust tripped over himself constantly in her presence, subtly announcing to the world that he was enamored of her. He had asked her out a thousand times, and she had replied *no* almost as many, issuing a *yes* on only a few occasions.

Despite all the *no's*, Lucy knew Trust would keep asking. In two years, when he returned home from his mission, she would size him up. If he had improved in the ways she thought he should, then maybe she would utter another *yes* and usher in the beginning of what could be a lasting relationship.

Piece by piece.

She brushed her blonde hair for ten minutes. Then she studied her blue eyes in the mirror next to her bed. She was beautiful.

"Maybe Trust isn't good enough," she said to herself as she kneeled down to recite the same prayer with which she had vainly petitioned God for the last couple of years.

After her prayer, she laid down and pulled her comforter up to her neck. It wasn't terribly late, but she closed her eyes and beckoned sleep. She had two of her more important college classes tomorrow, and she wanted to make sure she got enough rest.

Sleep smothered Lucy like a big warm cat.

5

THELMA'S WAY, TENNESSEE

I tried to smile as Elder Boone and I shuffled into town along the small footpath. I squinted, as if doing so might mercifully pull hidden houses out from the surrounding hills and drag them into the clearing. We came to a stop at the center of town or, more appropriately, the pit. I sang the words to "Called to Serve" over and over in my mind, hoping it would help.

We were standing in front of a small boardinghouse and store. There was a big poster tacked to the front of the store informing everyone about the distant sesquicentennial celebration. Two older men sat on the front porch staring at us. One was extremely heavy—heavy beard, heavy glance, and heavy stature. He sat upon that porch as if he had been destined to do so, his large, fuzzy face flushed simply from sitting. The other elderly man was as thin as the wooden chair he was pinched into. His puckered-up head bobbed and dipped with each rocking motion, and a smoking pipe hung from his sliver-like lips. His pitch-black pupils looked like magnets, each one attracted to the other and coming together at the top of his nose. The heavy gentleman fanned himself with a faded hat, seeking relief from the warm afternoon.

"Hello," I said like some great explorer presenting himself to the natives. *Disappointed, I presume.*

Elder Boone introduced us. "This is Roswell Ford," he said, pointing to the skinny man, "and this is Feeble, his brother," he went on, indicating the heavy one. "They're twins."

They both sniffed the air, as if my presence had presented a new scent.

"Bet he's the new elder," Roswell said to Feeble. They then turned back to whatever it was they were talking about before. It had something to do with possum fur.

"Nice to meet you," I said to no one, thinking how very un-twinlike they looked.

In front of the boardinghouse, the footpath widened to the size of a large dirt road, circling around the house and then running off in a couple of different directions. It made this place the center of town, the crossroads of the backwoods. To the east was our church building, a big, run-down wooden cabin with a new sign out front announcing the meeting times. It had a bell on top and a roof made of mismatched pieces of rough wood and sheet metal. Its wooden walls were dry and cracking, and weeds filled the flowerpots that were sitting out front. The entire thing had "service project" written all over it.

To the west of the boardinghouse was a school. It was

flat-roofed and leaned to one side. It had no front door, so I could easily see inside. Each desk was currently occupied by a wiggling child. A short woman with thick arms was standing in front of a chalkboard pronouncing the word "offspring."

I looked away from the school toward the sprawling meadow. It was full of wildflowers and weeds, and stitched with small paths where people had trampled down the growth to move across it. Two rusted and rotting pioneer-type wagons lay in the center of the meadow. Their metal bindings were bent and corroded, their wooden bodies splintered and dry.

Elder Boone saw me gazing at the wagons and spoke. "That's sort of the town park," he said. "During lunch and recess the school kids play on those."

"Fun," I commented dryly.

Elder Boone pointed to a small, outhouse-looking shack off in the distance. "That's Wad's shop," he informed me. "He's the town barber."

"Wad?"

"You'll understand once you meet him."

I wasn't sure I wanted to understand.

"He cuts the missionaries' hair for free," Elder Boone added.

What a perk, I thought.

Way past Wad's place was a bridge that spanned the mouth of the river, looking like an awkward set of braces. Though the bridge was far away from the boardinghouse, I could see that it was burnt and unusable. I didn't have the courage to ask what the story behind it was.

We picked up our feet and walked past the church and then past a small cemetery that lay between the church and what turned out to be our house. The cemetery ran back and over beyond our place, touching the river with its backside. Headstones and flowers dotted its layout like a poorly finished paint-by-number. In the middle of the cemetery was a big cement mausoleum with the name "Watson" carved into its top. The mausoleum was surrounded by trees and bushes, and in front of it stood a large statue of a woman. It looked to me like more people had died here in Thelma's Way than had lived.

Our place was wedged between the cemetery and the river. It was a small cabin with very little besides two beds and a hard dirt floor. There was a round table to eat on and a washbasin with a mirror above it. In the center of it all was a black iron stove for cooking and heating the place. A thick quilt was hanging on a wire, providing some privacy to whoever was standing behind it.

"Primitive," I observed.

"Home sweet home," Elder Boone clarified.

"Where do we keep our food?" I asked, noticing that there was no refrigerator.

"In the winter we can hang it out the windows, but for now we keep it over at the boardinghouse. Roswell and Feeble don't mind."

I thought maybe I did.

"We can shower at the boardinghouse and do our laundry over at Bishop Watson's place," Elder Boone continued. "It's not perfect, but hey, President Clasp just opened this area back up."

In my humble opinion, the area should have remained closed. This was nowhere, nothing, and no way all wrapped into one. This was the edge of the earth, the end of civilization, the dropping-off point for all things backward and isolated. Dirt floors, wood walls, and bugs the size of those in any foreign mission flashed before my eyes as I tried to find the silver lining in this very dark cloud. I pretended I was in some exotic country, living out in the uncharted forest. It helped a little.

"Toilet's out back," Elder Boone said. "And all mail gets delivered to the boardinghouse. President Clasp promised he would look into making improvements on this place, but I can't imagine either of us being here long enough to see any of them."

Elder Boone was skinny—too skinny. He had green eyes and a posture that the elitely prim would have been complimentary toward. He stood straight, walked straight, and talked straight. At the moment, however, I wished that he would make up a few crooked lies to help disguise the unpleasant truth. The truth being that I was stuck in Thelma's Way for at least a month.

I took a few steps into the cabin and set my backpack down on the bed. I was just about to sit down myself when a horrible noise rang out from outside. It sounded as if someone had just sucker-punched a hyena. The noise grew louder and louder until it eventually ended up on our doorstep, taking the shape of a little blonde girl with long braids and big feet. She was wearing a small, baggy dress and ankle-high boots, and her big head rotated in circles as she hollered.

"Elders, my dad is . . . ! He needs . . . !!"

Elder Boone grabbed the girl by the arm. "Calm down, Narlette," he ordered.

Narlette? This town needed a sensible baby-name book.

"But my," she wailed, "my . . . it's awful!"

She had that right.

"There's water in that pitcher, and a cup!" Elder Boone instructed me loudly, pointing over his shoulder.

I looked. Against the wall was a small shelf with a big bowl, a pitcher, and a glass on it. I grabbed the pitcher, quickly poured a glass of water, and ran back to my companion.

"Give it to her," he shouted.

Had I taken a second to think about it, I would have administered it differently. But, caught up in the movement of the moment, I threw the water into her face.

For a second she was silent. Then the calm was shattered as her young brain instructed her small vocal cords to stop holding back. She wailed, hollered, screamed, and yelped all in one incessant and steady shriek.

"To drink!" Elder Boone snapped. "Give it to her to drink!"

It was, of course, too late for that.

Elder Boone picked the girl up and set her on his bed. "Narlette," he said kindly, "I can't help you unless you calm down."

She looked at me with dislike and took in air. "My father is hurt bad," she finally managed to say.

"Should we get a doctor?" I asked, wanting to help.

"Not the bloody kind of hurt," she cried, shaking water off her like a dog. "Satan's got him again."

"Let's go," Elder Boone said authoritatively. He took Narlette's hand and pulled her out the door. I considered just waiting around and resting while he went out, but then I remembered I was a missionary. I will go; I will do. For the next two years I would be tied to my companion.

We stomped past the cemetery. We stomped past the church. We stomped past the un-identical twins Roswell and Feeble Ford. Feeble shifted his weight and yelled out, "Things okay, Narlette?"

"Daddy's in trouble again," she yelled back, having regained her composure.

"Tell him hello," he offered.

We crossed into the meadow and wove down one of the stamped-out trails. The long meadow stretched on for a few hundred feet along the river. Then came the trees, followed by the slope of the mountains. We hiked up through the forest, Narlette leading the way.

We soon came to a big home with a nice new roof and a freshly painted porch. There was a picture of Christ taped up in one of the front windows, and a dog with only two legs lay on the ground. The dog was chewing on something that I couldn't identify, although at first glance it sort of reminded me of my homesick stomach—mangled.

Narlette led us back around her house and up to a good-sized chicken coop. Loud fowl and colorful language came from within. We stopped a few steps away and just stood there listening.

"Brother Heck," Elder Boone finally hollered.

There was a brief pause, then an answering yell, "Who's out there?"

"It's the missionaries. Your daughter brought us."

For another moment there was silence.

"Go on your way," a voice finally yelled back. "I ain't fit for you to waste your time on."

I would have been happy to obey. Apparently, Elder Boone felt differently.

"We're not leaving," he informed Brother Heck.

"Send Narlette away," he yelled out from the coop. "I don't want her to see me like this."

Narlette skipped off as if this were suddenly just a big game.

"She's gone," Elder Boone hollered.

I was born a member. I had grown up singing "I Hope They Call Me on a Mission." I had grown a foot or two—topping out at a couple of inches over the six-foot mark. I had seen dozens of videos, taken classes, and read sacks full of books on the missionary experience. I had been prepped and readied. Or so I thought.

Brother Heck stepped out of the coop and stood there. He looked to be about forty-five years old, and he wore no shirt or shoes, just a pair of ripped and ragged pants. He was covered in blue paint and feathers. His painted hair was sticking up in clumps and matted in strips. There were bits of straw and dirt and feathers all over him. His round belly contracted and expanded like a blue balloon with each breath. As he stepped out of the coop, he was followed by a flock of spotted blue chickens. He hung his head dejectedly.

"What have you done?" Elder Boone asked.

Brother Heck looked up at the two of us and then hung his head back down. With his voice and gaze directed toward the ground, he spoke. "I see you got yourself a new companion."

"This is Elder Williams," Elder Boone introduced. "We just got into town."

"Nice to meet you," Brother Heck mumbled, still looking at the ground.

"Good to meet you," I replied, trying hard not to smile.

"Have you been smoking again?" Elder Boone asked.

Brother Heck glumly nodded. "I'm helpless."

"And . . . ?" Elder Boone prodded.

"And I felt so awful about indulging that I tarred and feathered myself. 'Ceptin I didn't have no tar, so I used paint."

We stood there silently for a moment.

"Patty's going to be awful sore," he said. "She was planning to use that paint on the house."

"There are other ways to repent," Elder Boone offered.

"I'm just so carnal," he moaned. "Weak as taffy."

The chickens grew bored and wandered off to find something more exciting to watch. Brother Heck took a seat on an overturned paint can. He put his head in his hands, smearing more paint on his face as he did so.

"Where is Sister Heck?" Elder Boone asked.

"Virgil's Find," he replied. "She went after some fabric. Narlette needs a new dress."

We sprayed Brother Heck off with a hose and then helped him clean up the paint in the chicken coop. During the cleanup we gave him a lesson on repentance and respecting ourselves enough not to paint our body-temples. He seemed forlorn and overly willing to change. It was obvious he had been through this sort of thing before. He showed us where he hid his cigarettes, and we burned them in one of the metal trash receptacles out back.

We left before his wife, Patty, came home. As we walked down through the forest and into the meadow, Elder Boone told me about the other times he had been summoned out here to help Brother Heck. Once they had to coax him out of a tree after Brother Heck had exiled himself to its tallest branches. On another occasion he had taped his legs to the spigot out back and then commenced to whip himself on his bare back with a fly swatter. As a form of punishment, that one was largely ineffective. Folks never knew what Brother Heck would submit himself to after a moment of nicotine-tinged weakness. Elder Boone also informed me that Brother Heck was one of the more active members in the area.

We came down out of the forest and into the meadow. The place was now alive. School was out, and children ran around, climbing through the two aged and dilapidated wagons. Like small mounds of earth, they would rise and crumble above the long grass. Collectively they gave the meadow a soul. We walked past Roswell and Feeble again, past the cemetery, and home to our abode.

I lay down on my bed and stared at the ceiling.

"Really, it gets better," Elder Boone said.

"It gets better, or I get numb?"

"Some of both, I suppose."

One thing was for sure, I couldn't see it getting any worse. I was so homesick. I closed my eyes. Darkness helped. With my eyes closed I could almost imagine myself on a normal mission. I inventoried the few things I had going for me. My companion seemed like a decent person. If I had been put with anyone else, I would probably have been unable to suppress the urge to simply run away.

My gloomy thoughts were interrupted by a knock at the door.

Elder Boone opened the door to skinny old Roswell Ford, who was dancing with anticipation.

"What's up?" Elder Boone asked.

"Feeble's having a vision," he hollered. "Come quickly, I'm betting this one's a big'un." He ran off.

"Feeble's having a vision," Elder Boone repeated to me.

"What?" I asked.

Elder Boone ignored me and ran out the door. I followed.

Thelma's Way was moving. Waves of people washed across the meadow and lapped against the boardinghouse. Soon the place was surrounded by kids and adults of all makes and models. The feature attraction: Feeble Ford.

He was on the porch, standing with his arms outstretched. He was dancing a little jig. I was amazed. Feeble had looked so planted in that chair of his; now here he was wiggling about like an over-stimulated teenager. The crowd was humming with excitement.

"Look at Feeble."

"Feeble's on one."

"What's Feeble going to say?"

Feeble was stamping his feet and shimmying as if he heard music playing. He waved his hat around, and then kicked one of the porch chairs for effect. It was very dramatic.

I came to a standstill behind Elder Boone. The crowd stood quietly, watching Feeble's every twitch and slither. Finally he stopped, clapped his hands, and sang, "Praise God, from Whom All Blessings Flow." Then he pointed at me.

At me!

His arm shook, and his feet stamped. Then, as if they had been poured into the top of his head, words ran out of his mouth. "Things are going to change!" he yelled. "Things are going to change. Don't take life at face value. A nickel can appear to be a dime." He clapped his hands and fell back into a chair, closing his eyes. His red nose sizzled. His vision was completed.

Everyone turned to look at me. I looked behind me, hoping they were focusing on something else. My short brown hair felt as if it were contracting, and my face was painted red with the blush of prophecy.

The townfolks gawked, eyeing me like fuzzy food that had been left in the back of the refrigerator. Seconds later, almost in unison, they turned their attention from me and began the work of critiquing Feeble's vision.

"Awful short."

"Not much substance."

"He sure got all fired up for just a few words."

"I liked his last one better."

Roswell spoke. "Has Feeble ever been wrong?"

The crowd collectively shook their heads no.

"I'd wager anyone of yous that Feeble's words will come true," Roswell ranted. "Anyone?"

No takers.

"Chickens," Roswell spat. "Afraid of a little bet."

"What the heck did Feeble mean?" a woman shouted, ignoring Roswell and getting back to the vision. "Things are always changing here."

Folks went on speculating for a few minutes. I saw Brother Heck through the crowd. He had Narlette in hand and was wearing a big pair of overalls. I could see spots of blue in his ears and on one of his elbows where we had failed to wash him clean. His graying hair was wet, and his foggy eyes looked full of thoughts he wasn't properly thinking. He was tall, and his wide shoulders gave the impression of constant attentiveness. He was actually a rather distinguished-looking man, if you could mentally get past the first impression he had so vividly painted.

The crowd broke up. People wandered off pondering Feeble's prophetic words. Brother Heck sheepishly sidled up to us. "Elders," he acknowledged.

Narlette smiled.

"Feeble had at it," Brother Heck commented. "I hope this vision don't make everyone crazy again."

Again?

"He didn't say much," Elder Boone pointed out.

"Appears he's taken a shine to this'un," Brother Heck said, nodding toward me. "I guess big things are in store for you." He stuck out his hand and introduced himself, as if this were the first time we had ever met. I suppose he was wanting to start anew. I couldn't fault him for that.

"I'm Brother Ricky Heck," he said proudly.

"I'm Elder Trust Williams," I responded, shaking his hand.

Brother Heck took Narlette's hand and walked off.

"I think he likes you," Elder Boone said.

I couldn't do this. This was not right. I must have gotten the wrong mission call. That was it. My real call must have gotten mixed up in the mail. I had to tell someone. Right now there was some elder in France who should be here, someone who had a command of backwoods etiquette. Someone who was fluent in 'ceptin's and ain'ts.

Elder Boone patted me on the back as we walked back to our home. "I'm glad you're here," he said.

I missed Southdale.

I missed civilization.

6

GREEN EYES

Grace Heck was clairvoyant. She could sense and tell things about others that were unknown even to them. Grace's father figured this was a result of her having accidentally hit her head against a large piece of limestone down by the Girth when she was seven. Her mother saw the gift as coming directly from God at her birth. Either way, Grace was pretty perceptive. Unfortunately, she couldn't seem to see her own future too clearly these days.

When Grace had turned twenty, her whole world had changed. Her reflection in the river looked unfamiliar. She had grown up being liked by pretty much everyone, but at the moment she didn't even know if she cared for herself. For the first time, she saw her life as lacking. What place did she as a woman have here in Thelma's Way?

She had hoped that having missionaries would be good for the town. But so far they had proved to be little more than an irritant—a new set of outsiders to look down their noses at everyone. Elder Frates had treated Thelma's Way as if he were the master teacher, and they were all the same slow child who couldn't quite grasp what he was saying. His act of trying to pompously reorganize the town was too much for Grace. She had promised herself that she wouldn't return to church until the full-time missionaries were a thing of the past.

She closed the cupboards and sat back in one of the wooden chairs. She looked around the quaint little home and sighed. A few months back, she had discovered this small cabin hidden deep among the thick mountain trees. She observed it for a while before bravely trying the door handle and finding it unlocked. Curiosity took her inside.

It was a nice place, though clearly abandoned. She had cleaned it out and fixed it up a bit. She spent many days and nights in it hidden away from everything besides her books. She was always checking out books from the Virgil's Find public library in hopes of broadening her universe. She dreamed about life outside of Thelma's Way, about any life different from the one she knew.

Grace was moving and simple in appearance. Her most recognizable features were her dark green eyes and her thick red hair, which was usually tied back behind her neck. The oldest of the three Heck children, she loved her family, although she found herself being more and more compelled to stay away these days.

What with the shelter of her newfound cabin, it was becoming increasingly rare for her to leave the sanctuary of the forest and wander into the open meadow, and now, after what she had just witnessed, she was determined never to come down. She had been secretly watching as her painted father had humiliated himself in front of the missionaries. She had looked on in horror as the elders had hosed her dad off and then lectured him on the Word of Wisdom. *Embarrassed* was too mild a word.

She had considered storming out of the trees and insisting that the elders leave her father alone, but something in her seemed to snap. The emptiness that had been creeping up on her for months was suddenly upon her in full force.

All she could do was watch.

Later, from behind the boardinghouse, she watched Feeble prophesy and point at the new elder. Curiosity wiggled through her veins, her mind flipping back and forth like the adjusting blades of a mini-blind. The new elder intrigued her. He was good-looking. Grace feared the new womanly feelings that were growing inside of her—feared and fanned.

After Feeble finished prophesying, she slipped through the back of the cemetery and down to the Girth River. She sat down on the edge of the ground and stuck her feet into the water like prongs into a socket. Her body jolted to the touch of the water. She washed her hands and took her hair out of its tie.

"Missionaries," she whispered.

Grace was lonely.

7

IT STARTS

Saturday, our early morning companionship study was interrupted by reveille. I looked out our window to see Roswell blowing a bugle in the middle of the meadow as the sun rose. It was pre-planning meeting day. We went outside, hurrying over as if something important were actually happening. A small crowd had already gathered by the time we got there. Roswell put down the bugle and caught his breath.

"We will now hear from Sister Watson," he announced.

Sister Watson, the bishop's wife, stepped up beside Roswell.

"I expected more of a crowd," she said.

There weren't too many people in the meadow. Feeble's vision a few days back had been a much bigger draw. But then, Feeble had had the courtesy to prophesy at a reasonable hour of the day.

"I'm certain our ancestors are disappointed," Sister Watson scolded. "Here it is the pre-planning meeting for our sesquicentennial, and you're all that have shown up."

I couldn't tell if she was insulting us or not.

"Some may say, 'But Sister Watson, the celebration isn't for almost two years.' To that I respond, 'Remember the slow turtle.'"

Everyone nodded as if they knew exactly what she was talking about. Having nothing to lose, I nodded too.

"I feel inspired," Sister Watson continued, "to have the full-time missionaries come up and give you all an impromptu lesson on participation. Elders."

I looked at Elder Boone. He was too busy pushing me forward to meet my eyes.

"You go do it, Elder," he said, smiling. "It will be good for you."

I wanted to protest, but Elder Boone *shhhed* me. The tiny crowd split. I reluctantly walked through and to the front. Sister Watson glanced at my tag to make sure she was remembering my name correctly.

"Some of you may remember Elder Williams from Feeble's last vision a couple days back. Well, Bishop Watson and I had the opportunity to meet with him the other day, and I can honestly say that he seems to have fewer flaws than the last missionary the mission sent us— the one with the funny, puffy booklets. With that, I give you: Elder Williams."

I looked at the small group. Brother Heck was there, and Feeble, and a few other folks I was beginning to recognize. Elder Boone smiled at me. I really hated public speaking.

"Well," I began. "I know that participation is

37

important. I think that people need to participate in things that are worthwhile.

"I came out on my mission a little later than most elders. I attended some college before coming out. It was a big decision for me. I am now happy to be serving on my mission and participating in the work."

Digby Heck, Brother Heck's teenage son, yawned. Sister Watson tapped her watch, indicating that I had taken enough time.

"In closing, I guess I would just like to say that I know participation is true, and—"

"Thank you, Elder Williams," Sister Watson interrupted.

I walked back to my companion. This time the gathering didn't split, so I had to sort of push my way through.

"Thank you, Elder Williams," Sister Watson repeated when I had settled back into my place. "I think we all need to remember that Elder Williams here is real new to the mission field. Anyhow, I was hoping for a larger crowd so that we could get the preparations to this pageant off with a bang."

BOOM!

I thought for a moment that my head had exploded. My ears vibrated and rang. I looked to the side of me and saw a man pointing a gun toward the sky.

"Yes, ma'am!" he hollered.

"It's a little early for firing that thing, Pete," Brother Heck said.

"Sorry," Pete replied.

"Normally you all know how I discourage Pete from

shooting that thing off," Sister Watson said. "But I'm happy to see a little enthusiasm this morning."

Elder Boone leaned into me and whispered, "Pete loves guns."

I moved to the other side of my companion.

"As we all know, there has already been some arguing over who would play what in our sesquicentennial play," Sister Watson continued. "But I want you all to know that those people working behind the scenes and building the stage are just as important as those who play the leads. To make things easier, I've decided that when the time comes, my husband and I will play the two main parts, and we'll put the rest of the assignments in a hat and draw names. That way everything's fair."

No one protested.

"As most of you know, the celebration is about twenty months from now, on the exact date of our town's inception. We are starting preparations early because we want to make sure that we do things right. We have a lot of props to build, as well as a stage. The play itself, tentatively titled "All Is Swell," should be completed in a few months, and at that point we will begin handing out parts. There will be songs to learn and costumes to make. I would have had the entire script finished by now, but Paul stealing the Book of Mormon has caused me to have to rewrite." Sister Watson took in air. "This isn't going to be as simple or as easy as our usual town plays. But don't get discouraged— we will have our ancestors on the other side of the veil pushing us around. Any questions?"

An older lady I didn't yet know raised her hand.

"Yes, Teddy," Sister Watson pointed.

"Will there be food?"

"Lots of it. This is going to be the celebration to end all celebrations. Plus we're going to open ourselves up to the world. All the surrounding towns will be invited, as well as anyone else who would like to come. This will put us on the map."

Pete Kennedy shot his gun off again.

BOOOM!

"Yes, ma'am!"

Roswell raised his hand and asked, "Do you have to be an active Mormon to participate?"

"No," Sister Watson answered. "The only requirement is that you have Thelma's Way blood coursing through your veins."

Everyone looked at their arms.

Brother Heck stepped up. "I'd like to say just a couple things, if'n that's all right."

Sister Watson nodded.

"Now, I never been a fancy word user. In fact, me and English just ain't real cozy. But I don't want some of you thinking that this is just another one of Sister Watson's silly plays. This is a pageant extra-ganza. And just 'cause it's got a three-dollar word like *sesquicentennial* in front of it, is no reason to not take it seriously. That's why we voted to start preparing so soon. We want every stranger that comes to the celebration in two years to walk away with a dazed look on their face."

"Thank you, Brother Heck," Sister Watson said. Brother Heck stepped down. "Now, we here in attendance are the fortunate few. We're getting in on the ground floor of this. As the day gets closer, more and more people are going to want to get involved, and—"

BOOOM!

"We're on the ground floor!"

Everyone looked at Pete. Sister Watson held her startled hand to her heart.

"Anyhow," she continued, "as the time gets nearer there will be more and more to do. I hope I can count on all of you to do your part and then some. I promise you that if you do, this will be a pageant the people will never forget."

Everyone nodded, congratulating each other for getting in on the ground floor. I think I was the only one who was nervous. Thankfully, it was none of my business. Some other unfortunate missionary would have to deal with it twenty months from now.

I was deluded.

8

It's a Small Ward after Paul

I had been told by President Clasp that the Thelma's Way Ward was small, despite the fact that virtually everyone in the surrounding area was Mormon.

President Clasp had lied. *Small* is measurable. The ward consisted of Bishop Watson and his wife; the Heck family—Brother and Sister Heck, Narlette, and her older brother, Digby; Sister Teddy Yetch, an older woman who lived across the Girth River; Miss Flitrey, the grade-school teacher; Feeble Ford; and us.

"It's a small ward after Paul," Elder Boone sang as I sat there looking at our tiny congregation.

Paul Leeper was the infamous, dishonest, local apostate. Heavy on the *local*, heavy on the *apostate*. I had been briefed on him by my companion.

Six months ago Paul had won a free trip to Rome from the Savin' Town grocery store over in Virgil's Find. Paul was shopping for anti-lice medicine and ended up being the one-millionth customer, thus procuring himself a clean scalp, a one-week, all-expenses-paid trip to Rome, and a lifetime 20 percent discount on all nonsale items at Savin' Town.

Rome wasn't ready for Paul.

Paul spent the first half of the week there perpetuating every ugly-American stereotype the Romans had ever had of us. He demanded that his waiters and servers speak English. He took pictures in places that were off-limits, and when people tried to stop him, he screamed about his rights under the U.S. Constitution. He talked loudly, walked loudly, and made fun of everything from their dilapidated coliseum to the stupid-looking currency the Romans used.

To make matters even worse, Paul had somehow confused Rome with Ancient Egypt. He became enraged when one of the local taxi drivers refused to take him to see the pyramids. Paul called the driver a couple of America's choicest words. In turn the driver ran over his foot, breaking all five of his toes and ruining his best pair of travel shoes.

While getting his foot worked on by one of the Roman doctors, Paul overheard someone talking about the finger of Thomas. Apparently the Vatican had the finger of Thomas the Apostle on display in its museum: the very finger that had once touched the Master after Thomas had refused to believe.

Well, Paul had his doubts. But he hobbled to the Vatican to see this finger for himself. There with his own two eyes he saw it, encased in glass and pointing toward him. It was an epiphany for Paul. It was a miracle, a life-changing event. Actually, it didn't really change him all that much, but it did afford him a whole new level of self-righteousness. He had seen the finger.

Paul was touched, and not like usual.

He was mugged by a couple of rough men on his way back from the Vatican. They took all his money and kicked him a few times. Paul saw this as a sign that Satan was personally trying to prevent him from making it back to Thelma's Way where he could testify that he had seen the finger of Thomas.

Penniless and stuck in Rome, Paul went to the American Embassy and demanded that he be given a few dollars for souvenirs and meals, seeing how he was a red-blooded American and all. The Embassy didn't give him any pocket change, but they did help him get an earlier return flight home.

Paul returned home to Thelma's Way two days sooner than he had planned and with an attitude that he was now better and more righteous than anyone there. Yes, he had stood next to the finger that had once touched the Master, and this, in Paul's mind, made him as important as any biblical figure, except maybe Moses or Abraham or that one guy who was in the fish.

The first thing Paul did was return to Savin' Town, the grocery store that had given him the trip, and demand some compensation for the two days of Rome he was forced to give up. Well, not only did the store refuse, they informed Paul that they had miscounted and he was not really their one-millionth customer. Their accountant, who was really the owner's nephew, had been off by a couple hundred thousand. Savin' Town revoked Paul's 20 percent discount and threw him out the door. Paul stood in the parking lot and prophesied that Savin' Town would rue the day they had tossed out the self-made apostle. Three days later the Savin' Town dumpster caught fire, causing the store to close for four hours.

Coincidence?

Paul thought not.

In his mind, this proved he was a full-fledged prophet. He left the LDS church to strike it out on his own. The only thing he needed was a congregation. Sadly, he found one in the Mormons. He led almost all of the members away from the Church. In the past Paul had been known as a chronic liar. One of his most famous lies was that he was actually the top-secret fourth Nephite not mentioned in the Book of Mormon. There was also his claim that as a youth he had spent two summers harvesting cookies at the Pepperidge Farm. But unlike before, this time Paul had proof of his brush with greatness. You see, he had brought back a postcard of the finger of Thomas, a relic of his own. He used it as token of his authority and his Savin' Town prophecy as the proof of his power.

The members flocked.

The People of Paul began to construct a small chapel on the other side of the river. They organized a choir, bought a bell, and watched their congregation grow as the gullible locals and their fascination with the parable of the finger drove them from the ward. The heavens appeared to have smiled on the People of Paul. But fate served up the final snicker.

Before the big desertion, the Thelma's Way Ward was doing pretty well. It was good sized and relatively normal, despite its relatively abnormal members. Bishop Clem Watson and his counselors, Feeble Ford and Toby Carver, were moving the work along at a perfect pace for the area. Then along came Paul, and the ward fractured like clay pigeons in the sight of God.

Bishop Watson tried desperately to keep his ward together. He pleaded with the members to pray and stay focused, but they seemed to like the blur. People didn't want to focus; they were too swept up in the momentum of Paul's new church. Even Toby Carver, the second counselor, deserted the Thelma's Way Ward. Bishop Watson was devastated. He petitioned Church headquarters for full-time missionaries to be assigned to Thelma's Way. He felt that with a little help, he could bring the deserting members back to their senses. The Church considered his request.

As Bishop Watson prayed for his wayward members' souls, Paul badmouthed Bishop Watson until he was red in the face. Then, during one of his tirades, Paul became bold enough to predict that bad things would befall the active Mormons. Two nights later someone broke into the church building (an act of minor difficulty, since it was never locked) and stole the Thelma's Way Ward community Book of Mormon.

At first I had no idea why these people were so concerned about a missing Book of Mormon. I was quickly informed that the stolen book was not your average, free, blue-covered copy. It was in fact a first edition that Parley P. Pratt had given the Saints when he had passed through Thelma's Way more than a hundred years ago. It was the most treasured possession in the entire town. It was the Mormons' stamp of approval—validating them, as it were. Parley P. Pratt had donated it to the town as a gesture of his appreciation for all the kindness and compassion they had shown him when he had become horribly ill from some bad meat, and the entire meadow area had helped nurse him back to full health. He had signed that Book of Mormon with the inscription:

With sincere appreciation, Parley P. Pratt

Not just appreciation, but *sincere* appreciation. It was quite a tribute to the backwoods town of Thelma's Way. The book was kept in the bishop's office and brought out to rest on the small table next to the podium each Sunday.

No longer. The book was gone. Someone had stolen the last thing the Mormons had to feel good about. The few members who had stayed faithful during the apostasy ordeal had always found additional strength in that old Book of Mormon. Now they didn't even have that.

The town was aghast. Thelma's Way prided itself on not having to lock its doors, on being able to leave a pie on the windowsill or a melon in the field without worry. What good was a neighbor if you had to keep an eye on him? Geoff Titter once left his good rake on the porch of the boardinghouse for a whole year before picking it up. No one ever touched it. That's the kind of people that populated Thelma's Way: mellow, Mormon, and honest to a fault.

Not anymore. The ugly crime of theft had appeared. And much like the mole on Tindy MacDermont's arm, the deed seemed to stick out and get attention. It was a big, hairy deal. Thelma's Way had its theories, or, more befitting, its theory, as to who had done it.

Everyone suspected Paul. They had found him to be a little too prophetic. They all figured he had done the deed so that his anti-Mormon prophecy would come true. As an ugly, final gesture he had stripped the Mormons and the town of their most prized possession. It wasn't enough that he had already driven everyone away—now he had, in a sense, stolen their soul.

Well, faster than they had joined him, Paul's people deserted him. They burned the bridge that spanned the Girth River and broke out the windows of the unfinished People of Paul chapel. No one wanted a leader who was a thief. He was completely dethroned, stripped of all the prestige his wacky prophecies had once afforded him.

Nowadays Paul spent his time in relative shame, working on his house in the forest across the Girth River. Neither Elder Boone nor I had as yet actually seen him. He still claimed his innocence, even though everyone knew he was guilty.

There being no real proof, however, Paul went unprosecuted for the crime, and the mystery of the missing Book of Mormon lingered like a goofy local legend. Paul's cabin had been searched, but the book wasn't there. Here in these hills there were a zillion places a person could hide a book. Most people figured he had either thrown it into the Girth River or burned it. Both possibilities were equally horrific and hideous.

Sister Watson took up with a couple of other civic-minded women and formed a small action group called M.A.P., Mothers Against Paul. It was a good name until Frank Porter, ever the wave maker, insisted on joining the group. Since he wasn't a mother in the true sense of the word, Sister Watson changed the group's name to P.A.P., People Against Paul. But then old conspiracy-minded Pap Wilson thought their group was out to get him personally. So Sister Watson changed the name once again, and P.I.G., Paul Is Guilty, was formally formed. Yes, young Digby Heck tried to make an argument for all the local sows, but his voice was not heeded. *P.I.G.* stuck.

So far, P.I.G. had made very little progress in its efforts. Its goal was to bring Paul to justice, or at least to give him a whipping or burn his house down. Justice worked differently in Thelma's Way.

Meanwhile, the Saints who had left the ward to join up with Paul never came back to our congregation. So now the hills were filled with inactive Mormons who were either too lukewarm, too lazy, or just too embarrassed to come back. Our job as missionaries was to rebuild the ward. We were to find the ninety and nine who had fool-hardily left the figurative one in this secret basin community filled with less-active Mormons.

Here it was, another Sunday service in Thelma's Way, and the enormity of the task ahead was giving me a headache. Elder Boone and I sat on the stand with Feeble and Bishop Watson. We were trying to make it look as if we had some sort of leadership authority.

Bishop Watson was a little old man. He stood just under five feet tall and walked with a limp. He had no hair and usually wore a shirt with sleeves that were entirely too long, and a tie that was too short. He had gray eyes and a big smile that made him look at least an inch and a half taller than he actually was. He was kind and spoke with a booming radio announcer's voice that didn't really match his physique. Everything he said sounded like an advertisement or news flash.

"Church at eleven."

"Don't miss out on tithing settlement."

"Be the first one to pick up your new manual."

Bishop Watson's wife was considerably taller and thicker than he was. She wore a dark wig over her light hair and spoke without really moving her mouth. It was actually a rather amazing and unnerving thing to witness. They made an interesting couple.

After church, Elder Boone and I had lunch over at the bishop's house. Sister Watson served up meat loaf, tossed salad, bean sprouts, peas, and some local delicacy called "ramp."

"It's the best thing around these parts," she bragged about the odd vegetable.

"One of the real perks of living here," Bishop Watson added.

I tried to smile as I ate.

"So, are you elders excited about the upcoming pageant?" Sister Watson asked.

"Well," Elder Boone answered, "it's still an incredibly long way off. I'm sure neither of us will be here."

"We're getting a real jump on this one," Bishop Watson boomed.

"I'll be finished with the script in a few months," Sister Watson announced. "The story is based on Parley P. Pratt coming here and getting nauseous. Of course there will be a lot of singing and dancing. Oh just think of it, Elders, our very own outdoor pageant. A pageant can really put you on the map, you know? Look at the Hill Cumorah, look at Nauvoo."

Bishop Watson looked around as if searching for Nauvoo.

The conversation drifted. Sister Watson began telling us in detail how she had helped to deliver the very cow we were now eating. Brother Watson provided color commentary. I found myself sculpting my portion of cow into the shape of Lucy with my spoon. It started half-heartedly but soon drew my attention. I glanced up nervously, but no one had noticed I wasn't listening. I pulled the table centerpiece in front of my plate to hide what I was doing. I stabbed a few pieces of lettuce from Elder Boone's plate when he wasn't looking and rigged up some clothes for my sculpture. I spied the peas across the table. They were green, but they would have to do for eyes. I asked Sister Watson if she would kindly pass them.

"Hand me your plate and I'll scoop some out for you," she offered.

I sat there for a moment, not sure what to do.

"Uh, actually, I like to scoop myself."

"Nonsense," Bishop Watson said, his radio announcer's voice booming through their dining room. "Sister Watson will set you up fine; hand her your plate."

I decided to skip the eyes. I backpedaled.

"Well, to tell you the truth, I'm full."

They both stared at me for a few moments, but soon they returned to their meals. Things would have been fine if I had not noticed Bishop Watson's sprouts. They would make perfect hair for my Lucy. I just couldn't resist. I commented on an antique-looking clock on the wall. While everyone was looking the other way, I stabbed the sprouts from off of Bishop Watson's plate.

No one noticed.

It was not enough. Lucy had thick hair. I complimented the tole-painted watering can that was sitting on the shelf behind them. But before I could successfully extract any more of Bishop Watson's sprouts, everyone turned back around.

"What are you doing?" It was Elder Boone. I covered my plate with my hands.

"Is something wrong with your meal?" Sister Watson asked.

"No," I replied.

"Then why are you covering your plate?" Bishop Watson questioned.

I slowly moved my hands to reveal a mound of misshapen meat loaf adorned with a lettuce dress and stylish bean-sprout hair. I felt my face go flush. Any moment the Watsons would throw me out of their home for displaying such awful table manners. But Bishop Watson just went on and on about how lifelike the likeness was, and Sister Watson passed me the peas with new understanding.

I sheepishly applied the eyes.

Elder Boone shook his head in disgust. I realized for the first time that I just might fit in here.

Sister Watson served ice cream for dessert, and Old Bishop Watson, in the spirit of competition, made a snowman out of his portion.

My mission was taking shape.

9

DRIFTING

Trust had been gone for more than five weeks but Lucy was adjusting. She shifted in her skirt and practice smiled at herself in the mirror. It wasn't often that her father set her up with dates, let alone a non-Mormon boy.

Lucy was looking forward to it. Gentile, beware.

Trust's letters were getting shorter. He complained less about the backwards people he was serving.

Lucy was concerned.

It was good to minister, but attachment could be catastrophic. What if Trust picked up unsophisticated mannerisms or a few awkward habits? He was supposed to grow up and out of his childish traits and ways, to come home ninety percent done, so Lucy could finish him off.

But Lucy's ability to refine, even by her own high estimate, could do only so much. Trust was a hardening ball of clay that needed to be molded further. Now, as his character stiffened, other people besides Lucy were there shaping him—people with names like Narlette and Feeble. It was all there in his letters.

Lucy furrowed her brow.

A mission was supposed to be regal and prestigious. It developed the finer arts of communication and persuasion. It was upper-class training, the first in an orderly sequence of steps leading to a foreign ambassadorship or overseas business appointment.

Lucy thought she would make a perfect ambassador's wife.

But stuck in Thelma's Way, Trust was about as likely to become sophisticated as she was to break out. Lucy had added the petition for his being transferred to her nightly prayer. So far, the request had gone unheeded.

"Oh, the trials I am forced to endure!" she moaned.

The doorbell rang—Lucy's blind date. The door opened. There stood Lance Fitzgerald with his square gentile jaw and dark gentile eyes. Lucy felt her body temperature rise.

Lucy was adjusting.

10

ONE UP, ONE DOWN

◆

WEEK SEVEN

I realized in my first couple of weeks that Roswell and Feeble Ford were really the heart of Thelma's Way. It wasn't necessarily a healthy heart, but they seemed to keep the town exactly where it was at.

Both Roswell and Feeble were Mormon, but only Feeble was active. Roswell had been inactive ever since Paul showed him the picture of Thomas' finger and bid him follow. He left the church and took up smoking all in the same week. Roswell felt a pipe made him look more mature, which was no small feat, given that he was over eighty.

Inactivity fit Roswell. He was tired of living under the substantial shadow of his hour-older twin. He liked the freedom and independence that inactivity provided. He liked to hear people say things like, "Feeble would never go inactive." It made him feel like a true individual. Yes, at eighty-some years old he had finally found himself. Unfortunately, his inactivity helped foster the town's indecisiveness. People felt better about not doing what they should be doing because Roswell wasn't. Roswell was old, you see, and supposedly wiser than most. If he wasn't going to church, then the rest of them could stay home, too. Roswell basked in the lukewarm glow of his newfound leadership position.

Of course, the few active Mormons used Feeble as their inspiration. Feeble had always been the good one, and smart. Feeble had read the Book of Mormon at least three times, the Doctrine and Covenants twice, the New Testament once, plus he had reread the Sermon on the Mount on at least six additional occasions. He had even started the Old Testament and gotten past First Kings. He was quite the scholar.

Feeble was definitely the more righteous of the two, what with his visions and all. Everyone felt that the only reason he had not already been translated was because he was so heavy. The heavens just couldn't heave him up. Most people believed that he ate so much just so he could remain overweight and stay here on earth to administer among the people. Such sacrifice. This theory, however, redefined the word *administer* to mean sit around and prattle. And it called attention to Roswell. After all, Roswell was so skinny that had God wanted him back, a slight breeze would have been enough to lift him home. His still being here in his eightieth year was a pretty good indication of where he stood with the heavens.

Roswell and Feeble were the last of the Ford clan to still be living in the state of Tennessee. According to Roswell, there was a cousin named Stubby who owned a pawn shop in Virgil's Find, but aside from him, they were it. What nice representatives they were. Roswell and Feeble spent all their time sitting on the front porch of their boardinghouse, Feeble commenting on the world around them, and Roswell making petty bets.

"Bet it'll rain this afternoon."

"Bet the raccoons'll be back tonight."

"Bet Tindy's sores take a good two weeks to heal."

"Five bucks."

"You're on."

The boardinghouse was a nice center of town, despite the fact that it wasn't much of a boardinghouse, or much of a town for that matter. There were a couple of rooms on the second floor that could have been used as a place for weary travelers to rest, but they were filled with old furniture, Roswell's collection of Woodsman Weekly magazines, and Feeble's "Great Men of the World" pewter figurine set, seventy-six four-inch figures in all. A complete set, all in perfect condition except for Thomas Edison's missing arm—on account of Roswell throwing Edison at a pack of noisy dogs one cold November night.

On the bottom floor of the boardinghouse there was a large all-purpose room and a small store that didn't have much to offer. You could buy bags of rice, beans, or flour and tubs of lard. There was also a glass cooler filled with soft drinks.

Feeble and Roswell had one of the few TVs in Thelma's Way. (Only about two-thirds of the homes in Thelma's Way even had electricity.) Their TV sat on a rolling cart in the middle of the store, and people from all over would come to watch football games and *Days of Our Lives*.

Feeble and Roswell were an institution, as close as Thelma's Way got to a Blockbuster Video or a high school basketball team. And to look at them rocking peacefully on the boardinghouse porch, you would never have guessed that their time had come.

It was early September and the seasons were beginning to rub up against each other. Elder Boone and I had just returned from the other side of the river where we had been visiting Sister Teddy Yetch for breakfast. She had a couple of new recipes she had wanted to try out on us. Her peanut-butter pork dumplings had not been too bad, but her fried widget recipe needed some tweaking.

Sister Teddy Yetch was about seventy years old. She was at the point in her life where her skin was turning from polyester to 100-percent cotton, wrinkling at every bend and crevice. She had thin gray hair and brown eyes that seemed to sag within their sockets. She didn't actually have a full set of teeth, but she did have most of the important ones in front. Teddy was kind, and she was the only active member who lived on the other side of the great Girth River. Apostate Paul lived across the Girth, deeper back in the trees, though to this day neither I nor Elder Boone had actually met him. There were a few other less-active members and Paul's abandoned chapel, but it was Teddy Yetch that we went to see.

To cross the wide Girth River you had to drag one of the community rafts to the part of the river near the high end of the meadow, right by the burnt-out bridge, and then

59

paddle quickly with one of the community paddles across the strong current. However, if you used your head, you could manipulate the current to push you to the other side. If you didn't move fast enough, the river would pull you down past our place, past the back edge of the cemetery, through some rapids, and eventually down over Hallow Falls. It was quite a sight to see old Teddy cross the Girth. She put us young elders to shame.

Elder Boone and I had just dragged our raft back up to the starting point for the next user and were stomping across the meadow when we noticed people were running to the boardinghouse, shouting and crying. I looked at my watch to see what time it was. I figured folks were just holding another unnecessary meeting to discuss their pageant that was still so far away. Or maybe they were all just throwing a fit over the current plot twist on *Days of Our Lives*.

I was way off.

I heard Feeble's name hollered a few times by different people. I thought then that he was just having another vision and people were talking about it. We picked up our pace and ran to the boardinghouse.

Feeble was lying on his stomach, his right arm stretched out, holding one of his pewter statues. His face was in the dirt, and it looked as if he had been in stride walking towards the meadow when he had simply fallen to the earth. Brother Heck was down next to Feeble searching for signs of life. Feeble's days of prophesying were over.

"What happened?" I asked as everyone else just stood around stunned, not knowing what to do.

"He's moved on," was all Brother Heck said.

Miss Flitrey's curiosity had gotten the best of her so she let her school kids out to see what all the commotion was. The horde of children joined the ring of folks that was now circling Feeble. The sky above clouded as if on cue. There was a heavy stillness in the air.

"Are you sure he's dead?" I asked in disbelief.

The entire ring of people nodded back, as if they too, by virtue of just knowing him, now knew him to be dead.

Toby Carver burst through the crowd and fell down beside Feeble. Toby was a kind person. He was always red cheeked and flustered. His square body was blocky and wooden, and he always had his sleeves rolled up, as if he were about to do something. He had a long thin beard and a pointy forehead that seemed to extend out past his nose. Toby was sort of the town's unofficial doctor. He had no medical training, but years ago he had twisted his ankle so badly, he had had to get it looked at by a clinic in Virgil's Find. The attending physician gave Toby a stretchy Ace bandage and a big bottle of pills for the pain. As things worked out, no sooner had Toby's ankle healed, than CleeDee Lipton hurt her wrist harvesting wildflowers east of the meadow. Toby trotted over to CleeDee's place, wrapped her wrist with his bandage, and gave her a couple of his pills. A week later she was fine. Well, from that point on, whenever anyone had an ailment or condition, Toby would hustle over and wrap it. He eventually ran out of the pills, but that bandage would be good forever. It had helped heal everything from Bishop Watson's pulled thigh to Digby Heck's swollen glands.

Toby knelt there next to Feeble's body, his Ace bandage clenched in his hand. It was too late. Toby cursed the heavens for not giving him more time. Toby could wrap Feeble from head to toe and it wouldn't make any difference now.

Then someone asked, "Where's Roswell?"

Everyone looked up.

Roswell rarely left Feeble's side. They were inseparable, everybody knew that. It had been difficult for Roswell to go inactive because it meant time away from his brother every Sunday. As much as he wanted to be his own man, Roswell needed his twin. Now here was his Feeble lying alone on the ground. It didn't look right. No one said it, but when it came to leaving this life, everyone had assumed the two would go together. Brother Heck and Digby raced into the boardinghouse. A few moments later they hollered for everyone to join them indoors. We all scrambled inside and into the bedroom, pushing and shoving for best position.

There were two twin beds about six feet apart from each other in Roswell and Feeble's room. One was sagging in the middle, sheets untucked, pillows on the floor. The other looked almost new. It wasn't difficult to guess whose was whose. Roswell's pillow was indented as if a head still lay on it. His blankets were folded neatly back. Next to his bed was a pair of red slippers, ready for Roswell to step into.

One problem. No Roswell.

Brother Heck and Digby searched the rest of the house while everyone else just stood there staring at the beds.

No Roswell.

"I knew it," old Briant Willpts exclaimed as we stood there bewildered. "I had a dream 'bout it and I warned Feeble. He laughed me off. Thought he was the only one who could have any visions. Well I say to you all, look who's laughing now," he spat.

Everyone looked at Briant to see who was laughing now.

"Well, I'm not laughing, laughing," he covered. "But inside I'm a big wad of righteous snickery."

Briant Willpts was an orphan. He was one of the few residents of Thelma's Way who had not actually been born in town. Because of this he felt he could misuse or make up words and then explain them by saying that these were words used in the outside world and people here just hadn't heard them before. Due to a bout with polio as a teenager, Briant walked as if he were trying out for the Hunchback of Notre Dame, his long arms swinging wildly whenever he stepped. He was about sixty years old, and used a cane whenever he needed sympathy.

"In my dream," he continued, raising his arms for dramatic effect, "I saw both Roswell and Feeble being lifted up to heaven on a liffy. I told Feeble to start preparing to lixidate this life. Pack your bags, Feeble, I says. Clean up your life and prepare to meet your creatoriums. Did Feeble take me seriously?"

Could anyone take him seriously?

"I'll answer on behalf of Feeble," Briant rambled, "seeing how Feeble is deceased and there is no way that he could properly respond to my incisive and indicament line of spectorial questioning. The answer is . . . Nope."

I couldn't even remember the question.

"Now, let me tell you all what happened," Briant waved his hands in front of himself, indicating that he would now lay things straight. A couple of people attempted to sit down on the beds, weary from standing and hoping to hear the explanation in comfort. Briant quickly scolded them and, as kindly and succinctly as he could, asked them please not to disturb the scene. So we all just stood around the beds while Briant spun one huge pile of yarn.

"Late last night after Roswell and Feeble retired to bed, a heavenly visitor came in a white robe. He came down and visited them here in this bedroom."

People looked around as if they were suddenly standing on holy ground.

"I know this to be an enveloping fact because around nine last night, I was walking past the boardinghouse and saw a strange glow coming from out of that window."

He pointed with his cane.

"It was a beautiful blue glow, brighter and more simshinery than any color I've yet seen before, and I've seen a lot of colors. Red, blue, green, brown, red . . . and some more I'm sure, I just can't remember right now. Anyway, I knocked on the front door but no one answered."

"I should have knocked longer," he added glumly.

"That heavenly visitor must have been informing Feeble and Roswell that they were about to be translated. He must have lifted Roswell out of his bed and tossed him up to heaven. It's obvious to the trained and scholaticable eye that this is what happened. Take a look-see. Slippers still neatly by the bed as if Roswell had never gotten out or up. Feeble, like we have suspected all along, must have been too heavy to yank topside-up. The way I see it is that this angel must have struggled with him, which would explain the messy bed. Then in frustration he must have given up. Feeble, desperatic to not be left without Roswell, ran outside in hopes of following this visitor. The visitor was so filled with compassion that he must have struck Feeble dead to end his heartache."

Everyone was nodding as if it all made sense.

"So you're saying that Roswell was translated?" I asked in amazement.

Everyone looked at me with one collective "Duh."

"That seems a little absurd," I observed, my blue eyes trying not to laugh.

Briant Willpts ignored me. He just stood there as if receiving fresh revelation. After a brief pause he opened his eyes and walked out of the room. He shuffled to the porch and then did the unthinkable. He planted himself in Feeble's good sitting chair.

Everyone gasped. They let out a collective murmur of approval. It was a sign—proof of Briant Willpts' authority as messenger. It was apparent to all, except me, that the spirit of Feeble had rested upon the hump of Briant Willpts.

"I don't think it's right," Brother Heck ventured. "You sitting on Feeble's chair as he lies there on the ground."

Leo Tip and Toby Carver, as if on cue, went to pick up

Feeble and lay him somewhere more dignified. One tug, however, told them they weren't men enough to do it. Toby waved over Brother Heck and Pap Wilson.

One per leg. One per limb. Still not enough.

Gun loving Pete Kennedy and Ed Washington joined them. They wiggled their arms underneath Feeble's belly, and locked hands. Then with one mighty heave, all six of them lifted him up off the ground. A pewter statue slipped from Feeble's grasp, making their load one pound lighter but still not easy by any means. With red faces and buckling knees they shuffled him over to the porch where they attempted to lay him down in dignity. Unfortunately the two porch steps got the best of them. Leo Tip, who was carrying the left leg and walking backwards, missed the second step and fell flat on his back. Brother Heck and Pap Wilson, literally at the head of this endeavor, pushed Feeble on top of Leo trying to keep their balance. Feeble's off-kilter weight twisted Pete Kennedy and Ed Washington's arms, giving the latter a burn he would complain about for years. The two of them fell towards Leo and onto the porch. Feeble's dead body rolled off of Leo and came to a stop in the center of the porch looking upward. Though deceased, Feeble wore the biggest smile I had ever seen him sport.

Everyone gasped. I guess folks had never seen Feeble smile before.

"He looks so happy," Sister Watson gushed.

"Downright peaceful," Bishop Watson added.

"Let there be not doubt as to what happened here today," Briant Willpts said, still sitting in Feeble's chair.

"The heavens took two strong pillars from our community. One went in a golden chariot, body and all. The other? Well, see for yourself."

I wanted to cry foul, to stand up and make a protest. But as a missionary, I felt it wasn't my place. Thelma's Way had its mind set, and its mind was set on believing that Roswell had been translated and that Feeble had passed away in some sort of botched attempt by heaven to bring him home. Whatever the truth really was, that is what they wanted to believe.

Amidst the commotion, Toby Carver's youngest boy, Lupert, slipped away from the crowd and picked up the pewter statue still lying in the road where Feeble had dropped it. He examined it carefully, then ran off into the meadow, apparently unnoticed by anyone but me. The ring of people began to dissolve as folks remembered unimportant things they needed to tend to. Miss Flitrey tried to gather her brood and herd them back to class, but most of them were too hyped-up from all the excitement to heed her.

"It's a miracle, I guess," CleeDee Lipton whispered in disbelief as she turned to go.

"I'll say," Briant replied. "I'll say." Which, of course, he already had. And with that, Briant Willpts was silent.

11

CLOSE ENOUGH TO TOUCH

◆

Grace had always liked Feeble considerably more than she liked that brother of his. Her heart sank when she saw him lying there on the ground. As the circle of townsfolk looked on, Grace looked away, her green eyes blinking back the hurt. Within her the seasons were already changing, and she could feel herself gearing up for a long, hard freeze.

As she glanced away she noticed the missionaries coming up from the river. She slipped back to watch. By now Grace had learned the newer one's name.

Williams. Elder Trust Williams.

She took his name as a good omen. With a name like Trust, he couldn't be all bad. From her vantage point in the hills, she had watched him closely over the last month. She knew he was struggling to fit in.

His brown hair and blue eyes were as familiar to her now as Lush Point or the Girth River.

Grace scolded herself for feeling like some kid with a crush. She wasn't going to fall for some missionary who would most likely leave in a couple months, never to come back. She was smarter than that.

The missionaries joined the circle of people looking over Feeble. Trust asked Grace's father about Feeble, and her father stated the obvious.

"He's moved on."

Grace followed the crowd as they walked into the boardinghouse. She stood behind Trust as he listened to old Briant Willpts prattle on.

She breathed in. Someone smelled nice. Pleasant body aroma was not something everyone around here had. She watched Trust as he listened to Briant stretching his story out long and tall. She could see Trust wasn't fooled.

She stepped a little closer. The ends of her red hair brushed against the back of Trust's arm. It was Trust who smelled nice.

She stepped back, turning to go. Maybe spring would come sooner than she thought.

12

HALF EMPTY, HALF FULL

There were no law officers in Thelma's Way. They had never really needed any. There had been no crime here until Paul pulled his stolen Book of Mormon stunt. I thought it would be good for someone in some sort of uniform to look into the missing Roswell, dead Feeble situation. But no one did. The closest thing was when Jerry Scotch, who worked at the Corndog Tent at the mall in Virgil's Find, showed up in his work outfit and pronounced the case closed.

Oh, the peace of mind.

I thought we should search the area for Roswell. People were offended, hurt, and confused by how disrespectful I could be of the so recently deceased. Elder Boone and I tried to get someone to toy with the idea that maybe, just maybe, Roswell had *not* been translated. Maybe he was alive somewhere, smoking his pipe or crying for his brother for all we knew, and that we should look for him. No go.

In the big collective consciousness of Thelma's Way, Roswell had been lifted up just like Briant said, and his brother Feeble had died of a heart attack running to catch up. I wrote President Clasp and asked him if it wouldn't be better for us to try to get these people to join another church so we wouldn't have to associate with them anymore.

We didn't really have a funeral for Roswell and Feeble. We had a ward service project. It took us all Saturday to dig holes big enough for the two of them. Thanks to some foresight Roswell and Feeble had grave plots already picked out. Two nice sites, right on the back edge of the cemetery, touching the river. I complained a lot about making anyone dig a grave for Roswell, seeing how there really was no body to bury. Folks began giving me a hard time about my lack of faith.

"John was translated; Enoch was translated."

Roswell was hardly an Enoch or a John.

"I bet *they* didn't have graves," I quipped.

"If you want to have people join the Church you had better start showing some appreciation for the spiritual things," Sister Yetch scolded.

"Roswell is not dead," I stated bluntly.

"Hush," Brother Heck intervened.

I continued to dig.

As missionaries we had clocked in an awful lot of service hours in Thelma's Way. It seemed as if the only time people wanted us around was when they needed help around the house. Digging the graves was just such an occasion. Everyone professed to love and admire Roswell

71

and Feeble, but the instant someone mentioned digging everyone suddenly had bad backs.

We finished the excavation (there's nothing else to call it when you're digging a grave for Feeble Ford), covered the coffins, and offered a dedicatory prayer. Instead of sending for headstones, Briant Willpts just had Roswell's and Feeble's porch chairs cemented to the ground at the head of their graves. A nice piece of granite can set you back a chunk of change, and besides, people would need a place to sit while visiting the twins. He figured he'd kill two birds with one stone. Pardon the expression.

Afterwards there was a small buffet in the boarding-house for those who had known the deceased, which, of course, would be everyone in town—except for maybe Joey Carver, Toby Carver's nearsighted brother who lived with their sister behind Lush Point. Joey spent his days making beautiful leather wallets that his sister took into Virgil's Find to sell. Word was he didn't particularly care for people. Everyone left him alone.

As it turned out, even nearsighted Joey knew the twins. He stood in front of me in the funeral buffet line. Things would have been a lot neater if I could have served myself first.

After everyone had finished eating, Sister Watson stood and proposed a toast.

"To the twins."

We all toasted.

"And to our future sesquicentennial pageant."

Most toasted.

"And to me, for having to rewrite whole sections of

'All Is Swell' seeing how Feeble is dead and won't be able to act."

Brother Watson raised his glass. Sister Watson sat down.

As I got into bed that night, I started to thank my Heavenly Father for everything I had. But then I got to thinking and decided I didn't have much. Maybe it was Feeble's death getting to me, or the town's refusal to believe Roswell might be alive. It seemed that my whole life I had planned for my mission. And now, here I was almost two months into it and I felt useless. I had hoped to be one of President Clasp's up-and-coming elders. I had hoped to be a district leader, or a zone leader, or a trainer. Instead, I was a big zero. I was lost in Thelma's Way. Lost and forgotten.

God needed to work with me.

13

A LITTLE
OFF THE TOP

◇

Six days a week we hiked the hills knocking on doors, teaching lessons to less-actives, and preaching to those who would lend us an ear. But every Monday was P-day. Preparation day. We would use our Mondays to do laundry over at the Watson house, go grocery shopping in Virgil's Find, and take care of all the things that didn't fall into our daily missionary routine.

It was Monday, and I was about to receive my first Thelma's Way haircut.

The last time I had gotten a cut was in the MTC right before I left for Tennessee. A tall man with big hands had buzzed off any and all pieces of hair foolish enough to grow longer than a quarter inch. But now my hair was starting to look shaggy. Something needed to be done.

Wad, the barber, was short, dark, and so weathered that it looked as if life had gnawed on him and spat him out.

His name suited him to a "T." His barber shop was an old outhouse shell that he had dragged down from his home once he had gotten indoor plumbing. It was filled with scissors and brushes.

When I showed up for my trim, he pulled a folding lawn chair out of his shack, planted it in the grass, set me down, and went to work. He wasn't shy about his work. He hovered around me like a wrinkled fly—buzzing and clipping as if his hands were intimately acquainted with my head.

For the full cut I was the center of the community. Everyone who walked by commented on what a good or bad job Wad was doing. Out in the open like that, I was fair game.

"He'd look better with more off the top," Toby Carver said on his way to the boardinghouse.

"It's uneven on the left," CleeDee Lipton advised, passing through the meadow.

"Not entirely symmetrical," Miss Flitrey, the school teacher, said as I sat there getting pieces of hair all over myself. Wad quickly took her comments into consideration.

The big secret, or the best known rumor around town, was that weathered old Wad had eyes for Miss Flitrey. He cut her hair for half the price he charged Sister Watson, used big educated words when he spoke to her, and would spend what some folks considered to be an inappropriate amount of time dusting her neck off with his softest brush after the do was done.

The guarded affection was reciprocated. Miss Flitrey

would bring baked goods to Wad and was presently tutoring him in math. Private lessons. Well, that is, if you consider the boardinghouse on a Saturday when the whole town is there watching television "private."

Miss Flitrey was a big, sturdy woman. She had taught school here in Thelma's Way for some twenty years. Her hair never looked the same, thanks to her frequent trips to Wad's scissors shack. She wasn't very tall, and her smile was like a comet—it appeared only once every hundred years and even then was difficult to spot. She was a workhorse and as stubborn a woman as I had ever met.

We had helped Miss Flitrey a couple of times at school by substitute teaching for her. It was a great way to give service to the community. Once when she had food poisoning, we filled in for a full day, teaching her school kids their times tables and alphabet. I would never forget how confused little Opie Wilford was as we sang the alphabet song. Every time we would sing the "l-m-n-O-P" part he would glance around nervously, thinking we were calling his name. I had the students sing the song a few extra times just so I could watch his reaction. Actually, his response had been the first indication to me that my heart was changing.

Don't get me wrong. I still wanted to be transferred out. But for the first time I was seeing these folks as the kind, simple, big-hearted people that they were. Maybe they didn't all have aspirations to own large homes. Maybe they weren't working towards owning a boat and a new pair of water skis. No, these people did things like put up chicken wire, chop wood, and shoot the breeze until the air was fatally wounded.

Wad snipped around my right ear.

"You liking it here?" he asked me.

"Sure," I replied. "What's not to like?"

Elder Boone was sitting on the ground next to the pile of old magazines Wad would put out for his waiting customers to read. He looked at me as if I were pulling Wad's leg.

"I like it here," I defended.

"Beautiful country," Wad said, "beautiful country. Makes a man want to take up painting."

I nodded in agreement. Wad jerked my head back, bothered by my moving it around.

"I've always dreamed of trying my hand at painting. I've got the artistic touch, you know. Right now, however, your head is my only canvas."

"Thank you, I think," I said.

"You've got such lovely hair, too," he went on. "So thick, so soft. My fingers love to touch it. Look at my fingers rejoicing," he said as his fingers celebrated within my hair.

I was about to tell him to please have his fingers rejoice elsewhere, when he set down his scissors and brushed me off.

"Well, you're done. What do you think?" He handed me a small mirror to look at myself.

My eyes were still blue, and my nose was still centered. Oh, and my hair was short.

Tindy MacDermont was strolling by as I stood up.

"Looks good, Wad," she complimented.

Wad sort of curtsied.

I offered to pay him, but he refused.

"I like to help out the missionaries," he blushed.

"How about coming out to church then?" I asked kindly.

"I sleep in on Sundays," he said, making his excuse and suddenly acting overly busy while putting his tools away.

"Church doesn't start until twelve-thirty," I rebutted.

"Like I said," he said, "I sleep in on Sundays."

Elder Boone and I headed over to the boardinghouse so I could use the shower and wash off all the tiny hairs that would otherwise stick into me for days. The town decided to turn the boardinghouse into a sort of co-op. Roswell and Feeble had left no will. Since the funeral, Briant Willpts had moved in to keep things going, but Briant had no objection to us using the facilities.

"We're never going to reactivate these people," I mourned, referring to Wad.

"Never's a long time," Elder Boone replied.

He was right.

14

A-LOT-O-LANCE

◇

Lucy liked Lance. Their relationship was so easy. It didn't require a lot of depth or thought for her to be with him. Lucy liked that. Trust had been so enamored with her that he was constantly trying to talk about important things, trying to sound more interesting.

Lance, however, didn't need to talk to be interesting.

Not that Lance wasn't as enamored with Lucy as Trust was, it was just that Lance expressed it so much more elegantly.

Gifts.

Yes, in Lucy's eyes Lance was about as close to being perfect as a man could be. He had wealth, reputation, and stunning good looks. True, he wasn't a Mormon, but Lucy felt she needed to become a better person by looking beyond that.

"Didn't someone once say 'every member a missionary'?" Lucy asked herself.

Well, Lucy felt she was doing the lioness' share by

continuing to be with Lance, and by setting such a high standard. Lucy made the Mormons look good.

Trust would understand, Lucy reasoned.

After all, Trust was also about the work. Lucy was simply doing her part. Could Lucy help it if Lance was right, and ready to harvest?

15

THE ROAD TO DON'T-ASK-US

◈

THREE AND ONE-HALF MONTHS

The path from Thelma's Way to Virgil's Find was remarkably unspectacular. For hundreds of years it had served as the townsfolk's only way in and out. And for hundreds of years no one had made a single improvement or upgrade to it. Despite the number of bare feet and dirty shoes that had traversed its dusty sprawl, it still remained nothing more than a skinny brown line that lay as a lazy guide from Virgil's Find to Thelma's Way, or more appropriately, to nowhere.

The people had petitioned the state for a road, but in the entire town there were only two registered voters: Sister Watson and Feeble Ford, now deceased. The state politicians didn't see Thelma's Way as a vehicle that would further their political careers. They saw it as an unknown pock concealed by forest, pleasantly forgotten by anyone who was anybody outside of Thelma's Way. Besides, turning the path into a road would require backhoes and dump trucks and risked offending the local environmentalists who wished to keep the parts of Tennessee that they didn't actually live in personally in their somewhat natural state.

Virgil's Find was a good-sized town with all the amenities that Thelma's Way was short on—movies, a mall, and plenty of paved main and minor roads. Its growth had covered what was once a big chunk of rural Tennessee, libraries replacing barns, banks replacing bars, and supermarkets replacing ranches and forcing the wannabe cowboys to spend their Friday nights sitting atop the grocery cart corrals, wishing for what once was well before their time.

We had to hike into Virgil's Find at least once a week. Thelma's Way just didn't have it all; in fact it hardly had any. It was a pain having to walk four miles to buy deodorant. The path was always either too muddy or too dusty. I wished for a road or a real trail. I wished for a legitimate out. I wanted a couple of well-marked exits, someplace where the ground was striped with black asphalt and orange dotted lines, with cars whizzing past me. Sure, Leo Tip had a car in Thelma's Way, but it didn't really count. Leo had built his car piece by piece, packing in old rusted parts from the Virgil's Find auto salvage yard, and assembling them in the dirt lot next to the school. Eventually, Leo had himself a real working automobile. Actually, what Leo had was four wheels hooked together by two bucket seats and a lumpy engine that ran only when it wasn't raining and if you greased the spark plug before you turned the starter over. It wasn't much to look at, but it did run, and Leo held his head high, perched in that bucket of bolts. It didn't matter that there were only about two hundred yards of actual dirt road in Thelma's Way. On a nice day Leo would drive that two hundred yards back and forth and around the boardinghouse again and again. At a cruising speed of five miles an hour he would wave at the local kids and nod at the occasional passerby who was usually walking faster than his piecemeal transportation could even go. If you were really lucky and caught Leo in an excessively unselfish mood he would pull up right next to you and pat the passenger side seat invitingly. I had yet to be invited.

I had less of a chance now then ever, seeing how Leo had cut back on his driving time ever since he had begun courting CleeDee Lipton. CleeDee didn't like the feel of the wind against her extra-sensitive face. CleeDee chapped easy. At five miles an hour, a stagnant breeze could suck every bit of moisture out of her chalky mug and leave her scaly and unable to smile. And, as even the most ignorant local knew, CleeDee's best and only feature was her smile.

The only other motor vehicle in Thelma's Way was Digby Heck's ancient dirt bike. Teddy Yetch had given it to him the year before on his sixteenth birthday. Teddy was too old to ride on it any longer—operating the clutch did a number on her arthritis, and the vibrating of the engine caused her teeth to slip out.

Digby loved it. There was only one problem: Digby had tiny ears. Sunglasses just wouldn't stay on his face as he rode. He tried taping eyewear on, but pulling the tape off all the time was making him prematurely bald.

Well, necessity gave birth to one odd invention. Inspired by a bowl of leftover casserole in his family's refrigerator, Digby went down to the Virgil's Find Shop and Save and bought him a couple of rolls of clear plastic Saran Wrap. A stroke of pure genius. Digby simply wrapped it around the top half of his head, covering his open eyes and voila, his sensitive peepers were protected. His mother even made him a little leather pouch that hooked onto the handlebars and held an economy-sized roll of the wrap. It was quite a sight to have Digby pull up next to you, his hair matted down by the wrap and his wide brown eyes pressed completely open.

At the moment, Elder Boone and I were on the path on our way to Virgil's Find to attend zone conference with President Clasp. I always liked getting out of Thelma's Way and meeting with other elders. Since the meeting would run late, Elder Boone and I had made plans to stay the night with Elder Minert and Elder Nicks in Virgil's Find.

We were about half-way there when we spotted an unknown person coming the other way. Having been in Thelma's Way for over three months, I thought I had at least seen most of the locals, but I didn't recognize this gentleman. He had dark black hair that didn't bounce or move as he walked, making it look like he was wearing a helmet. He wore a flannel shirt, blue jeans, and boots that topped off well above his ankles. His straight nose and tiny brown eyes looked silly the way they were placed on his face, as if God had decided to try something different and arrange his features unevenly. His big mouth gaped open to a smile as we came near to him.

He stopped in front of us, in the middle of the trail. He folded his arms in front of him. Not thinking much of it, Elder Boone and I broke to go around him, but he stretched out his arms to hold us back.

"Excuse us," I said politely as I tried to walk around.

"Do you know who you're talking to?" he asked, and without waiting for an answer, "I shall be recognized."

"I'm Elder Williams," I said, sticking my hand out.

"You are a child," he snipped, refusing to shake my hand. "I am an adult. Show some respect."

I think he wanted me to bow to him or something.

Elder Boone gave it a go.

"I'm—"

"Can't you see the light around me?" he interrupted. "Can't you?"

We both looked at each other and shrugged.

"Of course you can't," he sizzled. "You're numb to the spirit, and withered on the bush. Lock horns and be gone."

The clear doctrine, the compassionate delivery, the feeling of utter and complete peace. I suddenly knew who I was talking to.

"Paul?" I asked. "Paul Leeper?"

"The truth has been manifest unto you. Drink and go home bloated," he blessed me.

This was Paul. I was standing before apostate Paul. The havoc-wreaking, Book-of-Mormon-stealing, town-splitting, lies-spewing, reason-I'm-now-in-Thelma's Way, archenemy Paul. Larger than life, yet at least three inches shorter than I.

Elder Boone gritted his teeth. "You're Paul?" he asked.

Paul sort of curtsied.

"The Paul that went to Rome?"

"Saw the finger," Paul boomed, pulling out a postcard from his back pocket and flashing it before our view. The post card was worn and bent, but you could still see the finger, encased in glass, looking as if it were just floating in midair. Paul smiled smugly.

What Paul didn't know was that I had done my homework. About three P-days ago, Elder Boone and I had gone into Virgil's Find to do some grocery shopping, and we stopped by the public library to find out if they really did have the finger of Thomas on display at the Vatican. I found out that there was a finger on display, but that most real scholars didn't believe it was actually Thomas's finger. For all practical purposes it was probably some common schmo who had lost his finger dicing up beets and then discovered his loose digit could make him a few bucks.

I told this to Paul. Surprisingly, he was not at all grateful for having been enlightened. His face turned red and his hair actually seemed to darken.

"You're him," he said suddenly, holding his trembling hand over his big open mouth and pointing at me with the other. "You are the detractor I prophesied about."

"Now wait a second," Elder Boone jumped in. "When did you prophesy about—"

"Elder Williams," Paul interrupted. He had a hard time

letting others get a word in edgewise. He looked at my name tag and gasped.

"Williams. Moments ago as I was walking, I was prophesying to myself, and voices told me to beware of a coming detractor for he would do the will of the underworld." He stepped back for dramatic effect. "Williams . . . Will . . . Will of the Underworld."

I tried not to smile.

"Will of the Underworld," he screamed, his misplaced eyes bulging from his head. Then again, more quietly, as if he were pronouncing a title upon me. "Will of the Underworld."

He kept repeating the phrase in a gradual crescendo as he scrambled off the trail and into the forest.

Elder Boone and I just stood there for a moment.

"Nice guy," Elder Boone joked, breaking the silence.

"Wow, I feel so important," I said.

"Will of the Underworld," he said, and he bowed.

We made it to Virgil's Find without anymore incidents, unless, of course, you consider forty-year-old Ed Washington running past us wearing nothing but shorts and shoes and yelling for his mother, an incident.

16

GERONIMO

◇

Grace had been fine with her life.

All right, that wasn't completely true. She had a few concerns. Growing up in Thelma's Way had not always been easy. There had been times she wanted to strike it out on her own. She dreamed about traveling to distant countries. She thought about college, out-of-state, anything that was a ticket out.

It wasn't that she was embarrassed by her heritage; she just wanted to try something new, something better.

On the other hand, Grace liked things simple. She sometimes felt it should be enough that God had given her a brain to think with, two legs for walking, the forest around her for beauty, and the Virgil's Find public library. Things could be worse and she knew it. She shouldn't be waiting around for handouts.

But Trust Williams in Thelma's Way was something like a handout.

He was different from the rest. Her whole life Grace had been able to see into people's heads, get vague impressions of their thoughts. Trust was a stranger; his mind was harder to view, but the slivers she caught glimpses of were promising. No doubt he sensed he had fallen off the back of the planet landing in Thelma's Way, and he was right. But there was something within him that cared, whether he knew it or not, something willing to learn. It was honesty. She was giving him the benefit of the doubt.

Grace had yet to meet Trust face-to-face. She knew he wouldn't be stationed in Thelma's Way for long, not if Paul could have his way. He was currently going about door to door with that nonsense about the "Will of the Underworld." Paul must have sensed it too. Trust Williams was a threat.

Grace had never really cared for Paul and his lying ways. Others in town seemed willing to let it slide. He had, after all, wooed away two-thirds of the local branch. Sure, they had deserted him after he stole that Book of Mormon, but Grace wasn't so sure he couldn't do it again.

She opened the door to her hidden cabin and walked inside. She placed some wildflowers in a vase on the table. She set her books on her chair. She had promised herself that she wouldn't go back to church until the missionaries were gone, but she was considering breaking her vow. She could get a better glimpse of Trust at church. She had to find out more about him before it was too late, didn't she?

Then she thought better of it. What possible future

could there be for her with some rule-bound missionary from far away?

"Grow up, Grace," she scolded herself. "It's all or nothing with you. Only heaven can intervene."

And heaven has a way of taking its own sweet time.

17

THE INTRODUCTION OF GRACE

MONTH SIX

Reports came in. Paul was using his "Will of the Underworld" prophecy to try to scare people into avoiding me. CleeDee had been walking across the meadow when Paul all but materialized from behind a clump of grass.

"Will of the Underworld," he told her, pointing to our cabin. "Will of the Underworld. Beware."

He was trying to scare us, too. He wrote threatening things in the dirt in front of our cabin and threw rocks at the outhouse when I was in it. He pinned notes to our door with hieroglyphic scribbles on them. I later found out from Pap Wilson that Paul was working on his own alphabet and language.

I could think of a few words I would like him to translate.

The town had held another sesquicentennial planning meeting a few weeks back. Things were still moving along slowly. Sister Watson had not yet completed the actual script. She claimed her work with P.I.G. was really blocking the creative inspiration that this particular pageant required. Toby had finished the blueprints of the stage, and Patty Heck had begun sewing some costumes. I was starting to see the wisdom in allowing so much lead time before the actual play. This town moved slowly.

Summer had become winter, and winter was trying to outdo itself—flexing its cold, hard muscles and smiling its brittle teeth. The days had become shorter but felt longer. The nights had grown lengthy, and yet it seemed as if my head barely hit the pillow before morning poked its obnoxious nose around. Like the seasons, my soul was locking up. I didn't feel like I was becoming the missionary I should be. I needed to try harder. I felt as if the only thing I had to show for myself were my worn-out shoes and the beginnings of a backwoods accent.

Bishop Watson and Brother Heck were doing a pretty good job of holding our fifteen or so members together. They missed the Parley P. Pratt first-edition Book of Mormon that had sat as the ward's keystone and foundation for so many years, but they were coping.

Sister Watson and the members of P.I.G. had made a formal request of Paul asking for the book's return. They had offered to forgive him of all wrongdoing if he would simply give it back. They invited Paul over to the boardinghouse where they all gathered around a couple of long banquet tables. Sister Watson placed an empty basket next to a plate of cookies that Sister Teddy Yetch had brought for after the meeting. The members of P.I.G. told Paul they would turn off the lights and then, under cover of darkness, whoever had stolen the Book of Mormon could place it in the empty basket and be done with it.

Sister Watson turned off the lights. There were sounds of movement and shifting. She quickly flicked the lights back on. The basket was still empty and now Teddy's cookies were missing. Everyone sat there with full mouths as Sister Watson looked on in disgust. Well, if she had been disgusted by them all swiping cookies, she must have been even more grossed out when, moments later, everyone's taste buds told them to abort. People began spitting and coughing as they tried to obliterate the taste of Teddy's Spicy Raisin Mustard Snaps. Teddy, of course, went home offended, and the Book of Mormon was no closer to being back where it belonged.

One personal mission discovery so far was the realization that my mother had a weird flare for sending creative care packages. Mom and I were close, but sometimes I didn't feel like she really knew me. Part of the problem was that she was fairly timid and reserved. The moment any real emotion began to surface, she would scurry away like a frightened lizard. At last, it seemed, she had found a way to express herself.

She sent me new shoes, and old shoes other people in the ward no longer wanted. Forget the fact that most of them weren't my size. I guess she knew we were really hard on our footwear. She sent me cookies by the pound, and big posters with cute animals saying positive things. She sent me can after can of bug repellent, and notebooks filled with photocopied crossword puzzles and dot-to-dots for those times when I was discouraged. I had already completed most of the puzzles—discouragement was a familiar feeling these days.

We were finding work to do, but it was busy work, unproductive work. I had all my discussions memorized down cold due to the fact that I had given them to every inactive who would lend an ear. Despite the distraction of Paul, people apparently still liked hearing me ramble. Time and time again they would invite my companion and me over to present the discussions. Then, when we had taught them and challenged them to commit to Christ and become more active, they'd ask us if we had any free videos (which most of them couldn't even play) and shoo us out the door.

Thankfully, we had one person in our teaching pool. We were working with automotive expert Leo Tip. He was twenty years old and had been raised in a Mormon home. His father had passed away years ago, and his mother had died just last spring. He lived alone in a rather large house up on top of Lush Point, a small hill that overlooked the meadow. His father had invented a twisty wire with which you could tie off rope or cord. The invention was called "The Pincher." Leo had shown me one once. I thought it greatly resembled a garbage-bag twist tie, but what did I know? Anyhow, Leo still received small royalty checks in the mail every month from the sales of his father's invention.

Leo had never been baptized into the Mormon church because his father was a rather large man who didn't feel comfortable getting wet in white clothes. And instead of getting someone else to baptize their son, the Tips just kept on postponing it until Father Leo lost weight. Well, the size of his grave plot in the Tip family corner of the cemetery stands in testimony to the fact that Brother Tip never did master the weight issue. After his passing, talk of Leo getting baptized never came up again—that is, until we were going over the ward records with Bishop Watson and discovered that, technically, Leo was still not a member—a real, live, honest-to-goodness nonmember right there in Thelma's Way. It was a glimmer of hope.

The glimmer was fleeting.

Leo humored us by letting us teach him, but really he had his heart set on waiting until the next life where he knew his father would be thin and then having him perform the baptism. I tried to explain that things didn't work that way, but there was no budging him. It was a family thing. I was confused.

On the personal side, things were equally confusing. Lucy was writing me less frequently, and in her last letter she had dropped the name of some guy named Lance.

. . . *my car is being serviced, but Lance has been kind enough to drive me to and fro. I don't know what I'd do without him.*

That was all she had said, but I was now in utter despair over her state of mind concerning me. Was this Lance some ninety-year-old uncle who had nothing to do but drive his niece around? Maybe he was a fifteen-year-old kid who had just gotten his driver's permit and needed someone to ride along with him as he gained experience. Or maybe it was some creep gaining experience of a different kind. Lucy was *my* girl. I knew that, and I had worked most of my life to get her to at least think about knowing it. I could feel our would-be relationship crumbling.

Things looked grim.

Elder Boone had obviously been living more righteously than I, because he had received a transfer out. It came; he went; and now I was companions with Elder Sims.

Elder Sims was short, quiet, and bossy. He had the charisma of a well-groomed dirt clod. He rarely spoke any louder than a mumble, and he insisted on never being more than a foot and a half away from me. He was from New Plymouth, Idaho, a town not too much bigger than Thelma's Way. I was having a terribly hard time getting along with him. He seemed to flutter around me like a mumbling pest.

It was late January in Thelma's Way and, I suppose, in the rest of the world as well. We had gotten a little snow and lots of cold. The ground was brown and white, but the evergreen trees and bushes kept their color all year long in Thelma's Way. The meadow was dead, blanketed only in snow and checkered with footprints and trails.

I looked out our front door at the dark meadow. It was late in the evening, and Elder Sims and I had just finished our companion study. We had read a potpourri of scriptures all with the common theme of enduring to the end. I was feeling discouraged. This was not how I had imagined my mission would be. I felt like I had been cubby-holed. Set aside. President Clasp had simply put me here and was now refusing to deal with me until later.

These people, bless their souls, were no more interested in coming back to full activity than I was in picking out a plot here and settling down. We had taught countless discussions and new-member lessons, eaten with these people, mended their fences, plowed their grounds, canned their food, and baby-sat their children; all with zero results. People saw us as nothing more than two kind boys with way better clothes than they had. Besides, with so few non-members, it was hard not to feel we lacked real missionary purpose.

Bishop Watson was somewhat helpful, and Brother Heck was supportive to a point. But both of them were pretty much resigned to the fact that things would never get better.

"Let's wait until the Lord comes," Brother Heck said. "He'll straighten things out."

It was useless. I kept writing President Clasp and suggesting that perhaps he should close the area. We were doing no good. We could serve better someplace else.

Elder Sims came up and stood behind me as I looked out the door at the black night.

"It's dark," he commented.

"I'm going to go pray," I said.

Elder Sims frowned.

There was an old tree stump behind our house that I used to pray on. It wasn't the most comfortable place to kneel, but I could be alone. The little window at the back of our cabin looked out over the stump so my companion could keep a constant eye on me. Elder Sims would watch me go out the front door and then follow me so he could see me walk along the length of the cabin. Then he would run back inside and up to the rear window so that he only had me out of his sight for a couple of seconds.

I would pray for hours out at that stump just so I could have some space. And always when I would look up, there would be Elder Sims, his face pressed against the back window, keeping a constant vigil on me. It was unnerving, or comforting, depending on the definition of those two words. Elder Boone had been big on always getting up on time—that was his favorite rule. Elder Sims was big on the never-let-your-companion-out-of-your-sight rule. I knew it made him nervous to have me out of his view for even an instant. In his mind it must have been possible to do all the worst sins and a couple of the minor ones in a blink of the eye.

I walked out of our place and headed towards the stump, grateful just to be out of the house. Elder Sims followed me and then scurried back inside to watch me through the back window. It was a dark and cold night. A light snow had begun to fall. I had on my coat and gloves—I was bundled up for as long a prayer as it was going to take for me to feel right with the world again.

I knelt down and poured my heart out over the cold snow. The words came easily, even if they didn't make a lot of sense. I prayed for warmer weather, but thanked God for the cold that kept the bugs down. I thanked Him for the chance to serve, and begged for the chance to serve elsewhere. I prayed for patience to endure Elder Sims, but asked for a new companion.

There was a dull sensation of time passing. Every once in a while I would hear Elder Sims tapping on the glass, which did nothing but increase my resolve to lose myself in prayer. And lose myself, I did.

I can't remember falling asleep, but when I woke up my body was shaking. I was covered from head to toe with a two-inch blanket of snow, but through the snow muffling my ears, I could hear a voice.

"Wake up. You'll freeze out here."

I murmured, mumbled, and shooed.

The voice shook and spoke louder, a new sense of cold creeping over my sleeping body.

"Get up. You'll sleep yourself to death."

I opened my tired, cold eyes. My head was still resting on my arms. There were about two inches of snow covering me. I wanted to stand and shake myself off, but I could barely move. I had drooled into my arms and it was now frozen and sticking to my face. My legs were not only asleep, they had gone into hibernation. I tried to will them back to life.

"You've got to get up," the voice said again. "We need to get you warm."

I managed to move my drool-caked face a little to the right to see who was speaking to me. I felt like "Slobbery," the eighth and unknown dwarf as I stared up into the moonlight.

It had to be about two o'clock in the morning. The snow had stopped, and a huge moon was hovering over the layer of clouds that were resting just above the ground. The moon lit the gray clouds with a soft white. Here and there a ray of moonlight had poked through and was kneading the new snow on the ground with its bright hands. One of those beams of light was resting on whoever it was that had woken me and perhaps saved my life.

From where I knelt she looked tall. She had on leather boots. She was wearing a big wool coat with a hood over her head, and red hair spilled out from beneath it in such amounts that I could barely see her face. The moonlight made her look like a ghost, or an angel.

"Who . . ."

She didn't let me finish. She grabbed me by the arm and pulled me up. My legs cracked in protest. She helped me brush snow off of myself. I suddenly remembered Elder Sims. I looked towards the window and there he was, staring at me with closed eyelids. I assumed he was asleep. Had he been awake, he would have already screamed and run out to rescue me from this girl.

She helped me walk back around our cabin and to the front door. She pushed open the door, and I could see that she wasn't wearing gloves. She had long fingers that seemed to flutter as she moved them. With the sound of the door opening, Elder Sims was instantly at attention. His mouth gaped large enough to cram a cantaloupe into it.

"Elder," he screamed, being more vocal than I had ever heard him.

I thought he was concerned for my health. I thought he

was worried about my frozen condition. I thought he could see that I was mangled and shivering.

But all he could say was, "You're with a girl!"

The oil lamp was still burning, keeping the cabin nice and bright. I turned my head to get a better look at her. She stood just inside the door, her right hand holding my left elbow. Her coat was wet with snow, and her cheeks were red with cold. She tried to turn away as I gazed at her.

She wasn't beautiful, but she wasn't ugly either. She had dark green eyes, and her skin was pale, unlike anything I had ever seen before. She didn't smile. There was something mysterious about her. Maybe it was just that my neck was stiff and I was staring at her crookedly. Her large coat made her look big, but the tiny bit of shin showing just above her boots and below her coat told the real story.

"What are you doing with a girl?" Elder Sims asked. He was flustered and concerned.

"I fell asleep while I was praying and she woke me up," I explained.

"You were sleeping," he moaned.

"It was an accident."

"Most sins are."

I turned to my visitor to say "Sorry, he's nuts," but she was gone. There was nothing but an empty door and the chill of the night.

"Where'd she go?" I said, almost to myself.

Elder Sims answered me by running and closing the door. He latched it, locked it, and then stood with his back against it as if he alone were keeping all evil at bay.

"I knew I shouldn't have let you pray alone," he mumbled. "I knew it."

I walked over to the stove, put two logs onto the dying embers, and then stood there shivering and trying to warm myself up. Heat slowly escaped the old iron stove as it sweated and crackled, the new logs giving it a fresh fire in the belly.

"I'm going to write President Clasp," Elder Sims informed me.

"Tell him hi," I said.

I knew that I should be kinder. I knew I owed him an explanation. I owed him an apology. I knew all this, but I chose to ignore it, at least until morning, maybe until one of us got transferred. I was cold, cranky, and intrigued by the mysterious girl who had just helped me. After about fifteen minutes, I crawled into bed. Elder Sims still sat there on his bed scribbling away. President Clasp was going to receive one long letter.

Good, I thought as I drifted off to sleep. Maybe my companion's concerns would get me transferred. It struck me, however, that I wasn't as gung-ho to leave Thelma's Way as I had once been.

Odd.

Very odd.

I fell asleep seeing red.

18

SEEK AND SEEK

In the morning, I sat down to a breakfast of cold cereal and bread. Elder Sims sat down next to me. He had already eaten.

"Who is she?" he demanded.

"I don't know," I answered.

"How long have you two been meeting?"

"I'd never met her before."

Elder Sims guffawed. "Come on, Elder," he said. "I *am* the senior companion."

This was true. I had hoped after Elder Boone had been transferred that I would get to be a senior companion, perhaps even train a new elder, but instead Elder Sims was sent here to be my big brother and leader. It was his position to call all the shots.

"I've known her for about four months," I lied.

"And?" Elder Sims prodded, ready for the sordid details he had already imagined.

"And that's not the truth. I just met her last night."

He *arrged*.

"What's her name?" he asked harshly.

"I don't know."

"Is she Mormon?" he demanded.

"I don't know."

He sat up in his chair.

"Holding back potential investigators?" he asked, even more furious. "Waiting until I get transferred so you can teach her and count her as your own?"

"What?" I asked, amazed. "Listen. I fell asleep while praying last night and she woke me up and brought me in. That's it."

Elder Sims watched me chew and swallow a big bite of cereal.

"So, is that your secret meeting place?" he finally asked.

"I've never met her before," I said, exasperated.

"Do you pull the blinds down over the window to signal her to meet you there?"

This was ridiculous.

"We don't have blinds on our windows."

"Do you stand in front of the windows then, and flash hand signals or maybe do some sort of love dance?"

"Elder," I demanded.

"At least I'm fit to wear the title," he said, standing up. "I'm now going to kneel and pray for you."

I watched him kneel beside his bed and ask for forgiveness for me. I tried to be appreciative. I had a lot of things I needed forgiveness for, but the situation last night was not one of them.

When he was done, he got up and wanted a hug. I

refused. We read D&C section 132 together and then headed out.

Snow had covered everything. Our shoes crunched as we stepped along. We stopped off at the boardinghouse to say hello to whoever might be there. Despite the cold, Ed Washington and old Briant Willpts were sitting outside on the porch arguing about how many inches had fallen.

Elder Sims and I stopped and made a little bit of small talk with the two of them. Then I asked, "Are there many folks around here with red hair?"

Elder Sims shot me a dirty look.

"Now, let's see," Ed thought. "Toby's got red hair on his arms but black on his head."

"Other way around," Briant corrected. "Other way around."

"Don't mother me," Ed warned him.

Ed had a rather bad mother complex. Sister Washington refused to let him be his own man. Though he was about forty years old, he still lived at home and at her beck and call. Ed had thick hair that left him no forehead and no neck.

"What about women?" I asked.

"Don't know much about them," Briant admitted.

"No, what about women with red hair?" I clarified.

"I suppose they act similar to those with black or brown hair."

This was pointless.

Elder Sims grabbed my arm and pulled me off the porch.

"We've got work to do," he said to Ed and Briant.

We walked across the meadow to Bishop Watson's home. Sister Watson was the only one in at the moment. She was working on the infamous pageant script. The Watsons had no children and ran a little mail-order business out of their home. They sold handmade soap in fancy handmade packaging. Sister Watson made the soap, and Bishop Watson packaged it up and delivered it to Virgil's Find, where it was sent out around the world. Their house always smelled like lye.

Sister Watson invited us in and gave us a half a chicken that she and her husband hadn't been able to finish off. I took the wrapped chicken and put it into my backpack. We had been meeting with the Watsons and challenging them to pray for one of their friends so that the Spirit might soften their hearts and prepare them for us to come over and help reactivate them. Sister Watson was pretty nervous about forcing us upon one of her inactive friends. She claimed she was being more courteous than coward. I explained to her that her husband was the bishop and that it was their responsibility as well as ours to reactivate these people. She told me that she would feel more comfortable just waving at them when she walked by their homes. The ward was doomed.

"Maybe when you're talking to people about the sesqui-centennial pageant, you could also encourage them to come out to church," I suggested.

"I never mix politics with religion," she replied.

"It's not really politics," I pointed out.

"I guess you don't understand all the behind the scenes work this pageant involves. There's a definite underbelly to it. Lots of lobbying and politicking. I had to give Mindy at the Virgil's Find library two free bars of soap in order for her to hang our flier on the community bulletin board."

As we were leaving Sister Watson's home, I worked up the nerve to ask.

"Are there many women with red hair around here?"

Sister Watson just stared at me. "Is that anything for a missionary to be concerned about?" she asked, her mouth open but not moving as she spoke.

"Well, I was—"

Interrupted.

"Forgive my companion," Elder Sims jumped in. "He had a rather late night."

Sister Watson adjusted her wig as if she were tipping her hat to us. Then we stepped outside and headed up the hill towards the Heck home. We were giving the lessons to Narlette. She was about to turn eight and be baptized, and her folks felt it would be good for her to have a better understanding of the gospel.

Brother Heck was doing all right. He had had a tobacco relapse about two months previous, but nothing since then. Elder Boone and I had had to stop him from digging his own grave in an attempt to bury himself alive. It was a close call.

We reached the Heck home and knocked on the door. Sister Patty Heck let us in. The Hecks had a nice house. It was clean, fairly modern, and big. Sister Heck worked for a laundromat in Virgil's Find. She did all of their altering and specialty mending. Once a week she would hike into town and pick up a bundle of clothes. Then she would haul them back home and work on them. She was a master seamstress. There was not a pattern she would not attempt, conquer, and then somehow improve. She made all her family's clothes, was in charge of the costumes for the sesquicentennial pageant, repaired the Thelma's Way official flag after it was struck by lightning, and stitched up Digby after their dog, Limpy, bit him.

She was a small woman with a big head, and she always wore a skirt and a determined look on her face. She had a way of looking past you. It was as if she were constantly looking over your shoulder at something far more interesting and important. She had long, dark hair and strong, tiny hands. She wasn't mean, but she wasn't necessarily nice. She was a neutral personality. She was Sister Patty Heck. She was asking us to sit.

Elder Sims and I sat down on their couch and waited for Narlette. Narlette was one of the many mountain kids who was home schooled. Her parents took her out of school a few years back after Miss Flitrey suggested that Narlette's own relatives might have been descended from apes.

The very idea.

The Hecks felt personally insulted. Sister Heck waited by the phone for an apology, but it never came. (Miss Flitrey was not one to back down.) So now, thanks to a large amount of righteous indignation and her own hard-earned G.E.D., Sister Heck was home schooling her children. The responsibility added immensely to her already hectic schedule, but she managed to find time between cuffing and mending. She also discovered that kids could learn while working. Narlette was improving her math by keeping her mother's books; and her older brother, Digby, had won first prize in the Heck family science fair for his assigned experiment of painting the porch to see if that would improve its resistance to rain.

Yes, home schooling was working out just fine for the Hecks. Brother Heck even helped out when he could, his livelihood providing him with a rather flexible schedule. Brother Heck, like so many others here in town, did odd jobs. He fixed roofs for food, repaired appliances for clothes, and dug trenches for a little spending money. He sold eggs at the Virgil's Find farmers' market and blood at the regional blood bank.

Narlette came downstairs and joined us in the living room. The lesson went rather well up until the point when Narlette lost all interest and began singing to herself as we taught. She kept getting louder until we gave up. I closed with my testimony and a challenge for her to read her scriptures with her family. She said she would and would we care to see the scar she had procured by falling off the old burnt Girth River bridge.

Fair trade.

As Sister Heck served us an early lunch of peas and ham, I decided to probe just one more time for information concerning my visitor last night.

"So," I said, "you must know just about everyone around here."

"Pride myself on being familiar with the community," she replied, passing me a big bowl of white gravy.

"There are a lot of different-looking people around

here," I declared, my observation sounding meaner than I had meant it to.

"God may not have put the best-looking folks here in the meadow, but he made them sturdy and simple."

Now she was on the offensive.

"What I mean is that there are a lot of different colors of hair."

Sister Heck, Narlette, and Elder Sims just stared at me as if I were dumb. I shoved a bunch of cold ham in my mouth, hoping to choke myself to death.

Sister Heck decided it would be best to change the subject.

"Do you elders think you'll have a baptism soon?"

My full mouth restricted me from speaking.

"Leo Tip is interested," Elder Sims replied.

"Leo will never go under," Sister Heck informed us. "He's permanently dry. Too much love for material things."

We took a few minutes to silently enjoy our meal.

"There's not a lot of people with red hair around here," I finally spoke up, hoping to steer the conversation back to where I wanted it.

Sister Heck eyed me suspiciously.

Narlette snickered. "Grace's got red hair."

"Grace?" I asked, feeling my heart rate quicken.

"Our daughter," Sister Heck clarified.

I had forgotten that the Hecks had an older daughter whom I had never met. She was sort of a local enigma. She was kindly spoken of, but in the last while she had become reclusive, adjusting to womanhood by pulling away. At least that was Toby Carver's assessment.

"Where is she?" I wondered aloud.

"Who knows," Sister Heck replied. "Silly girl keeps herself hidden up in the hills. Spends too much time in Virgil's Find."

"Doing what?" I questioned.

"They got that big library there. Books 'bout everything," Sister Heck informed me. "I think Grace is more comfortable by herself."

"Anyone else with red hair?" I asked casually.

"Not really anyone else," Sister Heck chewed. "Except old Randall down at Triplet Cove, below the falls. Of course, his hair is falling out faster than it's growing."

Digby came bounding down the stairs.

"I'm going out," he announced, ripping off a sheet of Saran Wrap and preparing to cover his eyes.

"Don't be gone too long," Sister Heck said. "You've got homework."

I guess there was something that still needed to be painted or repaired around their house. Digby blinked at us through all that plastic film and took off.

We left the Hecks and headed up to Leo's place on the top of Lush Point. Lush Point was so named because years ago Grandfather Leeper, apostate Paul's grandfather, had decided that the Word of Wisdom was an item-by-item restriction and it didn't list moonshine. So he set up a few stills on the hillside and brewed the stuff for about two years before the folks in town would no longer tolerate it.

It was a particularly boring time in Thelma's Way history. Pretty much everyone was doing what they should be doing—everyone except Grandfather Leeper, that is. With so many idle hands twitching about, they decided to stamp out Grandfather Leeper's stills. Done under the guise of a ward activity, they all brought bats and beat the heck out of Grandfather Leeper's equipment. Then they gathered down in the meadow for a light supper and poetry reading. The moonshine seepage made the grass grow wild and green and gave the place its name—Lush Point.

Grandfather Leeper had passed away years earlier, and his son had also gone the way of dust. Now the only remaining Leeper was Paul, and he had left Lush Point to live across the river. So far he, too, had not done the family name any favors.

Leo let us into his house and asked us to sit down. It was now around noon and obvious that Leo had just gotten up for the day. He wore a large nightshirt with a picture of Garfield the Cat on it, and his hair was sticking up and down all over. Leo had long blond hair and big teeth. He had blue eyes, the right one remarkably darker than the left. He was about two inches taller than me thanks to his fluffy hair, and he was missing the tips of his three middle fingers on his left hand. (Leo had learned early in life that squirrel traps are nothing to play around with.)

I could smell his morning breath from across the room as he lounged on one of his fake leopard skin couches. He was quite the picture of luxury.

Leo's mother had never allowed him to have a dog when she was alive, so at her death a year ago Leo mourned by going dog wild. He now had about twenty hounds that he let roam Lush Point and come through his doggy door all day long. Consequently Leo's place was always stamped with muddy paw prints and speckled with hair.

"Looks like you're doing all right," I commented to him.

"Ah, shucks," Leo replied. "I'm getting by."

We had been over a couple days earlier, and had challenged Leo to have daily scripture study. "Have you been reading your scriptures?" I asked, hoping to get an idea of how he was coming along.

Leo nodded. "It's been a while," he added.

"How long has it been?" Elder Sims seemed to demand. "Two days?"

"Few months," he replied.

I put my head in my hands.

"Do you remember last week when we asked you to read your scriptures every day?" I asked.

Leo nodded while one of his dogs came in from outside and began to lick him on the face.

"Do you remember saying yes?" I asked.

"Been meaning to," Leo replied, inviting the dog up onto the couch. "Shucks, CleeDee's been taking a lot of my time lately. You know how women are," he assumed.

"It doesn't have to take a long time, Leo," Elder Sims said. "Just try to read a few verses a day."

"I don't see what the gawl awful rush is," he pointed out. "I can't be baptized until I die anyways. Daddy's waiting in heaven to dunk me under. If I got baptized here on earth he'd be pretty sore."

"I think he wants you to be baptized here," I said. "He knows how important it is."

"Shucks, how do you know that?"

"I just know how he must feel."

"Seems awful bold of you to say so," Leo added.

"What about CleeDee?" I asked. "Don't you think she's looking for a husband who can take her through the temple?"

"Why, what have you heard?" Leo jumped up. "That girl's eyes wander like the birthmark on my back. I tell you I can't leave her alone for a minute without her looking at some other guy. Well, if I can't have her then no one can—"

"That's not what I meant," I interrupted. "Don't you think CleeDee is looking for *you* to take her through the temple?"

"Ah, shucks," Leo blushed. "CleeDee and I aren't serious."

I contemplated pulling out my hair strand by strand.

My soul had turned soggy and my existence was beginning to run down my leg, surrounding my feet with the muck of failure. I had to get out of Thelma's Way.

I slowly put my scriptures back in my bag.

"What's the matter?" Leo asked.

"We need to be going," I answered.

"But we're not done," Elder Sims said, pointing out the obvious.

"I don't feel well," I insisted while standing up.

"CleeDee's coming over in a bit," Leo said. "She could make you some soup."

"That's all right," I said, looking around for my backpack. It was not there. One of Leo's dogs had grabbed it and was dragging it outside. I guess he had smelled the half chicken inside. I tried to catch him, but the moment I advanced, he took off with my pack through the doggy door.

"Leo!" I complained.

"Shucks, don't worry none. Wanda will bring it back when she's done with it."

I could see out the back window that Wanda was on her way to being long gone—running swiftly, shaking my backpack in her mouth.

"That's all my stuff," I complained.

"Don't worry. Wanda will probably bury it someplace and keep it nice and safe," Leo informed me.

"I thought you said she'd bring it back."

"Dogs is fickle," he yawned.

Great, I thought. Just great.

19

HALF AN INCH DEEP

Lucy was far from flattered. There was a giant ring on her dainty finger, but that was to be expected. The diamond band looked brilliant against her tan.

Lucy and Lance had taken a vacation to the Caribbean to discuss the issue of becoming engaged. In the process Lucy's fair skin had darkened nicely, and she had procured herself a fabulous ring and a fiancé that most women would have died for. "Of course, they would have to die and then be lucky enough to come back as me," she mused to herself.

Lucy giggled.

"What a snot I am." She smiled. "And justifiably so."

She and Lance made one attractive couple.

Lucy did worry over Trust. She had mailed him the happy news a few days earlier.

She felt a tinge of guilt. She had sort of promised that she would be around when Trust returned.

Then she chastised herself, "Once again I'm thinking

of others when I should be concerned about myself. Oh, poo," she swore. "I've got to stay focused on what's important."

She went back to matching color swatches.

20

FORK IN THE ROAD

I was no dummy. I was not oblivious to the fact that Lucy and I had been sort of drifting apart. But I had thought that we would drift back together before the end of my mission. Certainly our relationship would be strained while I was gone, but I believed we would be stronger because of it. I had thought that no matter what, she would be there for me when I returned home. I was wrong.

Lucy was engaged.

I couldn't believe it, and I couldn't imagine a more cold-hearted way for her to break the news to me. I searched every inch of my brain trying to remember if she had always been so cold. True, she put me in a fog whenever I was around her, but had I really been so blind?

She sent me a piece of paper with two pictures taped to it. One was of Lucy and me at a high-school dance years ago. It had been my first such experience and I hadn't yet found a way to put the words "hair" and "style" together in the same place. My hair was parted down the middle and poofy, and my smile showed off my nice silver braces as they glimmered under the camera lights. Lucy of course looked perfect, even back then. The other picture on the paper was a photo of Lucy and this Lance guy on a tropical beach. They looked like a Club Med Vacation ad, like some fake ideal that no one could ever achieve. I practically got an eating disorder just looking at it.

Below the snapshots were two lines of Lucy's perfect penmanship.

"I think it's obvious why you and I are off.

The wedding is set for this coming April. Lucy"

I took one last glance at the picture of the two of us at the dance and then tore the paper into shreds. Enough was enough.

I pulled my suitcase out from under my bed and began throwing clothes into it. Elder Sims was frantic.

"Elder, this too shall pass," he nervously reasoned.

"I've been waiting over six months for this to pass," I moaned. "I'm going to Virgil's Find until President Clasp transfers me."

I fumbled with my shirts and socks.

"Elder, this is not the answer," Elder Sims whined. "C'mon, let's go to the boardinghouse and call the Mission Home."

I slammed the suitcase shut.

"I'm out of here," I declared.

"You're going to regret this."

I wasn't even listening anymore.

Elder Sims grabbed his backpack so that he could follow me. There was no way he was going to be left there alone. I was going to self-righteously storm out the door and over to Virgil's Find to wait for President Clasp to send me my marching orders, but as I threw open the door Brother Heck was standing there. He looked at the suitcase in my hand and shook his head.

"I heard you got some bad mail," he said, solemnly offering his condolences.

"Yeah, well," I huffed, knowing that since the mail came through the boardinghouse, all news was everybody's business here.

"Can I talk to you fer a moment?" he asked me.

"I actually needed to get going," I explained.

"Won't take but a tick."

What was a tick in the eternal scheme of things?

I looked from Brother Heck to Elder Sims.

"All right," I said, setting down my suitcase and letting my shoulders drop.

I followed Brother Heck over to the front of the cemetery. Elder Sims sat down against the side of our cabin so that he could keep an eye on me as I conversed with Brother Heck. Ricky Heck and I took a seat on a log next to the statue by the cemetery gate. It was cold and gray. Wind, like emotion, swirled up my arms and around my face.

"Do you know who that is?" Brother Heck asked me, pointing at the monument.

I had never really paid the statue much mind. I had been living by it for over six months now, and I still hadn't taken the time to get to know my bronze neighbor.

"I have no idea who that is," I answered.

"Guess."

"Your mother," I tried.

"Nah, my mother was a lot heavier."

"Not literally, I hope," I replied. "That statue must weigh a ton."

"Guess again," Brother Heck went on.

I shrugged my shoulders. The last thing I wanted to do was play games with Brother Heck.

"That's Thelma," Brother Heck said, pointing towards the statue and telling me this as if he were sharing the secrets of the kingdom.

"*The* Thelma?" I asked.

"Nope, just Thelma."

"As in Way?"

"Yep."

I took a real good look. The statue was about five feet tall, and it stood upon a big wood base. Thelma had her right hand over her eyes as if she were looking forward, and her left hand on her hip. She had a bronze bonnet on and reminded me of some of the more famous Mormon pioneer statues I had seen in pictures. I had never really thought about the origin of the town's name. I just sort of figured that it, like the locals, wasn't supposed to make sense. I had no clue there had been an actual Thelma.

Imagine my delight.

"Have you ever heard her story?" Brother Heck asked.

I shook my head no. I was beginning to cool down.

"Actually the big pageant play will be kinda based on her life," Brother Heck began. "Thelma was a brat. She was the only child of a wealthy Mormon family back east.

Her full name was Thelma Fortsyth Palmer. Her parents and she had joined the Church when Thelma was only twelve. A year later they left New York state to join the Saints in Nauvoo. They set out with a big group of people. Called themselves the Palmer party. Maybe you've heard of them?"

I shook my head.

"Most of the Palmer party was poor, dirt poor. Done sold all their stuff to be able to afford the trip. But the Palmers weren't poor. Nope, not by a long shot. They had their servants make the trip with them. Thelma's own personal handcart was pulled by her butler while she fanned herself in comfort.

"Well, the trip became disastrous almost instantly. People's carts fell apart, the weather was bad, and there was lots of arguing as Sister Palmer bossed everyone around. They pressed on. Eventually, however, they got lost—somewhere in South Dakota, I think. Real lost. They made a camp and decided to hunker down 'til the bad winter was over. After three days of hunkering, Brother Palmer volunteered to go in search of assistance. They never saw him again. Sister Palmer assumed he had died in the cold struggling to find them help. Everyone else just figured he rode off to get away from her and Thelma.

"Well, Sister Palmer became real sick, and the party started to run out of food in their makeshift winter camp. So, they pulled up their stakes and commenced traveling while they still had strength. They traveled for weeks, not having a clue as to what point on the map they was occupying. They saw no one, no roads, no towns, nothing.

Finally a brother Dan Biggy organized a party-wide fast. It wasn't hard to do, really, seeing how they was out of food, but at the conclusion of the fast Brother Biggy felt inspired to head in a different direction. Sister Palmer was too sick to protest, but young Thelma was livid. How dare a poor person tell a wealthy person which way to go. Thelma demanded that they go her way. She said Brother Biggy didn't know squat.

"The party split.

"Those interested in following the Spirit went with Dan Biggy, and those who were too frightened by Thelma's thirteen-year-old rage to disagree with her went Thelma's way. Months later Thelma's party rolled into this meadow. Thelma took one look around and declared, 'This is a disgrace.'

"But Thelma's mother died while they were encamped, so Thelma refused to leave. A couple of people struck out on their own, but most folks stayed and put down roots right here, accepting the consequences of going Thelma's way.

"Once things were settled, Thelma used some of her money to commission this statue. She died two days after it was put up, trying to cross the Girth. They found her body down river below the falls."

"How come I've never heard this before?" I asked, still not sure if I should believe him.

"It's not the kind of thing we tell just anyone. Shoot, the kids here would be so disappointed if they found out Thelma was selfish and spoiled. Most of them think Thelma is Santa's wife."

"Why do they think that?" I asked.

"I told them," he said, embarrassed.

I shook my head.

"She doesn't seem like a very good person to look up to," I observed.

"Maybe not, but you've got to promise me that you won't tell anyone else what I just told you. I could get in real trouble, you understand? Don't even tell your companion. It's a secret, okay?"

"So why did you tell me?" I asked, confused.

"Because if you listen to those loud voices in your head, you could end up in the wrong place. But if you take time to let God guide you, you could end up in a much better mess. Brother Biggy listened, young Thelma didn't. Take heed."

"What happened to the Biggy party?"

"They made it to Nauvoo. Brother Biggy opened his own cabinet-building business. Made quite a nice living. I guess Thelma was wrong after all; he did know squat."

I sighed. The afternoon was collapsing. The sky was folding in on itself as winter chalked up another day.

"I know Thelma's Way ain't exactly paradise," Brother Heck said after a couple moments of silence. "But it could be worse."

I thought about asking for proof.

"We're real glad you're here," Brother Heck said shyly. "We might get under your skin, but we're real fond of you."

"Me?" I laughed. "Will of the Underworld?"

"Ah, Paul's just plain nuts. We all know that. I tell you

124

what, Elder, it's nice to have him pick on someone else for a change."

"Glad to be of service," I joked. Brother Heck was the most discombobulated, guilt-ridden person I knew, but he was wise in his own way, and I loved him for it. I couldn't remember my father ever taking the time to talk to me like Brother Heck just had. Any contact with my father had mainly taken place at the dinner table on Sundays, the one time during the week when we all got together. The rest of the week he was usually too busy to be part of things.

"There'll be other girls," Brother Heck said, referring to Lucy's letter. "I'm real sorry yours gave up on you, but the Lord will provide."

I smiled. It was hard to believe this was the same man who tarred and feathered himself with latex house paint.

"So, you gonna leave us?" he finally asked me.

"Eventually," I replied.

"Funny how life works, ain't it."

"Funny," I said.

21

LOST AND FOUND

Grace had been only slightly reluctant to pick the backpack up. She knew it belonged to Elder Williams. She had seen it slung over Trust's shoulder countless times.

The pack was ripped at the bottom of the side pocket, and pieces of grease-stained paper towel were strewn about. It was wet from the snow, and there were telltale signs of dog slobber. But the bulk of the backpack looked okay.

The previous night had been quite a night for Grace. She had only meant to take a late walk in the fresh snow. She had not expected to find Elder Williams frozen in prayer. She was not complaining, mind you, and now she had Trust's backpack.

Heaven was helping her out. She would return the backpack, but not before she took a peek inside.

She hiked down to the Girth River and sat upon a rocky ledge. She unzipped the backpack and looked inside. There were scriptures, some books, a couple letters, and a wallet. There was a small cassette player and a pair of headphones.

She poured the contents of the backpack out to examine them closely. She was having a good time until she saw the picture of Lucy in Trust's wallet.

One look was all it took. How stupid Grace had been to think Trust was different. She couldn't believe she had let herself feel something for a missionary that would have a girlfriend like Lucy. Lucy was beautiful. She was too beautiful. Her skin was polished and her smile was manufactured. She was everything Grace wasn't.

Disappointment swept over Grace like a violent storm. Her thoughts connected like lightning. She shoved everything except the wallet back into Trust's backpack. She pulled out the picture of Lucy and tossed it into the Girth River. She watched the mighty river drag it away.

"Good riddance," she sighed.

She walked over to the missionaries' home and dropped Trust's wallet in front of his door. Then she slung the backpack over her shoulder and hiked off through the forest. It would be some time before she wandered into the meadow again.

22

LATHER, RINSE, REPEAT

ONE YEAR

It had been about six months since I had sat with Brother Heck in the cemetery. Six months. Pete Kennedy had grown a beard, let it go gray, shaved it off, and begun another. The winter had turned to spring, and the spring had given way to a beautiful summer that was now almost halfway over. Life was warm, green and rainy. I had been on my mission for over a year.

I was still in Thelma's Way, and surprisingly to everyone, especially me, I was okay with this. I no longer checked off the days till official mission letterhead informed me it was time to pack my things. In fact, there were things here that I knew I was going to miss whenever I did get transferred out.

Astounding.

I had had a premonition I was up for transfer a couple months back when President Clasp and the Virgil's Find stake presidency came to Thelma's Way to get a look at things. Instead I got a new companion, they released Bishop Watson, restructured the tiny Thelma's Way Ward to be a tiny branch, and put Yours Truly in as the new branch president. Brother Heck was called as my first counselor with my new companion as second.

I was in shock for weeks. I had been hoping for the chance to train a new elder, or be a senior companion. Instead I was given a handful of full-fledged responsibilities, and it required coming to terms with the fact that I would be traveling nowhere fast. I had not known that full-time missionaries could serve as branch presidents. What a way to find out.

My new companion was Elder Jorgensen from Blackfoot, Idaho. He was almost seven feet tall and had the shiniest set of buck teeth I had ever seen. All his suits were too short for him, and his blond hair was wiry and abrasive-looking. He walked with a spring in his step, and was constantly talking about trucks and how to make them go faster. He was one of fourteen kids and the first in his family to serve a mission. Always up before dawn, he was the kindest, hardest-working missionary I had ever met. His parents were potato farmers who sent him boxes of spuds along with pictures of his truck, which they were washing regularly for him.

I had not heard very much more from Lucy. I assumed she was married and happy by now—while selfishly I hoped for neither of those things.

Months back, my mother had sent me a new backpack and a new set of scriptures to replace my lost ones. I guess

I was grateful. The backpack had a big pink rainbow stitched on the back of it, and the scriptures were my father's set that he never used. Of course, the set was so old that it didn't have the new references or page numbers. Mom had also soaked the backpack in dog repellent, hoping that would prevent me from losing it again. The thing was too pretty, too stinky, and too small. But I carried it around in honor of my mom.

I never found my old backpack. Oddly enough, the morning after I had lost it, I discovered my wallet lying in the dirt in front of our door. Everything was in it except for Lucy's picture. It was a miracle. I figured fate had removed her photo for me so I wouldn't have to suffer any further. Out of sight, out of mind.

I had not clearly seen Grace Heck since our life-saving encounter in the snow. The first thing I did when I was put in as branch president was to set out to find her. My records showed that she was now twenty-one and, as her branch president, I felt it was my duty to make sure she was having success in life. But Grace was too elusive. Even her parents couldn't round her up long enough for me to talk to her. I had tried dropping in on the Hecks and surprising them at dinner or other points when I thought Grace would be there.

She never was.

We were having some success where reactivation was concerned. We had managed to get a couple of people back to church. Ed Washington and his mother were attending regularly, and Toby Carver had been out twice in the last two months. We had also found an older woman named Nippy Ward over behind the Heck home who was now coming out to church. Nippy was as old as the hills and almost totally deaf. She never really understood a word of what you said, but she nodded a lot and smiled enough to make you feel like you were getting through to her.

The big news was that Leo Tip had decided to be baptized. He was going to be my first baptism. The event that pushed him over the edge was when Sister Watson and the members of P.I.G. held their first annual hand shadow contest to raise money to take Paul to court—Sister Watson really wanted to get some closure on this Paul mess so as to be able to fully focus on the coming sesquicentennial pageant. They held the contest at the boardinghouse late one night using Tindy MacDermont's powerful flashlight. Practically everyone in Thelma's Way threw their hands into the ring. Competition was fierce. Digby Heck almost won with his realistic eagle hand shadow, but then he made the mistake of looking directly into the flashlight and temporarily blinded himself. Teddy Yetch's turtle with retracting head was also quite spectacular. But Philip Green ended up winning the trophy, he and his eerie beetle hand shadow impression. Of course, he had a tremendous advantage due to the extra finger on his right hand.

At the end of the event people milled around in the dark eating refreshments that the members of P.I.G. had brought. Young Narlette got hold of Tindy's flashlight and waved it around making scary noises. Well, the whole thing sort of spooked Leo, putting him into a reflective mood. That night he dreamed he was drowning in a baptismal font. He could see his father looking down through the water, but he did nothing to help.

Leo was unnerved. What if the dream was prophetic? What if it was his father telling him to get baptized now or suffer the consequences? What if it was the two dozen of Sister Teddy Yetch's pickle wheat cookies that he had eaten at the hand shadow contest making him hallucinate?

Leo wasn't taking any chances. He scheduled his baptism for July 4th. The town was abuzz. CleeDee Lipton started coming back to church and talked of eventually going with Leo to the temple. There were those who had their doubts about Leo's resolve, of course, but today was July 4th and unless my eyes were deceiving me, Leo was wearing all white.

Most of the active members of the Thelma's Way Branch were gathered around the river next to the burned-out bridge. It had been raining all day, and the extra water had given the Girth a bloated, angry looking belly. We thought about postponing the baptism for a clearer afternoon, but Leo was ready now, and I didn't want to run the risk of having him change his mind.

Umbrellas were opened, slickers were pulled close, and mismatched boots stood in inches of mud. Just to be safe, Leo and I each tied ourselves to the frame of the derelict bridge before we waded into the Girth. The water was cold, especially for the middle of summer, and twice I felt the current almost knock my feet out from under me. We had to push out a good twenty steps to where it was deep enough for dunking. We then turned and faced the crowd. Everyone looked gray in the rain. Here and there a lit smile flashed, bright and cheery. Brother Heck and Ed Washington leaned out over the river to make sure Leo went completely under.

I said the words of the prayer and pushed Leo back. But his knees buckled as his head hit the water, and I fumbled to maintain my balance. It was no use, the water rushed over us and pulled us down river. Leo grabbed me and pushed me down, trying to climb above the water. The rope around my stomach went taut. I struggled to find my footing and stuck my head above the water, spitting and coughing. Leo was standing next to me breathing hard, his hands wrapped around his rope. We looked over at Ed.

"Sorry, it wasn't a complete dunk," he yelled above the noise of the water. "Leo's hand flew up."

I sighed, wiping the rain from out of my eyes. All that, and it didn't count. I thought back to when an older gentlemen named Myron was baptized in our ward back in Southdale. No one knew he wore a toupee, but when he went down, his hair didn't go with him. Someone screamed that he'd been spiritually scalped. One of the little boys in the front row reached out to grab it. His mother almost fainted, thinking it was a water rat. But Myron's girlfriend cried the loudest, never having seen Myron without his fuzzy top.

The local priesthood leaders began to debate whether or not it was necessary for a person's toupee to be submerged. They consulted the handbook, but there wasn't a section on bad-looking rugs. Just to be safe, they baptized Myron once more with him holding his hair in his hand.

Now here I was standing in the pouring rain in the

middle of a raging river, and Leo needed one more dip. We waded back upstream, feeling with our feet for firm footing. I tugged the rope around my stomach to make sure it still held. I wiped the rain from my eyes and pushed the short hair off of my forehead. Lightning crackled in the far distance. We needed to hurry. I threw a smile of encouragement to this branch I had grown to . . . love? Sister Teddy Yetch, her wrinkled face pinched in reverence to the event; Narlette, prancing on the shore with excitement; Bishop and Sister Watson, looking miserable in the rain; Digby Heck; Ed Washington and his mother; Nippy Ward nodding; and Grace Heck standing there next to the burnt-out bridge, her green eyes seeping out from under a yellow umbrella.

Her red hair was darkened by the wet air, and her white arms were cold and pale in the summer rain. I wanted to push Leo over and run back to shore. I just wanted to talk with her. She had been so elusive and now here she was.

I turned back to Leo. He was standing at attention, ready for baptism. I pulled my focus back to the moment and shut my eyes. I took his hands.

"Leo Tip," I said solemnly. "Having been commissioned . . ." I finished the prayer and pushed Leo under, holding on for all I was worth. This time Leo let himself go down. He came back up coughing and spitting water. We waded back to shore. I saw Grace slip away back behind the crowd. I almost called out to her, "Wait. Don't go." But I thought better of it, me being the branch president and all.

Folks congratulated Leo as they collectively stepped back from the crumbling river bank. Pete fired off his gun a couple of times in celebration and ruined his umbrella. Rain poured down through the holes onto his head.

"Do you think God's happy with my decision?" Leo asked, skeptical because of the rough weather.

Sister Heck handed him a wet towel to dry off with. "It's an Indian legend that God's happy when it rains," she explained.

"Paul says rain is a weapon God uses to smite the ingrates," Ed Washington chimed in.

Ed's mother flashed him a 'be quiet' expression.

"I don't know no Ingrates round here, anyways," Toby Carver observed. "Less yore talking about them private folks next to Tindy's place."

"It's not a name, Toby," Brother Heck corrected. "Anyone can be an ingrate."

"Not me," Toby scoffed. "I'm German."

"I think all this rain is just Satan playing his fife," Sister Watson said as our group began to wander away from the river and back towards the boardinghouse. "He can finger some pretty tricky tunes," she went on. "Heard him play 'Battle Hymn of the Republic' as I was deciding whether I should go to church last week."

Leo and I quickly changed out of our wet white clothes. Then we all crammed into the boardinghouse for the celebration. We had planned for fireworks to celebrate the Fourth, but thanks to the rain, that was out of the question. Besides, someone had taken the box of fireworks outside and now they were soaking wet. Elder Jorgensen dragged them back into the boardinghouse where Digby fetched a blow dryer to dry them out. I told him it seemed like a bad idea, but he wouldn't listen until one of the fire flowers ignited on his lap and singed a hole in his shorts.

The rain stopped about two hours later. We set up lawn chairs in the mud and attempted to light the rain-soaked fireworks. We tried to *ooh* and *ahh* as wet wicks sizzled and dudlike sparks spit out of the only slightly airborne fireworks.

There was a big sheet cake made by CleeDee in honor of Leo's baptism. CleeDee slit it up and passed out pieces on paper plates with plastic forks. Folks ate the lemon flavored cake with big smiles and loud laughs, as night became late-night, and the day just a memory. Elder Jorgensen and I relished every minute of it. It was our first baptism and it had gone over Thelma's Way style. Not with a bang, but with a pop and sizzle.

At CleeDee's suggestion, Leo pulled his old jalopy close, turned on the headlights, and pointed them toward us so we could see to talk. We told stories long into the night. We talked about the crazy Tennessee weather. We talked about the branch and the litter of Mormons who still refused to come back to church. We talked about Paul. We talked about his problem with telling the truth. And we talked about how the members of P.I.G. almost had enough money to get themselves a lawyer and take Paul to court. We reminisced about Feeble and Roswell. We talked about the pageant, and how it was creeping up on us, and whether or not people would come.

Eight-year-old Narlette fell asleep on her mother's shoulder. Mosquitoes buzzed around us like bad thoughts. Bishop and Sister Watson finally left the group to go home, the bottom half of their legs covered in mud like the rest of us. Ed and his mother eventually bid us adieu, carrying their two lawn chairs off into the dark. Soon it was just the Hecks and Leo and CleeDee and us. Leo's headlights were getting dimmer as his car battery drained.

"I saw Grace there today," I ventured.

The Hecks nodded, Brother Heck scraping his paper plate with his fork and cleaning off the last bits of his third helping of cake.

"She and Leo go way back," Sister Heck replied, swatting at the mosquitoes near Narlette's sleeping face. "I think Grace was sweet on Leo for a while."

Leo blushed. CleeDee looked on with pride. She had won her man. They smiled in silence for a minute or two. Then Leo looked at CleeDee's watch, said something about not wanting to haul another car battery in from Virgil's Find, and the two of them slipped off together, leaving us in the moonlight. The sky had cleared and the night was ablaze with stars.

"Grace seems like a nice girl," I observed.

"She is," Brother Heck said. "She spends too much time alone, but whatcha gonna do. She can be stubborn," he went on. "If'n I tell her to go south, she goes up. If I tell her that today is Tuesday, she'll argue that it's Wednesday."

"But it was Wednesday," Sister Heck said, reaching over to touch her husband's arm.

"Sure it was, that one time," he huffed. "But I'm still her father, ain't I?"

Sister Heck rubbed her husband's shoulder with her outstretched arm. I looked closely at Brother and Sister

Heck. Although they appeared different on the surface, they were worn to the exact same point. They were two peas in a rather weathered pod.

Sister Heck was proud of her man lately. Brother Heck had been doing so well controlling his addiction. So well, in fact, that I could see a point in the not-too-far-away future where he would be ready to assume responsibility for the branch. I know the idea of a twenty-year-old kid being over him was a blow to his backwoods pride. But he had handled things gracefully. As first counselor, he had stepped up to the plate.

Crickets moshed. Raccoons and critters were coming out of the woods. Every now and again eyes would flash in the moonlight. The meadow was ready to go to bed and we were keeping them up.

"Think Grace might be interested in coming out to church?" I asked, standing and picking up my muddy chair.

"I'm not sure," Brother Heck said. "She marches to a different pianist."

"Grace is just finding herself," Sister Heck defended. "If only she could find something to be interested in here," she said, heaving Narlette higher on to her shoulder and standing.

If only.

23

WET YOUR APPETITE

Grace slipped down into the meadow with her umbrella overhead and stood behind the crowd of spectators. She owed it to Leo.

She watched Trust and Leo mess up the first time and almost float off downstream. Trust looked different. A full year in Thelma's Way had changed him. His shoulders seemed wider, and his smile easier. His brown hair, wet from the river, was almost enough to make Grace like him again. She slid right up next to the bridge to observe their second try.

Since that night in the snow, when Trust's companion had assumed the worst, she had put Elder Williams out of her mind. The last thing Thelma's Way needed was another church scandal. And, secretly, she felt she would be doing Trust a favor by staying out of his way.

Never in a hundred years did Grace think Trust would

notice her standing there, but he did. And Trust's locked gaze was long enough to cause her to smile back at him.

Grace was no dummy; she was truly smarter than the entire town of Thelma's Way. The volumes of books she had digested made her a mental master on almost everything. She knew the whole idea of missionary romance was a contradiction in terms.

But she could not deny the feelings growing inside her. She ran off before Trust could climb out of the river, but she had seen how he was coming for her. So what if he was a missionary and, as such, just a fantasy. There was no harm in dreaming, was there?

24

DOOR NUMBER TWO

MONTH THIRTEEN

Sister Watson had finally completed the pageant script. She called a town meeting in the boardinghouse and, with great flourish, she presented "All Is Swell: The Story of Thelma's Way." Everyone applauded. She handed out copies to everyone interested in being involved. I took a copy and flipped through it. As I read a couple of the lines, I realized that the pageant would be even more ridiculous than I had anticipated. But knowing how important it was to everyone, I kept my opinions to myself. I slipped the script into my rainbow backpack, figuring it would make a nice souvenir.

Elder Jorgensen and I left to do some missionary work up in the hills. We had decided to investigate a particularly thickly wooded part of Thelma's Way that day. We had been systematically working our way through the woods, scouring every trail for lost locals. I kept having strong feelings that somewhere within these hills was someone no one knew about. An unknown nonmember. The Holy Grail.

We climbed over Lush Point and ran down through an arroyo for a few hundred feet. We hiked up a small hill and into a clearing

"This is where we left off last time," Elder Jorgensen said. It was only about three in the afternoon; we had hours before dinner. The trail stretched out in front of us, beckoning.

It was always surprising to me the number of homes hidden up in these hills. Most of the houses had been built years ago. According to Brother Heck, the community had really rallied together back in the good old days to help each other build.

Before long, we stumbled onto a house perched precariously on a small knoll next to a flowing stream. The place was old and looked to have been added on to about three or four times. It was the home of Corndog Tent employee Jerry Scotch.

Jerry was trying to be active. He had been coming out to church. Last fast and testimony meeting, he had testified about how he had almost lost his job. According to his testimony, Jerry had bought a candle for Jan, a girl that worked at the Teriyaki Carousel two shops down from the Corndog Tent in the mall. Jerry was kind of sweet on Jan and figured he would give her a scented candle because he had heard that people of Asian descent liked incense. Jerry bought the candle from a store on the upper level of the mall called Mr. Wick. Well, Mr. Wick charged three dollars for gift wrapping. Extortion! Jerry wasn't exactly getting rich working at the Corndog Tent. Luckily, Jerry thought up what he considered to be a fantastic idea. He took the boysenberry scented candle back to his work, dipped it in batter, and fried it up. He figured it would come out covered like one of his hot dogs.

Creative cornbread wrapping paper.

There were two problems with his plan . . . well, actually there were far more than just two, but the two most obvious were, one, just because Jan worked at Teriyaki Carousel didn't mean she was actually Asian. Jan, in fact, had been born in Virgil's Find to Inga and Swen Swenson. Problem number two was that candle wax melts when put into a big vat of boiling oil.

Who knew?

Imagine Jerry's surprise when he pulled that present up to find nothing there. Jerry ended up giving Jan a discounted calendar from the year before. Jan didn't even accept it, informing Jerry that her parents wouldn't allow her to date until she was at least fifteen. Jerry's boss never found out about his mistake, and people enjoyed boysenberry flavored corndogs until the oil was changed a few days later.

It had been quite the faith-promoting testimony.

Elder Jorgensen and I talked with Jerry for a few minutes at his home and then headed out to find somebody even less active. We hiked for another mile or so without seeing a soul. We were just about to turn around when Elder Jorgensen spotted a rock chimney hidden behind a thick wall of trees.

"Over there," he said, pointing like a happy dog.

I patted him on the back. "Good work, Elder."

We pushed through the trees and up to the cabin. It was small and weathered but cute. There were flowers in the window boxes and a front walkway that had been swept despite the fact that it was only dirt. The windows were clean and trimmed with colorful curtains. We stepped up to the door, feeling a little like Hansel and Gretel, our mouths watering over the possibility of teaching a first discussion.

I knocked. No one answered.

"Hello, anyone home?" Elder Jorgensen called out. He pushed his face up against one of the windows and peered in. "There's got to be somebody in there," he said, his buck teeth clicking against the glass as he spoke. "There's a half eaten apple on a table and a book lying open on a chair." He knocked again, harder this time.

One thing I had learned while serving in the backwoods was that if people didn't want to be interrupted, they wouldn't be. And if you continued to bother them after they had made it clear that they wanted to be left alone, you could expect a brandished shotgun or a couple of loose dogs.

"We'd better go," I said, about ready to head back to town. But Elder Jorgensen looked deflated.

"When I saw that chimney," he said, "I thought for sure it was a sign. There's just got to be somebody out here."

I gave in. "Maybe we should hike back a little further," I said. His face lit up, and he took off walking.

We had covered about a half a mile more territory when Elder Jorgensen hopped up on a fallen tree that was lying across a small crack in the earth. He proceeded to balance himself along, his arms outstretched, talking a thousand words a minute about back home.

"So Chet said, push the pedal harder. You'll get more torque if you just—" Elder Jorgensen was mid-sentence when I heard this huge snap and saw the log give way.

"Elder," I yelled, jumping down into the crevice where he and the tree were now wedged.

Elder Jorgensen was conscious, but his right leg was pinned by the folding tree—pinned and immobile, if not worse. His face was wrinkled by a grimace. He was in some serious pain.

"Can you pull me out?" he asked with the faith of one certain I could bring him back from the dead if I had to.

I pulled on the tree. I pushed on the tree. I kicked the tree until he began screaming.

"I've got to go get help," I said, wiping sweat off my forehead.

"But we're supposed to stick together," he moaned.

"Don't be ridiculous, Elder," I reprimanded. "This is an emergency. You're in real trouble."

"If I only had my truck . . . " he started to say.

I took off running before he could finish.

I'd never been great with direction. Standing next to the North Pole, I probably couldn't tell you which way was south without making at least three guesses. It was a serious flaw. I don't know why my perception was so bad. You could blindfold my mother, put her in an electric dryer for three hours, take her out, turn her upside-down, and she'd still be able to tell you exactly which way was north. My father was the same way. I don't think I had ever heard him use the words *left* or *right*.

"Look over there to the west, son."

"The fork goes on the east-hand side."

But my soul lacked direction, geographically speaking. This had been a real problem living in Thelma's Way. The forest and hills really threw me. I worked hard to establish a series of markers to help me stay oriented close to town. But deep in the woods, I was useless. I'd never make it back to the meadow alone.

I thought of the cabin nearby, the one with the unwilling occupant. It was my only hope. It took me a while stumbling around, but I finally spotted the cabin's rock chimney. I banged on the door begging for help. Nobody came. The handle was locked.

I considered trying to retrace my steps and hopefully find Jerry Scotch's place again. But I didn't think I'd be able to do it.

I took a deep breath. I forced myself to calm down, and then I did what I should have done earlier. Standing right there in front of that door, I prayed. I prayed for Elder Jorgensen. I prayed for his leg. I prayed for my mind to stop buzzing long enough for me to think clearly. I prayed for God to send help. I prayed that if he was not going to send help, he would at least let me know what to do. And while I was praying, I heard the door open.

It was a miracle. And it was Grace.

There she stood. She was the last person I had expected to see. And in the same moment that I realized I had discovered her secret hiding place, I also realized I had not been wrong about her. Her appearance was like the memory of a embarrassing pop song from my junior high years. I felt silly for being moved.

I stared.

Her red hair was long and loose. Strands of it were touching the right side of her face. She had on a summer dress and no shoes. She might have appeared to be just an average girl to anyone else, but I could see how the light rested upon her in the most unique way, giving her both sharp lines and soft curves. Not even Lucy had created such a visionary event for my simple mind. Don't get me wrong, Grace was no classic beauty. She wasn't the kind of girl you would see in a fashion magazine, or looking good in spandex at the gym. She was simple and complicated. It was as if she were a part of this lush landscape, her green eyes and pink lips being the best thing these hills had to offer. For me, it was kind of like staring at a psychedelic pinwheel.

Far out.

I was suddenly well aware of how companionless I was. Elder Jorgensen was in trouble and, by almost all measures, what I was now doing was against the mission rules.

I was alone. With a girl. The same girl as before, that night in the snow. I pulled myself together.

"My companion needs help," I stated.

"What can I do?" she asked calmly.

"Is there anyone else here?" I questioned.

"Only me."

Under normal circumstances Grace would be more than enough, but not at the moment. I needed a couple people to help me drag my companion out from under that tree.

"He's pinned down under an old tree," I began to explain. "His leg might be broken, and I don't know if he's bleeding or not."

"Did you give him a blessing?" she asked.

Good question. How dumb had I been? Here I was a full-time missionary and branch president and I had failed to do the one thing that could really make a difference. It took an inactive member to get me to even think of it.

"I didn't really think—"

"There's some rope inside," Grace interrupted. "We could hook it around a pulley and try to get the tree off of him."

I just stood there as Grace ran back inside collecting things that might be useful. Then we took off. The plan was to get Elder Jorgensen out from under the tree and make him comfortable. Then Grace would run into town and get further help. It was a pretty good plan, or would have been, had I been able to find him. We were lugging around the rope, the pulley, and some bandages. Our futile search soon became a pain.

"Can't you remember which direction you came from?" Grace tried to ask kindly.

"Over there," I kept trying to say with some confidence.

"What were you guys doing out here?" she asked.

"We were looking for investigators."

"No one lives out this far," she said. "The wells are bad."

I thought for a moment that she was saying the Wells

family who lived a mile behind the boardinghouse were bad people. Then I realized she meant the water.

"So is that your family's cabin?" I asked, knowing already that it wasn't.

Grace didn't answer.

"I've been looking for you for quite some time," I huffed as we climbed up a small hill.

"Why?" was all Grace said.

"I wanted to thank you for waking me up all those many months ago. In the snow," I further clarified.

Grace just shrugged.

"Plus, I wanted to talk with you."

"About what?" she asked skeptically, stopping in her tracks.

I didn't have an answer for that. I had just always wanted to talk to her. It was my turn to shrug my shoulders.

We trudged on.

I thought we were headed in the right direction until we came to a stream that I knew I had not crossed before.

"Shoot," I said, embarrassed at being lost.

I screamed Elder Jorgensen's name but no one answered.

We stopped again.

"Tell me what the area looks like where he got hurt," she said.

"It looked like forest," I joked. "There were some trees, and bushes, and a short gouge in the earth."

Grace turned and headed in the opposite direction. I

guess my poor description had been enough for her. A few minutes later, we were standing by the crack in the earth.

But Elder Jorgensen was gone.

"I don't understand," I said. "He was really trapped."

I craned my head around, but there was no sign of him.

"Don't be alarmed," Grace said calmly, sensing my panic. "I'm sure he's okay. He probably got himself out, or somebody found him. Let's head into town. Someone will know where he is."

"Which way is town?" I asked.

Grace answered with a point.

We walked towards Thelma's Way looking for Elder Jorgensen. We hiked up a few hills, across a few meadows, and down a few steep slopes. Neither Grace nor I spoke much. We were both uncomfortable. I started thinking about how this would probably be my only chance to talk with her. For over a year now I had been living and serving here in Thelma's Way and for all that time, Grace had remained hidden. Even though I was worried about Elder Jorgensen, I couldn't resist the opportunity to ask Grace a few questions.

"So you must like it here," I finally said.

She turned and looked at me like I was daffy.

"I mean, you grew up here."

She smiled at my poor communication skills. "This is home," she responded, her voice the sound of good news.

"How long have you been in Thelma's Way?" she asked me.

"Over a year."

"That's not normal," she observed.

I looked at her as if seeking clarification.

"Missionaries don't normally stay so long in one area," she added.

"Yeah," I replied wittily.

"Are you being punished?" she joked as we walked down through a small overgrown patch of ivy.

"Possibly," I replied, trying to keep up with Grace without appearing winded. "Heaven knows there's a long list of things I need to correct."

Grace smiled. "I find that hard to believe," she said, walking faster. "Do you think they'll keep you here until the pageant?" she asked.

"No way," I answered ignorantly.

Grace walked on in front of me, her bare feet stepping in all the right spots. I didn't know if I had romantic feelings for her or just feelings. I couldn't help but see her in a different light from the rest of the citizens here. It was as if she were purely an emotion with arms and legs. I had no idea how to voice my thoughts, even in my head.

Let me attempt, however.

I remember being a kid and going down to the toy store with my friends. We would stand in front of the display of action figures and talk about which one we would buy if we had the money. My friends always drooled over the mean-looking ones, the ones with rows of big teeth and huge muscles. I secretly liked the nice ones, the dad-looking ones with parted hair and smiles.

On one occasion when I actually had money, I cowardly bought a tough-looking one with flashy guns and karate-chop action just to save face in front of my friends.

Had I been alone, I probably would have picked out the camping boy with working flashlight and first aid kit.

Well, that was Grace.

That's not to say that she was a boy, or that she carried a flashlight. She was just the kind of girl I would pick out if I were totally honest with myself. She wasn't like Lucy with all her bells and whistles. Grace was like the science kit that most of us pretended to loathe, but secretly worked with in our rooms—fascinated by all the parts, and constructing worlds, but not brave enough to admit that learning was fun.

I was ready to learn.

And yet, how weird it was to have met Grace here. I would most likely be gone in a few months, never to return. And I could already see myself comparing every girl I met after my mission to Grace. I only wished that I could really get to know her. Of course, there was really no good way for a missionary to get to know a girl while serving a mission. At least, there was no right way. The fact that I was alone with her now was more than most missionaries should ever experience. I felt a little guilty.

"So do you ever *think* about coming out to church?" I asked Grace, trying to feel more like a branch president.

"I think about a lot of things," she replied.

"It would be great if you did," I said.

Grace sort of smiled.

"You have a nice family," I commented, desperately trying to make conversation. "Your father is a great help to the ward."

"I'm happy you approve," she teased.

I smiled, liking this side of her.

"What's your family like?" she then asked.

"Oh, two parents, a younger sister, and a brother," I answered as if I were being timed.

"Do they have names?" Grace asked, pushing aside a long tree limb so as to slip through a tight spot in the forest. She let go, and the limb swung back at me.

"My sister's name is Margaret, and my brother's name is Abel," I informed her while dodging the branch.

Silence ensued.

"You like to read," I finally stated bluntly, knowing she spent a good deal of time at the Virgil's Find library, and sounding like an idiot.

Grace smirked. Except it wasn't a smirk. It was void of any malice or sarcasm—it was a sincere smirk.

"I love to read," Grace answered.

Silence again.

"How about you?" she then asked.

"I read lots of things back home, but here I concentrate on just reading my scriptures."

Grace blinked, her long eyelashes giving me something new to concentrate on.

"I'm reading the biography of Martin Calypso," Grace explained.

"Oh," was all I said, hoping she wouldn't ask me if I knew who Martin Calypso was.

Grace stopped. "Do you know who he is?" she asked.

"No," I admitted with a sorry little laugh.

"He was a man who was unashamed of his family

despite the fact that his debt-ridden brother eventually killed him."

"Mighty tolerant of him," I commented.

Grace laughed.

I recognized where we were now. A few minutes later the big meadow came into view. Kids were swarming over the rotted pioneer wagons, screaming and hollering as if they knew that summer was coming to an end.

The instant we stepped out of the trees and into the meadow, everyone looked up and took us in. I suddenly missed my companion more than ever before. Whether or not they were active, everyone in Thelma's Way knew that elders shouldn't be walking alone with girls, especially coming out of the trees.

A few adults gasped. Sister Teddy Yetch ran up to us as fast as her old legs could carry her. Briant Willpts shuffled right behind her. And Paul, who was passing the afternoon arguing with members of P.I.G., came sidling up as well. He wouldn't miss this for the world.

"What's going on here?" Briant asked.

"I lost my companion," I tried to explain.

"How can you lose your companion?" Teddy asked. "He's bigger than you are."

"Yes, how?" CleeDee snipped snidely as she approached.

Grace tried to slip away from it all, but Teddy wouldn't let her go.

"Hold on a moment, young lady," she scolded, and she grabbed Grace by the arm. "I think you got some explaining to do."

"I knew it," Paul exclaimed. "I've been telling you all for months, and no one believed me. Will of the Underworld."

The little kids playing on the pioneer wagons stopped what they were doing to watch us adults act like children.

"My companion got hurt and Grace was trying to help us," I said, hoping to quiet Paul.

"How condental of you," Briant said.

"That's not a word," Grace retorted.

Briant's ears sizzled. In all his years, no one had ever been so bold as to correct him. He had heard tell of folks whispering behind his back about his made-up words, but before now no one had actually challenged him to his face.

"Why, you little . . . ." he said, stopping to think up a new word. But before his thought process could be completed, he was interrupted by Brother Heck.

"Leave her be, Briant," he said, stepping in front of us. "Where's Elder Jorgensen?" he asked me.

"Yes," Paul hissed. "Where is your companion?"

"I don't know," I replied. "I was hoping he was here. We had an accident and he disappeared."

"Disappeared?" Miss Flitrey asked in amazement. "Sounds like a story with holes."

"Holes," the children all said in chorus, as if they were still in school.

"I have been telling you people for months that your church is corrupt," Paul raged. "And here is the main corrupter." He pointed at me.

"Calm yourself, Paul," Brother Heck clipped.

"Really," I tried to explain. "I was—"

A low moaning broke out about twenty feet away from us. We all turned that direction to look. I saw a hand rise above the tall grass and sort of wave. It was Elder Jorgensen's. He was lying on the ground, completely hidden by the thick growth the untrampled parts of the meadow had to offer.

I ran over and propped him up.

"What happened?" I asked.

He gasped a few times and then licked his lips. "I was able to push the tree off," he explained. "You know the one that was on my leg, the one that cracked?" He asked me as if it were so far back and so inconsequential that I had forgotten about it.

I nodded yes.

He went on. "Then I made a splint for my leg and fashioned myself a couple of crutches out of dead branches. I hobbled all the way back. Right before I got to the meadow, I ran out of steam. Crawled to this point here. I hope you're not mad. You were gone so long, I thought you might be lost."

"Why would I be mad?" I asked.

"For me taking off like that."

Elder Jorgensen was one faithful missionary.

I saw Toby Carver take off running, most likely to fetch his Ace bandage. Brother Heck and I picked up Elder Jorgensen and helped him over to our home.

Amidst it all, Grace was gone.

"Shoot," I said aloud as I laid my companion down on his bed.

"I'll be all right, Elder," he comforted me. "Don't you worry about a thing."

"I'm glad," I replied.

His leg looked bad. It was bent at a funny angle. Toby came and wrapped it with his bandage. While he was wrapping, he questioned me about being alone with Grace.

"So you two were just helping your companion?" he asked suspiciously.

"Yes."

"I guess we'll have to take your word on that," he added.

It was no secret that the town talked about me and Grace occasionally, even though there was nothing to talk about. The story of her rescuing me all those months ago in the snow was a favorite to retell. I was okay with this, as long as no embellishment occurred. I had never done, and never would do, anything inappropriate in regards to Grace Heck. I was here to serve a mission. True, I had begun to refer to our mealtime prayers as "saying Grace," but that was as close as I got to walking on the wild side.

Toby finished wrapping Elder Jorgensen's leg. Brother Heck and I laid him on a stretcher and carried him to Virgil's Find.

We only dropped him twice.

25

BOO

◇

Month Fifteen

Elder Jorgensen was looked over by a competent doctor in Virgil's Find. Prognosis: a bad break. We spent the
night near the hospital with the two full-time missionaries
stationed there, Elder Bess and Elder Jepson. The next day
Elder Jorgensen was driven back to Knoxville to heal.
President Clasp had done some quick shuffling to find me a
new companion. Elder Weeble and I returned to Thelma's
Way the following evening.

Elder Weeble looked like an egg. He was short and
compact. His head was tiny and his feet were big, giving
him a tremendous sense of balance. Weeble wobbled, but
he didn't fall down—at least not physically. His spiritual
balance was a different matter.

He spent all his time talking about how he wasn't worthy to be on a mission because he had done so many bad
things before he came out. Oh, he was no real rebel. His
pre-mission escapades consisted mainly of things like going

to 7–11 during Sunday School and talking back to his parents.

I felt Elder Weeble was just looking for attention and a way out of actually working on his mission. He pined about his girlfriend back home. He agonized over basic church doctrines, unsure of what he really believed. He didn't like climbing hills, couldn't teach a lesson if his life depended on it, and was horribly bothered by almost everyone in Thelma's Way. We didn't click.

Most irritating of all, he had the habit of asking ridiculous questions on a regular basis: "How come we have to work today? Why do we always have to wear white shirts? Do you think they accidentally left the page about afternoon naps out of the Missionary Handbook?"

Despite Elder Weeble, the branch was actually doing better than ever. I wasn't vain enough to think it had anything to do with my leadership, but ever since I was made branch president, Pap Wilson had started coming out to church. And Todd Nodd, the town wino—who used to come to church only because it was a warm place away from his vicious, alcohol-intolerant wife—had even attended once while sober. He sat in the front row and asked questions to the speakers during Sacrament meeting.

Plus, as Wad and Miss Flitrey became more and more serious about each other, Wad began attending the branch with her. The two of them looked quite cozy each week as they cuddled in their pew.

Even Grace Heck had been making an appearance, wandering down from her hideout in the hills. Her presence made my Sundays more fulfilling, but whenever she got within three feet of me, everyone in the congregation watched us like hawks. She would smile, and I would nod, and the air around me would start to thin. I had told President Clasp all about her, and how I seemed to have these unexplainable feelings for her. I thought maybe he would play it safe and finally transfer me. He didn't. I thought maybe he would command me to never think of her. He didn't. He simply admonished me to do the job and serve as I knew I should. He also told me to make sure none of my subsequent companions conveniently broke their legs, giving me a chance to be alone with her again.

Snow had fallen by mid-October that year, making it more difficult for us to get around. It was particularly treacherous crossing the Girth to see Teddy Yetch, but Teddy liked to have the missionaries in her home, and we liked to check up on her at least once a week.

We were actually teaching Teddy's neighbor in the hope of reactivating her. Sister Lando and Teddy had been good friends for years. She was small like Teddy, but heavier, and at least ten years younger. It seemed physically impossible for Sister Lando to talk without using her hands. She had gray hair and perpetual bad breath. She had bright hazel eyes and a pointed nose that seemed to collapse into itself at the tip. Elder Weeble speculated that over the years she had overused the expression "right on the tip of my nose" and, thanks to her talking so much with her hands, she had poked the tip of it in. Whatever the reason, it gave her a distinctive look.

Sister Lando had been inactive long before Paul had ever gone to Rome and returned to tear the ward apart.

Her reason for not coming out to church was simple: the Church didn't respect the fact that she came from a long line of supposed witches. Sister Lando could not understand how a religion that was so big on families being together could forbid her to wear her great-great-grandmother's pointy black hat to church. Sister Watson was allowed to wear her Easter bonnet, and Patty Heck received no reprimand whenever she donned her floral shawl. So why in the name of the good people of Salem couldn't Sister Lando wear her wide-rimmed, extra pointy black hat without getting guff?

Regardless of her ancestry, we wanted Sister Lando back at church. We needed her. I had told her that it still would not be appropriate for her to wear her hat in the chapel, but that she was welcome to wear it as she walked to and from the services. I even promised her that she could store it in one of the church closets for safekeeping. She found no comfort in this, seeing how Parley P. Pratt's first edition Book of Mormon had been stolen from right off the pulpit. I told her no one would be interested in stealing a musty old black hat. She told me to bite my tongue lest she be forced to turn me into a prune.

I laughed as if it were a joke. It *was* almost Halloween, after all, and everyone was getting into the spirit of things. The people of P.I.G. were leading the way. They had hit on a new money-making scheme and were busy making preparations for their first annual "Non-Satanic, Haunted Fun House."

Saints beware.

They had staked out a spot in the woods next to the

Watson's house. Toby Carver had hauled in some two-by-fours and rigged up a little maze. He stapled up plastic tarps for walls. For a week now the spot had been off-limits to anyone without a P.I.G. pass. I had cautioned all the people involved about not making it too scary, seeing how little kids would be going through and we didn't want to leave any of them emotionally scarred. Of course my words of caution did nothing but fall on deaf ears—except for Toby Carver, who asked if it was possible to make fake emotional scars out of relish and glue.

One good thing had come out of this non-satanic haunted house so far. Sister Lando had an occasion on which to wear her witch hat. Of course Pap Wilson put up a fight, arguing that her hat sort of watered out the non-satanic part. Pap was acknowledged and then ignored. Sister Lando also helped Sister Watson make some of the decorations and loaned P.I.G. a number of her best brewing kettles.

It was late afternoon that all-hallows-eve when Elder Weeble and I went to the boardinghouse to check for mail. We stepped inside, shaking off snow and wishing winter were ending instead of beginning. Elder Weeble got one letter from his girlfriend, and I received a cassette tape from my family. Pete Kennedy was working the counter at the boardinghouse. He was busy scooping flour from a big bag into a tiny container.

"You guys going to the fun house?" he asked, dusting his hands off.

"Probably," I replied.

Pete snickered.

"What's so funny?" I asked.

"Nothing," Pete giggled.

"Something's funny," my companion said, displaying his lack of patience for these people.

"I just hope you two don't get too scared," Pete explained.

"You're leaving your *gun* at home, right?" I asked.

"Yeah," Pete said mournfully. "Sister Watson said I'm not allowed to bring it to public gatherings any longer. I can't even bring it to the pageant."

Elder Weeble scoffed. "You mean that play you guys have been laboring over forever?"

"Yep," Pete answered with pride, oblivious to the sarcasm in Elder Weeble's voice. "Sister Watson just posted the parts. The rehearsals begin in the spring."

Pete pointed to the bulletin board. I walked over to take a look. Sister Watson would be playing the part of Drusa, and Bishop Watson was going to play a rather frail looking Parley P. Pratt. Narlette was going to be Thelma, and everyone else was listed as "insignificants."

"How appropriate." Elder Weeble laughed.

We took our mail and went home to prepare for the night's festivities.

Our home was really coming along, too. We had new windows to keep out the cold, and the week before, they had finally hooked up the electricity. It was so nice to have electric lighting again. We found a second-hand microwave in Virgil's Find. It worked great. We even had a small refrigerator where we could store food and keep our condiments consistently cold year round. If all went well, in the spring we would get running water. I hoped not to be here for that.

I liked my branch president calling, and I really did have good feelings for this town, but I was becoming increasingly restless. I was feeling less like a missionary and more like a permanent fixture. I needed out of here and on to something else. It wasn't right, me being here for so long. I would have considered it all a big mistake if not for the fact that President Clasp wrote and visited so often. Always he would reiterate how strongly he felt that I should stay right where I was. I kept thinking that there had to be someone here that only I could touch. So I had written out everyone's name on a big sheet of paper and consistently prayed over them, hoping that heaven would show me the way. So far heaven had left me alone.

I just wanted to be somewhere where we rode bikes and tracted outdoors. I wanted my mission to have two parts: the unusual part when I was put here, and the after-the-unusual part when I was put somewhere to serve as I had once envisioned I would.

I hardly knew any of the other elders in the mission. I had seen nothing of Tennessee except for Thelma's Way, Virgil's Find, and a little bit of Knoxville. My after-mission slides were going to be sorely lacking—"and here's another shot of the rotting covered wagons, this time in the snow . . ."

"Do we have to wear our ties tonight?" Elder Weeble asked as we finished up our soup.

"Of course," I replied.

"Why would we wear ties to a haunted house?" he whined.

"Because we're missionaries."

"But it's Halloween. The whole point is not to look like what you are." Elder Weeble was speaking slowly, as if I might have trouble understanding.

"Forget it, Elder," I said.

Elder Weeble put his soup bowl in the big tub of water we had by the refrigerator. "I don't see why there has to be so many rules. Men are that they might have joy," he said, quoting his favorite scripture, and the only one he knew.

"Take it up with President Clasp," I said.

"I just might," Elder Weeble said boldly. "This mission needs some innovators."

I took the dishes out to the river and rinsed them off half-heartedly. I brought them back inside and set them up to dry. We then headed over to the festivities. It was still light, and snow fluttered as the ominous clouds scratched themselves, sending dandruff-sized flakes down through the air. As we walked through the meadow we passed groups of kids dressed up for Halloween. It looked as if most of them had chosen the copout ghost costume.

Paul was in the meadow as well, heckling all those who were heading to the festivities. We waved politely. He didn't return the gesture.

We walked back behind the Watsons' house and over to the improvised spook alley. Sister Watson was standing out front with what looked to be a glass fishbowl, collecting money from the line of people waiting to go in and be scared.

"Are we going in?" Elder Weeble asked me.

"I'm not sure," I replied, stepping up to Sister Watson.

"Good turnout," I commented on the long line of anxious patrons.

"Folks appreciate the effort we've put forth," she proudly said. "Should put us over the top as far as P.I.G. money is concerned. We'll get that Paul Leeper yet."

So far no one had actually been into the tarp-covered structure to be able to fully appreciate all of their efforts.

"This isn't going to give kids nightmares?" I asked her.

"The kids around these parts are accustomed to fear." It seemed like a logical reply.

"Is it appropriate for missionaries?" I asked.

Sister Watson scoffed as if she would never take part in any activity that was not appropriate for missionaries. We paid her four dollars and took our place in line. A few minutes later Tindy MacDermont parted a portion of the tarp and started ushering people in. Lupert Carver was the first to go into the haunted house. I expected to hear screaming or hollering coming from inside as he entered. But there was not a sound. What seemed like only a few seconds later, Lupert came around from the exit in the back holding a small dish of something and complaining.

"Is that it?"

Ed Washington quickly whisked Lupert away before he could say anything else. The next child to go in and come out looked a bit more frightened but still seemed dissatisfied. Every child after that had the same expression when they came out. And always they were carrying a small dish of something brown and a folded piece of paper. For those kids who could get a word in edgewise before Ed hustled them away, it was always, "That's it? That's the whole haunted house?"

Finally it was our turn. We were the first adults—well, semi-adults—to go through. I parted the tarp cautiously and crept inside. It was pitch black for a few seconds and then, as the tarp closed behind me, a light flashed on and there was old Bishop Watson sitting on a folding chair handing out pamphlets for the John Birch Society.

"Corruption is everywhere," he booed. "Beware."

Around the next corner was Toby Carver covered in ketchup and lying on a table. I watched him lick and taste himself when he thought we weren't looking. Just past him was Miss Flitrey serving up chocolate pudding from a big kettle. The kettle was labeled "mud."

"Have some dirt, my pretty," she said. Sister Lando was standing next to her, sporting her hat and cackling.

For the grand finale, Jerry Scotch sort of barked at us as Pete Kennedy escorted us out the back tarp.

I stepped back outside and just stood there, wearing the same expression as everyone else. P.I.G. had spent a week on that haunted house and that was all they could come up with. I looked at my John Birch pamphlet.

"Do you really know who your friends are?" it said across the front in bold.

Obviously not.

Elder Weeble came out complaining about the pudding.

"This stuff tastes like tar."

"What'd you think?" Ed Washington asked us.

"It was short," was all I could think of to say.

"But scary, right?" he added.

"In a sense," I replied.

"Are you going to eat your pudding?" he asked.

I handed him my pudding and walked off with my companion.

* * * * *

Those who had been through the haunted house already, and those who weren't planning to ever go through, had gathered at the Watsons' home to drink cider and socialize. I was pretty familiar with the Watsons' home, due to the fact that we did all of our laundry over there. We walked in and took a seat on their couch. People sat around talking about the haunted house, the John Birch Society, the coming pageant, and Paul, as kids smeared pudding over everything the Watsons owned.

I sipped my cider, enjoying the conversations and voices that had grown familiar to me. I was comfortable here. I would have helped myself to a second glass of cider, but Briant Willpts came into the room and informed us that they had used that same cider to play bobbing for apples earlier in the evening, and had anyone seen his teeth.

I stared into the empty glass in my hand with new horror when we heard Sister Watson screaming outside.

"It's gone!" she was yelling. "It's gone!"

Everybody ran out to see what was going on.

"What's gone?" Brother Heck asked.

"The money," Sister Watson sobbed, falling to her rear

on the porch and beginning to cry. Her wig slid to the back end of her head. "All of the money we collected. Gone. Gone. Gone."

"Can't be," Sister Heck insisted.

"But it is," she insisted back.

Money missing was something to be concerned about. There was no one in Thelma's Way who took money for granted. Sure, Leo seemed to always have enough, but even he still seemed to respect the almighty bill.

Grace's brother, Digby, pulled up just then on his motorcycle and unwrapped the Saran Wrap from around his head.

"Are you sure it's gone?" Pap Wilson asked Sister Watson.

"I looked everywhere," she wailed. "We were keeping the proceeds in Sister Lando's crystal ball, and I set it down to help. We were just cleaning up, pulling down the maze. I turned around and it was gone. The crystal ball was right where I'd put it, but the money inside it was gone."

"Who could have taken it?" I asked.

A giant, dimly lit mental light bulb cracked on in unison above the crowd's head.

Paul.

Everyone turned around.

As if on cue, there he was standing about fifty feet from the porch. He had been pestering everybody earlier, now he was suspect. He stared at us all in disbelief.

"What are you all looking at?" he asked in disgust, taking a couple steps backwards and away from us. "I didn't do anything. Truth is the wind that lets me soar."

These people would show him sore.

"Thief!" Briant yelled in response to Paul's wisdom.

"Where's the money?" old Pap Wilson demanded.

Paul didn't stick around to answer questions or dish out any more confusion. He raised his fist in defiance and took off running down to the meadow and towards the river.

Everyone stood there as if they were helpless. It was one thing to be outraged by what Paul had done. It was something else to actually exert effort to try to apprehend him.

"I'll get him," Digby yelled, jumping back onto his motorcycle and kicking it to life. Smoke burst from its rusty pipe. The crowd parted like the Red Sea, providing a place for him to cycle through.

Digby gallantly whipped out his roll of plastic Saran Wrap and haphazardly rolled a bunch of it around his head to protect his eyes. He looked like a clear mummy out for trick or treat. He revved his bike, nodded to the crowd with his now-matted noggin, and took off across the snow.

The chase was on. It was almost impossible to see Paul and Digby in the dark.

As luck would have it, Tindy MacDermont just happened to have her powerful flashlight with her. She flicked it on and spotlighted the spectacle, bright against the snow.

Paul was well over halfway across the meadow before Digby had even gotten started. If Paul could make it to the Girth River and onto a raft by the burnt bridge, escape would be certain. We watched as Digby closed the gap.

Digby's rusted motorcycle was no speed demon. It had a top speed of somewhere just above the double digits. So now as he sped across the meadow trying to catch Paul, it looked rather surreal, like slow motion. From where we all stood, we could see the back of Digby and the back of Paul even further off as he ran like the wind.

Digby was closing in.

Paul was heading straight for the bridge, his arms flailing wildly as he ran.

Digby was getting closer still.

Narlette began to chant.

"Go, go, go, go," she repeated over and over.

Everyone began chanting along.

Paul was getting ever closer to the river. It looked as if Digby might not be able to catch him. We saw Paul glance over his shoulder, see Digby, and move even faster. Digby was not about to give up. He needed to lighten his load. He reached over his shoulder, pulled off his backpack, and threw it down. Then, in one swift move, Digby lifted both feet from the pedals and kicked his boots off and into the air.

His load now lighter, he closed in on Paul. I don't know exactly what we all thought Digby would do when he got to Paul. I guess he could have run him over, or jumped off and wrestled him to the ground. Not knowing somehow made the suspense even greater.

"Go, go, go, go, go," we all whispered.

He was so close now. Paul wasn't going to make it. We all watched the back of Digby's head as he went in for the kill. Digby looked strong and heroic as he gallantly pursued Paul, his Saran Wrapped head shining in the light of Tindy's focused flashlight. He sat up straight on his motorcycle as he moved in for the grab. He put out his left hand, reaching. Then the back of his head began to wobble. His shoulders slumped as he suddenly put his hand back on the handlebar.

Something was going wrong.

Digby was slowing down! We saw him sort of bob from side to side as he decelerated. Then in one fluid movement he tipped over, bike and all. A patch of oil smeared against the snow marking his spot. Paul jumped down on the bank, grabbed a raft, and took off across the thickening Girth.

"What happened?" Sister Watson yelled.

I took off running with Brother Heck towards the spot where Digby had collapsed. Elder Weeble was right behind us. I could see instantly what the problem was. In his haste, Digby had plastered Saran Wrap around not only his eyes but also his nose and mouth, cutting off all air intake. I quickly pulled the wrap off of his head. He coughed and took in a huge gulp of air. He looked up at me.

"I almost had him," he whispered.

"Paul's fast," Brother Heck said, leaning over Digby and me, his hands on his knees.

I helped Digby to his feet and then let him lean on me as we crossed back over the meadow to the Watson's place.

"I almost had him," Digby told his father.

"I'm right proud of you, son," Brother Heck said.

Leo wheeled the motorcycle back to the Watson's porch and leaned it against the rail.

"Good chase," everyone said, patting Digby on the shoulder.

"What about the money?" Sister Watson cried.

"It's gone for now," Brother Heck said. "We'll give Paul a visit tomorrow."

"It'll be too late," Teddy Yetch moaned. "He'll have hid it up by then."

"Well, I for one ain't going to go stomping over to Paul's place right now," Brother Heck said. "Paul would shoot me and claim he couldn't see who I was."

"And to think I was ready to re-believe in him," Pete Kennedy said.

Once again Paul had botched everything. Everyone besides Elder Weeble and I shuffled back into the Watson's home. I guess they were hoping to salvage some sense of celebration. In my mind it was too late for that.

Elder Weeble and I left the crowd and headed into the night.

26

OPEN MOUTH, INSERT FUTURE

Elder Weeble and I walked back across the meadow to the boardinghouse and sat down on the porch. It wasn't often that the boardinghouse was vacant. Usually locals were strewn through it long into the night. But tonight the party was somewhere else. I could hear faint voices still coming from the Halloween celebration across the meadow.

"Why are we stopping here?" Elder Weeble asked, after we had settled onto the porch.

"It's kind of a nice night," I replied.

"It's Halloween and I'm cold," he complained. "If I were back home in Colorado I'd be hanging out with my friends."

I just stared at him.

"What?" he finally said self-consciously.

"After all that's happened today, that's all you can say?" I asked bluntly. "Why'd you even come on a mission?"

It was Elder Weeble's turn to stare at me for a moment.

"I don't know," he finally said stubbornly. "I guess my brother went to Russia, my sister went to Australia, and I'm stuck here."

I appreciated the family history, but his dialogue didn't exactly answer my question.

"So you went on a mission because your brother went to Russia?"

"No," he insisted.

"Because your sister went to Australia?"

"Don't be dumb," he said. "I came on my mission because I was supposed to."

"So why don't you try to like it here?" I asked. "These people aren't so bad, if you leave out Paul."

"This place is a dump," Elder Weeble said.

I looked at the black sky and the distant sparks of scattered houses lighting up for the night. I smelled the air as if it were a fine stew simmering in front of my hungry stomach. I looked at the porch steps and observed the knife etchings carved into its wood.

"Feeble was he . . ."

I assume it was supposed to say "Feeble was here." Feeble must have become distracted before he was able to properly mar the porch. I knew people who were dead here. That really made me feel attached.

I had barely gotten to know Roswell and Feeble, but I still missed them. Of course, in so many ways Feeble still was here. Thelma was still here. No one's spirit ever seemed to leave this place. The meadow seemed to trap the souls of all who wandered in. I already knew I would leave a large chunk of myself when I left. Elder Weeble just couldn't see it.

"This place really isn't so bad," I reiterated.

"Give me a break, Elder," he mocked. "You're just confused from being here so long. Besides, you like it here because of your weird girlfriend."

"What?" I asked sharply.

"Your girlfriend, the redhead," he explained. "Hope, Chastity, whatever."

"Grace?"

Elder Weeble snickered.

"What about Grace?" I asked.

"I've heard things. It's all through the mission."

"What kind of things? I hardly even know her," I protested.

"That's not what Elder Sims said," Elder Weeble went on. "He said you used to meet with her in secret. Even Toby Carver said you two were caught walking alone in the woods. Sounds awful cozy to me. No wonder you never want to leave. Although I can't see what you see in that backwoods horse."

I hated Elder Weeble.

It was an awful thing to feel, but I just couldn't stand him any longer. I don't know why my emotions boiled to the surface so suddenly, but I had a feeling that talk of Grace had something to do with it. I had never done anything wrong or improper. I had never even had an improper thought about her. But heaven be scorned, I did feel something for her, and in that respect I had been open and honest with President Clasp. I had done nothing to be ashamed of.

I had left Lucy, the most gorgeous girl in Southdale, and I had discovered that the world was bigger than her and her perfect smile.

Now, as I watched Elder Weeble sit, trapped in his box of pity and misunderstanding, I was sick. His mean words were both stupid and wrong. Grace was no backwoods horse. She was a confusing painting that took time and knowledge to truly appreciate. I was going to dispute what he had so callously said, but once again he opened his big mouth.

"Let's hear you stick up for your girlfriend," he slurred.

"She's not my girlfriend and you know it," I argued. "I'm a missionary, for goodness sake."

"Yeah, right," he said, standing up and wiping the cold from off his seat.

I don't know why I didn't tear into Elder Weeble. I wanted to throw him to the ground and make him take it all back. I wanted to call him names and maybe hit him a few times. I wanted to stand up and say, "Yes, I like Grace, and no, I do not like you." But I didn't do any of these things. We were companions. We were stuck together. I was the senior companion and consequently the one that should act with more maturity and reason. Elder Weeble was just confused. I needed to make this missionary experience good for him. I had a responsibility. It would do no good to drag things out. So I did the expedient thing and laid it to rest.

"Listen," I began slowly. "I do not like Grace. She's just

another part of this crazy town. We're here to do a job and that's it. We can leave this place better than we found it, or worse. If we want it to be better, then you should at least act like you care."

Elder Weeble said nothing.

I stood up next to him.

"Happy Halloween," I joked.

Voices drifted from across the meadow as the snowy ground lay silent and clean. The festivities were still in full swing at the Watson house. I felt my heart slump as my tired feet and soul recognized the end of another day.

"I'm tired," Elder Weeble informed me.

We headed for home.

27

PAINFULLY MARRED

Grace had not meant to hear. She had been walking through the cemetery when she saw Trust and his companion make their way back and sit down on the dark porch of the boardinghouse. She crept up to the wall and listened as they spoke. She couldn't resist.

Grace had meant to hear.

Grace had been wrong about Trust. Very wrong. How had her heart permitted this to happen? Grace's one ally, her own intuition, had turned on her, betrayed her, left her alone. Grace could not explain the feelings she had for Trust, and she could not brush them away; she knew there was something more at stake. It had seemed at times as if Trust had come to Thelma's Way just to give her hope.

So much hope. So much hype.

"I do not like Grace."

Five words from Trust's lips.

Grace stood there, her back against the side of the boardinghouse, her heart lying cold with the snow.

"I do not like Grace."

Five words. Nothing else.

It was just that she hoped for something more.

28

SLEIGH BELLS RING, I AIN'T LISTENING

Snow fell like shaved cheese—slices, wedges, and gobs—mixing together on the ground, and piling up as if God were Italian and earth was his lasagna. Just gratzi. We wouldn't be going anywhere soon. I looked over at Elder Weeble. He scrunched his face up against the window.

"Great," he said, raising a fist and pretending to curse Mother Nature.

It was ten o'clock Christmas morning, and the prospect of spending my day cooped up alone with Elder Weeble didn't exactly excite me. The snow was at least a couple of feet deep and still coming down. So much for Christmas cheer this year.

I was still in Thelma's Way, celebrating my second and last mission Christmas. We had put up a tiny tree in the corner of the house, and a few small gifts sat beneath it waiting to be opened. We had planned to spend the day at

181

the Hecks' home. They had invited us over for food and Christmas company. I couldn't help being excited about the prospect of possibly seeing Grace. Surely she would spend Christmas with her family. I had bought a little secondhand book in Virgil's Find to give to her. She had gone into deep seclusion the last couple of months, and I was simply hoping that my small Christmas present might make her feel welcome.

Yes, those were my intentions. Purely concerned.

The snow kept coming.

"Some Christmas," Elder Weeble whined, thrusting himself upon his bed in anger. "If I were home in Colorado, I'd be having a blast."

I pulled a chair up to the window and stared at the falling skies.

"Let's go do something," Elder Weeble complained.

The wind was really howling now, making the visibility about three feet.

"We can't go out in this," I replied.

"If I was in Colorado I would," he snapped.

I thought about starting a fist fight with my companion just for the sake of having something to do. Heaven knows he irritated me enough to bring me to blows.

I opened my backpack up and pulled out Grace's gift.

"Merry Christmas, Elder," I said, handing it to him.

"I didn't get you anything," he fumbled, suddenly gracious.

"No big deal," I replied, waving the whole thing off. "No big deal."

29

SPRING RUNOFF

MONTH TWENTY

I had never seen a more beautiful time or place. This year spring seemed to bring more than just renewed life, it brought new colors and textures. Even the air seemed freshly pressed and packaged. The Girth ran stronger than ever, and the meadow was alive with tiny green limbs and speckled yellow faces. The children seemed older and wiser, and the adults less absurd. The dirt seemed richer, the houses nicer, and the season longer.

Oh, and by the way, I had been released as branch president.

I was now just a regular missionary again. My days in Thelma's Way were numbered. I had not actually received word concerning my transfer, but I knew it would happen soon. I had served in Thelma's Way for twenty months.

I was grateful for my time as branch president. It had taught me a lot. The Lord had allowed me to really care for these people. I hoped they would remember me. And I had reason to believe I had worked my way into the local lore thanks to the Nippy Ward Incident, as it had become known.

A little while back I had finally talked the mission into putting out the money to buy hard-hearing Nippy a hard-hearing hearing aid. Nippy had been faithful in coming to church every week, and I felt that we owed it to her to help her hear what was being said. The mission put up most of the cash, and the branch members got together and tossed in the rest. We bought her a really nice one—an unbelievably tiny device that was supposed to let her hear every interesting, and uninteresting, thing we said without hardly being visible in her ear. The Sunday after we had gotten it, we all met at church early to make the presentation. When Nippy came in we yelled "surprise." It was loud enough for her to hear. Then I approached her and presented her with the little piece of technical wizardry. I put the tiny thing in her palm and promised her it would help her to hear. Nippy smiled, nodded, thanked me profusely, and then, before I could stop her, she swallowed the thing. Hundreds of dollars down the throat. She thought it was some sort of super hearing pill.

I don't think Nippy ever fully realized what had happened, but she graciously pretended that the pill had had a positive effect. Now she nodded with much more vigor. I knew that incident would not soon be forgotten. That, and maybe the job fair that I had put on.

I had wanted to help the members better their lot in life by teaching them how to find work and instilling in them a desire to be self-sufficient. I invited some of the more established members from Virgil's Find to come and talk to us about work habits and share their secrets for procuring a good job. It actually went pretty well. Average-looking Jerry Scotch, however, interrupted the speakers a lot, butting in with suggestions. I guess he thought his steady job at the Corndog Tent made him an expert on the subject. His suggestion about taping a piece of licorice to your resume as a treat for whoever would read it was certainly a novel idea. Well, the long and the short of it was that Pete Kennedy actually got a job as an exterminator in Virgil's Find. Later, of course, he did get fired when it was discovered he had been spraying the funeral home with his eyes closed, scared he might see something that would unsettle him. His indiscriminate spraying had killed a lot of expensive rose bushes and ruined a good portion of wallpaper. But the point was that being assertive brought results. I hoped he would remember the principle. Even if he never worked again.

Elder Weeble had given way to my latest companion. Elder Staples was from Texas, and he was big. His shoulders barely fit though our door. He had big hands, big feet, and a big voice. He had an appetite that an "all you can eat" buffet would be hard pressed to fill. He was writing to about twenty girls back home, and talked realistically about how he would someday play quarterback for the Dallas Cowboys. He was constantly calling me "Sport." When I went over the "Elder" rule with him, he began calling me "Elder Sport."

He liked to look in the mirror. Actually, he liked to look at anything reflective. Polished shoes, silverware, glass, he wasn't too particular, as long as the image reflecting back was his own. He worked hard enough, but he also enjoyed playing dumb pranks on the locals. When we knocked on someone's door he would turn around so that his back would be facing them when they opened the door. He liked to tell people that he was from China and a member of the U.S. shuffleboard team. He liked to play "Got Your Nose," "Your Shoe's Untied," and "Button-Button." He had wavy blond hair and blue eyes that were shallow and gleaming. He didn't like the fact that I was senior companion and was rather vocal about it. We were working to make our partnership productive.

Grace's father was put in as branch president. He had come a long way. Toby Carver was his first counselor, and Leo Tip his second. They were a good team.

The work was going well. We still had not recovered as many inactive Mormons as I had hoped we would, but the ones who had hung around had grown stronger. On a sad note, Bishop Watson had passed away a few days after Christmas. He went peacefully in his sleep. We laid him to rest alongside his predecessors in the Watson family mausoleum.

Sister Watson mourned for an appropriate time over the death of her husband. Then she lost herself in preparations for the upcoming sesquicentennial pageant. With no husband to hold her back she was moving forward with great effort.

I had not seen Grace since before Halloween. She seemed to have disappeared. Brother Heck said that even he and his wife hardly saw her. She came by to help her mother with the costumes for the pageant, but that was about it. The Hecks didn't know what she did with the rest of her time. I was tempted to seek her out, but I knew that would not be right. Besides, with my poor sense of direction, I wasn't sure I could find her place again. Toby Carver had seen her a few times on the path to Virgil's Find, and Leo said she stopped by every once in a while to visit his dogs. When I thought about leaving Thelma's Way, my thoughts always circled back to Grace.

I had even written my mother and dropped Grace's name. I had mentioned that she seemed nice, and that I thought highly of her. Two weeks later I received a copy of *The Miracle of Forgiveness* in the mail. Mom wasn't taking chances.

With Bishop Watson dead, and the leading role in "All Is Swell" now up for grabs, Paul Leeper had taken new interest in the town pageant. Despite what Sister Watson might think of him, he demanded the right to star in the show as the only other male in town with the spiritual charisma and presence enough to represent Parley P. Pratt. He took it very seriously. He even said that since the lead male was Parley P. Pratt, the part should go to him, seeing how Parley's middle name was Paul. I informed him that Parley's real middle name was Parker. Paul insisted that in German "Parker" meant "Great Paul." Apparently he now saw the pageant as a way for him to get his message about seeing the finger to a wider audience than even he had originally conceived. The world was his stage, and he was ready to act on it.

But, of course, it was for naught. Sister Watson said there was no way on earth that she would ever consent to a thief like Paul having anything to do with such a sacred enterprise.

When it became clear that Sister Watson would not give in, Paul changed his tune.

"I wouldn't be caught dead in such a silly, stupid show, anyway," he said. "The real Parley P. Pratt would roll over in his grave to know you were representing his life in a pageant. May the winds of disgrace visit your commode."

Sister Watson stood her ground. Pulling her wig down over her eyes, she bore solemn witness that, on the contrary, outdoor pageants had served a critical role in Church history. Each of the centennial parades in Salt Lake City had featured pageants. And just because Parley P. Pratt or Brigham Young had never been in a pageant didn't mean they wouldn't have leaped at the opportunity had it been presented. Brigham Young was reportedly quite a dancer.

Paul said she was full of hot air and Sister Watson challenged him to a duel. Well, not a duel, really, but a public debate on the subject of pageants. Paul agreed, and a date was set.

The town was abuzz. Finally, Sister Watson and Paul would go toe to toe, tongue to tongue, and testimony to testimony in the middle of Thelma's Way. There was some concern about Sister Watson taking on so much so close to the big pageant, but she felt strongly that she must do it. The time had come to put Paul in his place, P.I.G. money or no P.I.G. money.

The afternoon before the big debate, Elder Staples and I slipped out to finish canvassing the very last section of Thelma's Way that I had not yet gotten to. It was a portion of forest between Thelma's Way and Virgil's Find. I felt like once I had really gone through this piece of land then I could leave feeling as if I had done all I possibly could.

Elder Staples led the way. We found a couple of homes. One was vacant, the other was occupied by a hermit named Melvin who claimed to have known Joseph Smith personally.

"Used to bowl together."

When I suggested that perhaps he knew another Joseph Smith besides the one who had restored the gospel, he got offended.

"Nope, knew the real one."

I kindly pointed out the fact that had he really known Joseph Smith then he, Melvin, would have to be at least a hundred and fifty years old. Melvin simply said that the little bit of extra weight he carried around helped push out his wrinkles and make him look younger.

Melvin wasn't interested in ever coming back to church. He claimed that Joseph cheated at bowling and that he wanted no part of a religion that condoned that kind of behavior.

We checked the back forest line of the area and found one more home. A young kid answered the door and invited us in. I recognized him from the meadow. I had seen him a number of times playing on the wagons.

"My mother's an actress," he said as we sat down.

"Wow," Elder Staples replied. "I'm impressed."

"Is your mother home?" I asked.

The kid ran off without answering.

189

A couple of minutes later the actress, his mother, came out. It appeared she mainly starred in parts requiring frumpy-looking backwoods leading ladies. She had a robe on and curlers in her hair. She sat down on the chair across from us.

We introduced ourselves and asked if she was familiar with the Mormon church.

She was. Her deceased husband had been a member.

"You're not a member?" I asked, seeking clarification.

"No," she answered.

"You're positive?"

She nodded.

I thought I was going to hyperventilate. Here, before me, sat a true-to-life nonmember—a real rarity in this hidden pocket of Tennessee. I think I was most jealous of other elders in this mission because they had so many nonmembers to work with. Well, we had one now.

"I'm a born again," she informed us.

Hallelujah.

We slowly questioned her making sure she hadn't simply forgotten that somewhere down the line she had been baptized a Mormon.

She had not.

Her nine-year-old son, Greg, was not a member either. Elder Staples had not put in the kind of time in Thelma's Way that I had. Consequently, he was not as overjoyed as me. Sure there was a chance she would never join the church. But at the moment, she was a possibility. She was a single nonmember mother. Her name was Judy Bickerstaff, and she worked part-time in Virgil's Find as a secretary for a small business. Of course, as her son had pointed out earlier, she aspired to one day be an actress. Her son, Greg, attended school in Thelma's Way. According to Judy, she and Miss Flitrey were fairly good friends. I couldn't understand why Miss Flitrey had never told us about this good nonmember friend of hers before.

Greg played with some toys on the floor as we got to know Judy. He set up action figures on my knees so that he could shoot them down with his dart gun. One figure caught my eye. It was a little metal man. I recognized it from someplace. I held onto it and studied it as we talked. There was a name etched into the bottom. "Martin Calypso."

"Where did you get this?" I finally asked Greg.

"Lupert gave it to me," he replied, snatching it back.

"Lupert Carver?" I asked.

Greg nodded. "He got it from a dead man."

Feeble.

I remembered seeing Lupert pick it up after Feeble dropped it in the dirt all those months ago. It was one of Feeble's "Great Men of the World" pewter figures.

"Martin Calypso," I said aloud. "It sounds so familiar."

"Whatever," Elder Staples replied. "It's just a toy."

Greg ran off, bored by us, and Judy invited us to dinner in three days and promised she would at least consider listening to the lessons. When we finally left their place, Elder Staples was properly excited. I was excited, too, but there was something about the name Martin Calypso that made me somber.

"Get over it, Sport," Elder Staples said as we walked back home.

It was early evening, the day before the big debate.

We had found a potential investigator.

Judy Bickerstaff.

Martin Calypso.

I hardly slept that night.

I woke up Elder Staples at four-thirty in the morning and told him to get dressed. We were going to Virgil's Find.

30

FOOD FLIGHT

◇

By the time Elder Staples and I got back from Virgil's Find, Thelma's Way was primed for the afternoon debate. There was already a crowd gathering in the meadow.

Two long banquet tables had been set up in the meadow next to the rotting pioneer wagons and not far from the nearly completed pageant stage. One table had two chairs, one for Sister Watson and one for Paul; the other was covered with food that folks had brought for the pot luck that would follow the debate. President Heck was actually wearing a tie and standing in front of the tables trying to look official. Sister Watson was working the crowd, shaking hands and patting backs. It was a big day.

Out in the meadow, Wad was sitting next to Miss Flitrey, CleeDee was lounging on a blanket with Leo, and Teddy Yetch and Sister Lando were selling extremely moist looking pre-debate pineapple brownies. I watched Digby Heck pull up on his motorcycle, unwrap his eye protection, then use the same sheet of Saran Wrap to cover one of the brownies for later. Kids ran around, and adults brought down lawn chairs and tree stumps to sit on. Old Pap Wilson and considerably younger Sybil Porter dragged out a couple of cinder blocks from the boardinghouse and made a few benches by laying boards across them. Nippy sat down in a folding chair and prepared to nod. The air filled with anticipation.

The scheduled starting time for the debate soon passed, and Paul had not yet arrived. Briant Willpts offered to play the part of Paul and debate Sister Watson himself. Sister Watson declined the offer. She would wait for the real thing.

The afternoon sun warmed the tops of our heads and shoulders as we sat ringed around the rosy looking at Sister Watson. Smugness seeped from her smile as she glanced about, feeling like maybe she had already won. President Heck shrugged his shoulders and looked to Leo Tip for the time. Leo didn't actually wear a watch, but CleeDee did. In fact, it was rumored that the real reason Leo had begun going out with CleeDee was simply because she wore a watch.

Whatever the reason for their first date, they were now the talk of the town. Word was they would be getting married in the Atlanta Temple sometime in July. That would be after my mission, but I had decided I would fly back if it happened.

Leo looked at CleeDee, and CleeDee glanced at her watch. Words were whispered and then Leo declared Paul officially late.

Ed Washington and his mother got up as if to leave.

People shook their heads, disgusted with Ed's lack of patience. Ed's mother made his excuses for him.

"Ed's got some chores to do," she explained.

Poor Ed.

From the standing position Ed spotted someone down by the river coming their way. The crowd fell silent and parted to let him through. He was dressed all in black and strutting.

"It's Paul," Ed said, stating the over-obvious.

Any and all wind died and the sun clicked things up two notches. Paul stepped silently up to President Heck and nodded. President Heck answered with a similar nod. Paul took his seat at the table next to Sister Watson, and the circle of spectators closed in around them.

President Heck cleared his throat as Teddy Yetch popped open an umbrella for shade. Everyone glared at her, filled with shade envy. I saw Toby Carver try to scoot closer to her and procure himself some cover.

"A few rules," President Heck said. "There's no need to swear, 'ceptin someone says something really profound. In which case a respectful, 'I'll be darned' is perfectly acceptable.

"In the spirit of fairness," he continued, "we will let Sister Watson go first because she's a woman.

"Each person will be given a certain amount of time to speak their mind," President Heck said. Then he paused, using *his* mind to remember what amount of time that was. "I think a couple minutes a question is appropriate. Leo will be our official time keeper."

Leo lifted up CleeDee's arm, showing all the watch he would be using.

"And just so as we're all in the know, the stated purpose of this debate is to find out if, given the chance, Parley P. Pratt would have acted a part in our pageant," President Heck explained. "I'm assumin' he would have played himself."

Sister Watson nodded her approval. President Heck signaled Toby Carver, who blew a whistle.

The sun was warm. The sky was clear. The debate was on.

Sister Watson turned to Paul and shuffled a few papers in front of her. She adjusted her reading glasses and sniffed through her nose. She pondered and looked as if she were going to ask a well-thought-out question.

Looks can be deceiving. She went right to the jugular . . .

"Why should anyone believe anything you say about pageants since you were the one who stole the Book of Mormon?" Her lips had barely moved.

Everyone sat there, stunned. The debate had hardly begun, and Sister Watson had issued what seemed to be a certain death blow.

Paul didn't flinch. "I didn't steal anything," he replied.

"That's a lie," Teddy Yetch yelled out from the crowd.

There was no rebuke from President Heck, our unbiased official. Sister Watson smiled.

"Why did you steal the P.I.G. money?" Sister Watson fired round two.

"I didn't steal your dirty money," Paul replied. "I never stole anything."

"That's a lie also," Teddy yelled out again.

I saw Toby Carver begin making a noose out of his ace bandage.

"Where were you the night the Book of Mormon was stolen?" Sister Watson probed.

"I don't know. That was well over two years ago," Paul sniffed.

"Funny how your memory is so selective," Sister Watson jabbed.

The crowd *woooooed*.

Pete Kennedy stood up in the third row. "Paul, you 'member when we caught that big deer that turned out to just be Geoff's dog?"

Paul nodded.

"That was seven years ago," Pete added.

"Ten, actually," Paul corrected.

"Well, if you can remember ten years ago then how come you cain't remember two?" Pete craned his head around, startled by his own insight.

The crowd began to murmur.

"Thing being . . ." Paul tried to explain.

Leo held up his hand indicating two minutes was up.

"Next question," President Heck said. "Paul?"

Paul tried to collect himself. He stood to speak.

"No fair standing," Jerry Scotch shouted out. "Makes Sister Watson look short."

President Heck knitted his brow. Paul sat down again.

"Thing is," Paul began. "I never stole nothing. Are

these the hands of a thief?" he asked, gently spreading his palms before him. Sister Watson sort of opened her mouth, but Paul's words continued to fill the air. "True enough, these are the hands of an imperfect man."

Some of the spectators started licking their lips. Paul seemed ready for confession.

"But these imperfect hands," he continued, "have held infants that were sick, pulled friends out of predicaments, and paddled across the Girth in service. Take a good look at these hands. Respect the service they have dished up. Pull up a chair and feast from my sacrifice." Paul took out a hanky from his shirt pocket and started to wipe his eyes. "There is something I have not told you all," Paul continued, misty-eyed. "But I feel you have aged in wisdom."

The compliment melted like chocolate over the crowd.

"When I was in Rome," Paul went on, "all those years ago, I experienced something that I was told not to share. The heavens forbade me to share it with you. But it was revealed to me this morning as I was shucking corn that now is the time to let you know. I've been given clearance to impart the truth . . ."

Leo's hand went up.

"Next question. Sister Watson?" President Heck said.

Paul cursed himself, aware of how close he had come to swinging the crowd emotionally to his side. This two-minute time thing would be the death of him.

Sister Watson stood and looked down at Paul. She knew he had gained ground as it was. She pulled out all the stops. "Did you or did you not try to kill Digby Heck?"

She was passionate, at least as passionate as a person can be without moving her lips.

The crowed started to murmur again and craned their necks looking back at Digby.

Paul's tiny, poorly arranged face, puckered up.

"I . . . I never meant to hurt Digby," he claimed.

"Never meant to, meant to," Sister Watson repeated. "Just like Cain never meant to hurt Abel."

Folks wiped at their brows in awe of Sister Watson's powerful debating style. It was obvious from her last question that she had done research on the matter of murder.

Miss Flitrey raised her hand. "Do you really think it's necessary to drag the Bible into this?" she asked.

Sister Patty Heck, who was sitting behind Miss Flitrey and was still sore over her teaching her children about ape genealogy, shifted in her chair and knocked Miss Flitrey's legs out from under her. "Stop trying to remove the Bible from everyone's lives," Patty accused.

Miss Flitrey turned around with a raging face and said, "Nice skirt," snidely to Sister Heck, making fun of her homemade clothing.

Well, not everyone could afford to shop the Virgil's Find garage sales like Miss Flitrey. Her teacher's salary allowed her to live a little too comfortable for most folks. Besides, everyone knew that Wad was dropping a lot of his hair-cutting money on her these days. Yes, at the moment Miss Flitrey was the closest thing the town had to having its own Kennedy. Sure, Leo was well off, but he didn't flaunt it like she did. And yes, Pete actually bore the Kennedy name, but Pete was Pete, and Pete was poor.

Toby Carver bravely stood up for Sister Heck and her homemade clothing. "I think her skirt looks right smart," he said, tugging his beard.

"How would you know if anything was smart," Miss Flitrey bit back.

"Hey!" President Heck yelled. "This debate is for Paul and Sister Watson. If you two want to schedule time to have your own argument, that's fine. Although I must say right now that my wife is right, and Flitrey is wrong."

Miss Flitrey looked at Wad, wondering if he was going to stand up and defend his woman.

Wad remained bunched down.

President Heck brought things back to the debate. "Paul's up. Next question."

"Wait a minute, he never answered my last question," Sister Watson argued.

"Your time's up," Brother Heck officiated. "Paul's turn."

"You can't count your wife and flighty Flitrey's squabbling as my time," Sister Watson protested.

"Rules is rules," President Heck snorted.

Sister Watson sat back, steaming like a bowl of blushing chowder. In the spring heat her wig was starting to slide to the back of her head.

"Can I speak now?" Paul asked, flicking the tip of his nose.

President Heck nodded.

"First off, let me say I would never harm Digby. He and I are kindred spirits. In fact, he reminds me of my trip to Rome."

Nice segue.

"Quick count," Paul continued. "How many of you here have ever been to Rome before?"

Narlette raised her hand, but she was ignored.

"I guess that makes me the expert," Paul bragged. "You folks have no idea what I'm talking about, do you?"

Touché.

"Now listen up," he said. "I am going to share with you what happened and those of you who are touched enough to understand will know I speak the truth." Paul paused and breathed deeply. He was going to say it all in one breath.

"When I saw the finger of Thomas I also had a vision about how you all would one day doubt my words and try and drag me down and have this debate and not let me be in the pageant and persecute me and then finally come to understand my position on heavenly and important and mystical things." He sucked in air. "So what I am about to tell you has been prophesied. The ghost of Thomas . . ."

Once again Leo's hand went up.

Paul was furious. "Why can't you allow a visionary man to properly prophesy?" Paul demanded, his big arguing mouth taking up the bulk of his face. "Blasphemy is your ally."

"The floor is now Sister Watson's," President Heck answered, motioning for Paul to simmer.

"So, Paul," she began. "Why did—"

"Maybe we should let Paul finish what he was saying," Ed Washington's mother interrupted. "Sounded sort of important."

We all stared at Ed's mom.

"Sister Watson has the floor," Jerry Scotch argued, as if he knew what having the floor meant.

"Don't you mouth off at my mother," Ed Washington demanded, showing more spirit than I had yet seen him have.

Jerry Scotch smirked. Ed lunged at Jerry, but his mother stopped him.

President Heck waved frantically at Toby Carver, signaling him to blow his whistle. Well, Toby was too busy offering Teddy Yetch money so he could sit in her shade to notice Brother Heck.

Paul pounded on the table. "Silence!" he demanded.

Everyone shut up.

"I have come down from my home," he huffed. "I have crossed the Girth River and taken the time to come to this farce. Your disrespect is a tube full of pasty ill will. I decree that I will be patient no more."

Paul stood.

"President Heck here," he pointed, "and his Mafia missionaries have had control of this valley for too long. Look at what they have brought you. The amount of Christian love contained in this meadow could be measured in a thimble's thimble."

Most of the crowd looked at their fingers, sort of pinching the size a thimble's thimble would be.

"Look at me," Paul blared. "I am an agent of prosperity sent to dwell among you. Your attention is necessary to your salvation."

Everyone now focused on Paul. In fact, they focused so intently that they didn't realize Sister Watson was not only standing up next to him, she was swinging one of Teddy's empty brownie pans at his head. I guess she wanted to speed up the debate.

"Sister Watson!" I yelled, pointing at her.

I had hoped to prevent her from hitting Paul. Instead, my pointing caused Paul to turn towards her. Sister Watson whumped Paul square in the face, the brownie pan ringing out through the meadow. Even Sister Watson was stunned by what she had done. Paul fluttered and then fell flimsily onto the table in front of them. President Heck ran to him and lifted his head. Because of Paul's already discombobulated facial features I couldn't tell if Sister Watson had done any damage. Toby undid his Ace bandage noose and sidled up to Paul. Paul stirred. He was all right.

I figured it was time for me to stand and tell the world what I knew.

"Paul didn't take the book," I yelled out.

"What book?" President Heck asked, the entire ring of spectators now looking at me.

"*The* book," I clarified. "The Book of Mormon that Parley P. Pratt gave Thelma's Way."

Everyone kept staring.

I walked up to the table. "I know for a fact that Paul Leeper did not take the Book of Mormon."

"Listen, Elder Williams," Toby said. "We like you and all, but I don't think this is really any of your business."

"Yeah," said Briant. "You're a good kid, but you ain't stock. Everyone knows it was Paul that stole the book. Just ask Jerry."

All eyes focused on Jerry. "*I* think he took it," Jerry said sheepishly.

"If he took it, then how come I have it?" I unzipped my rainbow backpack and pulled out the first edition Book of Mormon with the special Parley P. Pratt inscription—the very same one Paul was accused of stealing all those years ago.

Everyone gasped. Children cowered behind their parents. People covered their mouths.

"I told you!" Paul hollered. "I told you I didn't take it."

Pete Kennedy yelled out, "It was Elder Williams all the time. Let's get him." He reached for his gun, or at least where his gun would be had he been allowed to bring it.

I think they were considering a lynching, but Sister Watson spoke out. "Elder Williams wasn't even here when it was stolen," she said, staring at the book in amazement. "He wasn't even on his mission yet."

Everyone paused to think about this. It was worth considering.

Elder Staples tried to help me. "My companion didn't steal this book," he said standing. "I just saw him buy it."

"He bought it!" Pete yelled, still furious. "Let's get him."

President Heck held his hands up to silence the crowd.

"Maybe you have some explaining to do, Elder Williams," he said to me. The crowd hushed. I set the book on the table in front of me.

"I know that this will come as a great surprise and disappointment to all of you, but Roswell Ford took your book."

"Come on," Briant Willpts booed. "How dumb do you think we are?"

I prayed he wouldn't force me to say.

"It's true," I argued. "Roswell knew everyone would blame Paul, since Paul had prophesied that bad things were going to befall the Mormons, and Roswell needed the money. He stole the book and sold it to his cousin Stubby in Virgil's Find."

"Roswell's dead," Sister Yetch yelled out. "We shouldn't be speaking 'bout the rotted like this."

I hadn't considered that translated beings actually rotted.

"Teddy's right," Old Pap said. "Disrespectful through and through."

I threw out my next bit of news.

"Roswell's not dead," I shouted. "His cousin saw him last week. In fact, I have reason to believe he also stole the P.I.G. money."

Everyone's eyes turned red as they glared at me. Elder Staples stepped right up next to me and flexed his chest. I guess he was acting as my security.

"Now, Elder Williams," Toby cautiously said. "It's one thing to tell wild stories, but it's an entirely different deal to slander the translated name of Roswell and Feeble."

"You people have sinned," Paul spoke up. "You have misjudged me and now as the truth rears its big fat head you will see me as your superior."

Jerry Scotch had had enough. He jumped up and ran towards Paul, ready to grab his neck. Brother Heck held him back.

"People, listen up," he demanded, struggling against Jerry. "There has to be an explanation for all this."

"Yeah, Elder Williams is lying," Briant Willpts shouted.

"I'm telling you the truth," I insisted. "Roswell sold the book to his cousin Stubby for two hundred and fifty dollars. Stubby then sold it to a woman who collects old books so as to appear educated. I bought it back from her this morning."

The crowd fell hushed. I couldn't tell why until Wad spoke up.

"Two hundred and fifty dollars for that old thing. That's a fortune!"

"Two hundred and fifty dollars," I repeated.

President Heck picked up the book. "Let me get this straight," he said. "This thing's worth two hundred and fifty dollars?"

"Actually," I said, "this book is worth far more than that. A man back in my hometown bought a first edition Book of Mormon for twenty thousand dollars. And this one here's in better shape, and it's signed by Parley P. Pratt. I bet you could get a lot more for it."

Everyone was standing now.

"Twenty thousand dollars?" Sister Watson whispered in unbelief. "I thought all that book had was spiritual value."

President Heck set it back down on the table as if it were a hot coal. Then he reconsidered his actions and picked it back up. He held it tightly to his chest.

The crowd started to drool. I watched the gears in the noggins around me calculate what they could do with twenty thousand dollars. The wind picked up, blowing honesty, decency, and Christian consideration out of the meadow, replacing them with a triple helping of half-crazed greed.

Sister Watson moved first. She grabbed at the book, wrenching it from President Heck. By then, Briant Willpts was swinging his cane at Sister Watson. She dropped the book to put her hands up. The book had barely hit the table before Jerry Scotch clapped it up and turned to run. Sister Lando stuck one of her sturdy legs out and tripped Jerry. The book went flying though the air. It landed on Leo and CleeDee's blanket. For a moment, everyone just stared at it lying there. Then in one collective grunt they dove for it. Hands flew, hair whipped, and legs kicked. I stood there speechless. I turned to Elder Staples to see what he was doing to help calm the situation. He was no help; he had Paul on the ground trying to pin him down. He wasn't about to pass up this chance to wrestle an apostate.

"Elder!" I hollered.

I held up my hands foolishly, thinking it would help. And, just at that moment, Teddy surfaced from the pile of scrapping fighters with the book in hand. She only had a second. She had to get rid of it or get toppled. I guess she took my hands being up as a signal because she tossed it to me.

Frustrated and gunless, Pete Kennedy picked up a plate full of potato salad and launched it at me. Warm pieces of potatoes and eggs flew through the air.

"My salad!" Sister Yetch yelled, as if she had given birth to it. She broke from the pack and dove over the food table towards Pete. Everyone else dog-piled me. Hands, knees, elbows, and feet danced upon me like popping rocks. I was being kneaded like a ball of dough. Those who couldn't get to me and the book started throwing food at me and each other. The air was thick with handfuls of casseroles, cookies, and homemade confections.

For a good five minutes food and feet trampled and flew over me. Then one by one people dropped from the fight, falling to the ground to lie by me in exhaustion. A few people crawled off and away from us all. I watched Digby get hit in the eye and Leo get tackled by Paul. Old Pap Wilson beaned Wad with a few franks, and Frank Porter nailed Geoff Titter with a tin of Patty Heck's shortbread cookies. Eventually everyone was down.

I sat up and surveyed the scene. It looked like a battle-field, one big messy mound of people.

"Who has the Book of Mormon?" I asked looking around for it.

"Patty took it from me."

"I saw Pap with it."

"I never touched it."

"Just great," President Heck complained. "It could be anywhere now. I saw at least twenty people wander off when the food started to fly."

"So then why worry?" I sighed. "It will show up."

"Twenty-thousand dollars," Sister Watson whined.

"Well, I don't have it," Paul insisted, trying to pull some frosting from his hair.

"Just great," President Heck said again.

I lay back down and listened to the heavy breathing of my war-weary brothers and sisters.

"So Roswell's not dead," President Heck eventually said as he lay there recovering next to me.

"Nope."

"I thought I had seen him a couple months back in the deep forest," Toby muttered. "But I didn't say anything out of respect."

"He's somewhere," I replied.

Sister Watson was on her hands and knees looking for her wig. When she finally found it, it was covered in pudding. But the chocolate treat seemed to work well as an adhesive. So she slapped it back on her head and took a seat on one of the overturned cinder blocks. We all looked pretty ridiculous.

Sister Lando was the first to laugh.

I sat up and saw her body jiggle as she lay there violently snickering. Teddy laughed next, her old cackle filling the air like the food had previously. Ed joined in the jovial giggling, and then the rest of us.

We laughed for a good ten minutes, wiping our eyes and trying to catch our breath. We laughed and picked food off each other. Even Paul was enjoying the group snicker till Sister Watson shot him a wounding glance. It was okay for others to laugh at her hair, but not Paul.

We picked up the tables and cleaned up the meadow. I was wiping what looked to be some sort of jam off of my white shirt, looking down at the ground, when I noticed two beautiful feet step into my view. The feet were adorned by skimpy sandals that left little to the imagination.

Could it be?

I looked up slowly, hoping beyond hope that these two feet were connected to who I thought they were. My eyes stopped at the face of Grace. She wasn't smiling, but she wasn't frowning, either. Everything continued to go on around us as we stared at each other. Folks cleaned up and picked at themselves, oblivious to the two of us.

"You," I finally stated.

"Me," she replied, her red hair pulled back into a tangled ponytail.

I didn't know what else to say. She popped into my life at the most unusual times. I couldn't believe she had just walked up to me, planted her feet, and stayed there to let me speak with her. I was almost convinced that the feelings I had had for Grace were one sided and unfounded. But here she stood, and the spring light made her appear more splendid than all the flowers nature could push forth. Her thin dress was long and blowing in the gentle wind. She looked taller than I had remembered. Her green eyes fluttered with the breath of life.

"Where have you been?" I asked.

Grace smiled by accident. She quickly corrected herself. "Why?" she asked.

"I just . . . well . . . I, you make me so nervous," I said, leaking more honesty than I had intended.

Grace took a step back.

"I make you nervous?" she questioned, putting her hand to her chest.

Maybe it was the springtime. Maybe it was the teasing of warm weather. Maybe it was the knowledge that I wouldn't be here for too much longer. Maybe it was Grace. Whatever the reason, for the first time in over twenty months, I felt completely alive. I had been relatively happy the last year or so. Thelma's Way had even felt like home a couple of times. But completeness had been fleeting. At the moment, however, my soul was a sanctuary, and contentment was grazing on the fields of my heart. I was a peg that Grace had hammered into the landscape, making me fit.

"Grace, I . . . "

I was too busy admiring the scenery to notice Elder Staples step up to us.

"So you must be Grace," he smiled coyly, sticking out his hand and interrupting us. "Sport here has told me all about you."

Grace's smile disappeared.

"Only nice things," I offered.

"The whole town knows he's sweet on you," Elder Staples blabbered.

I blushed responsibly.

Her green eyes let me know that she was on to me—in a good way.

"So, did you come to see the debate?" I asked, trying to sound sure of myself.

"No," she replied beautifully. "I just dropped off a couple of costumes I made for the pageant at the boardinghouse."

211

"Were they hard to make?" I asked, sounding like a fool.

"Not too bad," Grace responded kindly.

"Oh," was all I said.

"Like I said," Elder Staples butted in, "he's sweet on you."

Grace smiled, then she turned and walked off. Just like that she was gone. I couldn't tell if the conversation had ended well or weirdly. A little bit of both, I concluded.

"Way to go," I scolded Elder Staples. "I'm not sweet on her."

"What?" he asked. "I was just trying to help."

We went back to helping with the meadow clean-up until it was done. President Heck was the only one to ask me how I had figured all this Roswell, Book of Mormon stuff out. So, when everyone was gone, my companion and I sat down with him on the rotting pioneer wagons and we talked.

I told him how Feeble had passed away with the figure of Martin Calypso in his hand, giving us the ultimate clue. It had been Grace who had first informed me of Martin Calypso. We had gone to the Virgil's Find library that morning to research him out. It turned out that Martin Calypso was a gentle pig farmer who lived in the 1800s. He was best known for the saying, "Let man and pig fight for freedom as brothers."

"He wasn't real smart," I added. "Anyhow, Martin had been rather successful until his twin brother, Leonard, started gambling and depleting the family funds. In a desperate state, Leonard ended up stealing their rare family

Bible and selling it to a Dutch sailor named Rugger. When Martin confronted Leonard, Leonard killed him.

"Well, I got to thinking how closely this resembled Roswell and Feeble," I said. "And the pieces fell together. I remembered that Roswell had told me about his cousin Stubby who had a pawn shop in Virgil's Find. I looked him up in the phone book. Elder Staples and I then went to visit him. I just wanted to find out if Roswell was still alive, and if Stubby by some chance knew where he was. I found out much more.

"When we entered Stubby's shop I simply asked him where Roswell was. He said he hadn't seen him in a couple of days, realizing immediately after he had spoken that he shouldn't have told me. It was too late. I knew Roswell was alive. I asked Stubby if he knew anything about an old book that Roswell might have had. Feeling that he had already said too much, he told us more. Yes, he knew about the book. He even gave us the address of the woman he had sold it to, there in town.

"I couldn't believe it. We headed over to her place, and she gladly sold it back to us, claming that it didn't look as snooty as some of her other old books. She gladly took my out-of-state check. She obviously didn't know the value of the book.

"I was ecstatic.

"We raced back here, stopping only at the boardinghouse to check if the rest of Feeble's 'Great Men of the World' pewter set was still there. Of course, the figures were all gone. Roswell had probably been sneaking in and out of the boardinghouse, taking them to sell. I bet if we checked all the other Virgil's Find pawn shops, we'd find a few with a number of little metal men on hand."

"But why?" President Heck asked.

"For the same reason he stole the Book of Mormon. I guess it's like Martin Calypso," I said. "Remember how much Roswell liked to bet everyone?"

"I guess," he answered.

"Think," I said. "He was constantly saying 'I'll bet you ten bucks this, or that, will happen.'"

President Heck nodded.

"All I can figure is that he lost more bets than he won. He must have needed the money. And when Feeble caught on to the fact that Roswell had stolen the book, he probably threatened to turn him in. Feeble was pretty honest and, unlike his brother, an active Mormon. Maybe Feeble had a heart attack running after or away from Roswell that morning. Something must have happened."

"So he killed his brother," President Heck said, scratching his head.

"I don't know the whole story," I pointed out.

"Where's Roswell now?" President Heck asked.

"He can't be too far away," I said. "I figure he stole that P.I.G. money because he needed something to live on, or maybe he needed to pay some other debts. He must be pretty good at slipping in and out without being noticed."

Elder Staples yawned, bored with it all. "This is one goofy town," he commented.

"So Paul's innocent," President Heck said incredulously.

"Yep," I replied.

"Of course, he'll use all of this to build up his own religion again," President Heck pointed out. "He'll talk on and on 'bout how he was persecuted for the real gospel."

"Probably so," I agreed.

"We're right back where we started from," President Heck mourned.

The thought was thoroughly depressing. Any contentment I had felt earlier from the presence of Grace was suddenly gone. We got up from the old pioneer wagon and went home. Feeling that things were worse now than when I had entered the valley made me sick. I had turned this place back into what it always had been. Confused.

What was I thinking?

31

HALF BAKED

Sister Watson wasted no time. After getting permission from Ed's mother, she cast Ed Washington as Parley and called an emergency meeting to get him acquainted with the cast. Some folks thought she ought to have given the part to Paul after all, seeing as he didn't really steal the Book of Mormon or the P.I.G. money. But Sister Watson held her ground. Thief or no thief, anyone who claimed to have seen the finger was trouble. Besides, Paul had besieged her with hundreds of handwritten memos demanding changes to the script—changes that would emphasize similarities between Parley P. Pratt and Paul himself. They were both visionary leaders persecuted for their testimonies. They had both traveled to far away lands, that sort of thing. It didn't work. Paul was banned from the planning committee for good.

The morning of the emergency meeting, everyone awoke to find a giant loaf of bread sitting right outside the boardinghouse, in the meadow. It was at least seven feet long and four feet wide. The sight of it was rather creepy and surreal. Having served in Thelma's Way for so long, I thought that there were few things that would surprise me anymore. This did.

No one knew where it had come from. Some speculated that it had dropped out of a plane.

"A really big bakery plane," CleeDee said.

Leo suggested that it was an alien loaf.

"Maybe other species travel in bread," he said, his eyes getting wide.

"I've never seen anything like it," President Heck said.

But Sister Watson was a voice of reason.

"It probably came from Teddy," she said. "Teddy's always making new things. I'm sure it's just her way of helping with the pageant. We should be right grateful, it seems to me."

Everyone agreed that seemed to make sense.

Lupert Carver walked right up to it and pinched off a piece.

"It's good," he declared, and that's all it took.

President Heck went to get his tree saw and stood there at the butt of the bread cutting off chunks for people. CleeDee fetched some honey.

After everyone had eaten, it was time for the meeting to begin. There was still about three-fourths of the loaf left, and people began talking about freezing the rest, and questioning each other as to who had a freezer. President Heck was about to start dividing the thing into sections when Teddy Yetch showed up.

"Thanks for the breakfast, Teddy," Ed Washington

chimed. Everyone smiled and applauded until Teddy interrupted.

"I didn't make that enormous thing. Never been one
much for baking bread."

"I wonder who baked it?" Toby asked.

Suddenly it was quiet. Sister Watson spat out the wad
of bread she had in her mouth.

"What if it's Paul?" she said nervously. "What if it's
poisoned?"

"It ain't poison," Toby said. "Poison tastes sour. Besides,
if Paul had made a giant loaf of poison bread, you can bet
he'd be around to watch us eat it."

Everyone looked about quickly, then all at once every
eye, except for Tindy's lazy one, glanced back at the bread.
People began stepping away from it.

"Paul, you in there?" Brother Heck yelled.

The bread remained silent.

Teddy Yetch took a stick and drove it into the center of
the bread. Everyone gasped. Teddy pulled it out and posi-
tioned herself to do it again.

"Wait," I yelled. "If Paul is in there, you don't want to
kill him."

Teddy thought about this for a second.

"Paul's not smart enough to bake himself in a loaf of
bread," Sister Watson shouted. "Jab it again, Teddy!"

"Wait a second," President Heck said, holding his
hands up. "Elder Williams is right."

President Heck walked up to the bread and jammed
both his fists into it. He felt around in the middle for a few
moments and then struck something. He looked like a

breadenarian about to deliver a litter of loaves. He yanked hard and pulled out an ankle. Muffled protest began to emanate from inside the bread. Toby stepped up and helped Brother Heck pull Paul completely from the bread.

Paul lay on the ground coughing up bread for a few moments. He was completely covered in crumbs and mad about being discovered. He stood up and pointed at all of us.

"You and your secret meetings," he said. "I've a right to know what you're saying about me. I've a right to know about the pageant. But the joke is on you. I spent the last few months building a big hidden oven over beyond Lush Point. I knew it would come in handy. I wheeled this loaf out here and crawled up from the bottom and into it. And it would have paid off, too, if you'da just started your meeting on time 'stead of eating first. Greedy gluttons," he shouted, shaking his fist. He wiped some more bread crumbs from his face, turned around, and stormed off toward the Girth River.

We all just stood there. But Sister Heck was thinking clearly.

"Is the bread poisoned?" she called after him.

Paul turned back around and shook his head no before continuing on.

Elder Staples and I each had another slice before Sister Watson started her read through.

The pageant was coming.

32

PRACTICE MAKES . . . IF AT FIRST YOU DON'T SUCCEED

◇

About a week before the much-anticipated pageant, Elder Staples and I helped Toby finish the stage. This was no tiny structure. Toby had gone all out. The stage was on the far end of the meadow facing the boardinghouse. It was tall, wide, and fairly impressive. It had taken him almost the entire twenty months to design and construct it, but because of that, it looked as good as any church house stage I had ever seen.

With the stage completed, Sister Watson decided to do the first dry run of "All Is Swell," up on it. Elder Staples and I stayed around to watch. The play started with Thelma coming into the valley and settling. It then went on to tell the story of Parley P. Pratt coming to Thelma's

Way and getting sick after eating the bad ham. A lot of the play focused on a woman named Drusa who helped nurse Parley back to health. Sister Watson also wrote the play to tell the full story of the missing Book of Mormon. She had even added the recent debate scene.

It was a hard production to watch. Not even Sister Watson's vibrato could cover up the awful lyrics she had written. People were still stumbling over lines and Ed Washington had a mild case of stage fright that made him wiggle when he spoke. I asked Sister Watson about alternates but she told me that the idea was ridiculous. No one would dare back out of such an important production. As far as she was concerned, the only way out of the performance was by death. She cited the example of her late husband.

As Elder Staples and I were sitting there, Frank Porter walked up. Frank was playing the part of the wicked ham. He had initially refused to be in the play. He said he didn't want that many people looking at him, but Sister Watson talked him into being the ham, seeing how the costume was a complete disguise. She guaranteed him that people wouldn't recognize him by his feet. Frank took the part knowing that his role would be crucial to the success of the show.

The ham stepped up to us and stopped.

"So what do you think, Frank?" I asked. "Is the show going to be a success?"

Frank grunted.

"Has the pageant committee decided on what food they will be serving?"

Frank grunted again.

The pageant committee consisted of Sister Watson, President and Sister Heck, Toby, Teddy Yetch, and Grace. Grace was basically a member by default. Since she had helped her mother with the costumes, Sister Watson felt it necessary to include her on the board.

"Have all the invitations been mailed out?" I asked Frank the Ham.

He didn't answer me.

"How many people have they invited to this thing?" Elder Staples asked me.

"I don't know," I answered. "At least a few thousand. Digby put posters up on telephone poles in Virgil's Find and at the mall in Collin's Blight."

"Do you think anybody will actually show up?" Elder Staples laughed.

"I sure hope so," I replied, looking at the huge stage and realizing just how much effort had been put into this thing. My gut told me otherwise. What were the chances that any outsider, let alone a crowd, would be interested in coming to see "All Is Swell"?

The cast on the stage broke out in song. They all sang along until Ed forgot one of his lines. Everyone stopped to look at each other.

"What's my next line?" Ed asked Sister Watson in frustration.

Sister Watson began flipping through her script.

"The work is moving forth," I hollered out, offering my assistance.

Sister Watson located the line in her script. "The work

is moving forth," she said in amazement. "How did you know that?" she asked.

I shrugged my shoulders. "It's not that long of a script. I read through it a couple of times. It kind of sticks in your mind, I guess."

"Can we continue?" Ed demanded, his legs twisting under him. "The line just slipped away from me for a moment. It won't happen again."

"All right," Sister Watson yelled, "from the top."

Frank wandered off back behind the stage. We watched the next two scenes and then stood up to go to an early afternoon teaching appointment over at Judy Bickerstaff's home.

President Heck caught us as we were walking away.

"Have either of you seen Grace?" he asked.

We both shook our heads no.

"She put on Frank's costume to see if a person could walk with it on and never came back. I hope she didn't fall over and roll into the river. I think we're going to have to cut out a couple of arm holes in that ham. It's no fun falling over if you can't catch yourself."

Patty Heck stepped out from behind the stage and yelled at President Heck.

"I found her," she informed him.

"Never mind, guys," he said, walking off and away from us.

"So that was Grace in the ham," Elder Staples elbowed me.

"I didn't know," I pointed out.

"I'm sure you didn't, Sport."

"So, what did you think of the play?" I asked, changing the subject.

"I think it's even worse than some of the productions my sister used to stage in our backyard," Elder Staples answered.

"I hope this turns out to be a good thing," I sighed.

"Think of it this way," Elder Staples said. "Even if everyone hates it, at least it will finally be over."

I was comforted, I think.

33

LIVE AND LET ACT

Two nights before the sesquicentennial pageant there was a knock on the door. I opened it up to find President Heck standing there, his face sober and long.

"What happened?" I asked.

"There's been a problem with the pageant," he replied.

I looked over at the huge completed stage on the far end of the meadow. It sat there, just waiting to be poorly acted upon.

"What kind of problem?" I asked.

"I think you'd better come with me."

Elder Staples and I followed President Heck over to Sister Watson's home. We entered without knocking. There was Sister Watson sitting on the couch. Next to her was Patty Heck, Teddy Yetch, Toby Carver, and behind Toby was Grace. I would have been happy to see her, I mean them, if it wasn't for the grave expressions on their faces. My heart shrunk to the size of a grape, then shriveled to a raisin. I suddenly felt guilty for something I had never done. It was as if I had been caught and dragged before a jury. How did they know that ten minutes earlier, I had had a quick, safe and fleeting thought about Grace?

These people were good.

It had caught up with me. I had tried not to let the presence of Grace be a distraction on my mission. I guess maybe I had failed. It was pretty tricky of President Heck to fool me into coming over by claiming there was a problem with the pageant. Everyone stared at me.

"I can explain," I offered nervously.

"You can?" Sister Watson asked.

"My mission president knows all about it," I fumbled, trying not to look at Grace.

"He does?" President Heck asked.

"I've kept him informed."

"Of what?" Toby asked.

I looked around. Everyone was obviously confused. I decided that now was a good time for me to shut up. Grace looked my way.

"You can explain about Ed?" Sister Watson asked in disbelief.

"What about Ed?" I questioned.

"Paul got to him. We don't know how, but now he's refusing to do the pageant unless we give in to Paul's demands," Toby said.

"You're kidding?"

"Wish we were," President Heck said sadly.

"What are his demands?" I asked, bracing myself for the worst.

Sister Watson picked up a piece of paper in front of her.

"These are some of the lyrics Paul insists we use," she said.

> *God gave to all*
> *The gift of Paul*
> *So listen to his will.*
>
> *The price of cheese*
> *May rise and dip*
> *But Paul is with us still.*

Everyone grimaced. Paul made Sister Watson's lyrics sound almost normal.

"That's why we got together as this committee tonight," President Heck added. "Grace and Patty have finished the costumes, Toby's done with the stage, and the others are ready to act. But we can't do the play without the lead male."

"Just find someone else," I reasoned.

"Where are we going to find someone at this hour?" Patty asked. "No one knows the lines."

"That's ridiculous," I scoffed. "Surely someone knows them. Even I know most of them."

Everyone smiled.

I had been tricked, all right. Except these people weren't calling me on the carpet because of Grace, they were calling me on stage due to Paul. It was all a setup. I had warned Sister Watson about having alternate actors, now here was my own forewarning biting me in the un-thespian-like end.

"I can't—"

"Sure you can," Sister Watson said. "I think it would be only fitting to have you in our play. True, you're not blood, but you're the longest lingering outsider we've ever had here."

"I can't act," I pointed out.

"You just got to pretend you're someone else for an hour or so," Toby instructed. "It's real easy. I do it all the time."

"I think it's against my mission rules," I argued.

"We can call your mission president if you'd like," President Heck offered.

"There's going to be people from all over," I said, though I didn't really believe it. "You guys have invited the entire state. You don't want me going up there and doing a halfway job."

"If that's the best you can do," Patty said.

I looked at Grace, thinking that maybe she would help me.

"I think the people would love it," she smiled.

"The part requires singing!" I stated in a panic.

"All in favor say aye," Sister Watson sang out.

"Aye!"

"Don't I have a say in this?" I begged.

"Think of how this will help the missionary work," Brother Heck comforted.

"You've never seen me act," I said dejectedly.

"Well, I won't have to wait long to do so," he replied.

Sister Watson, Patty Heck and Teddy Yetch got up and went to the kitchen. Grace slipped out the back door, avoiding me as usual, and Toby laid down on the couch as if preparing for a late night nap on Sister Watson's sofa.

"I knew we could count on you," President Heck said, putting his arm around me. "I was the one that brought up your name."

"Thanks," I said.

"Don't mention it," he replied.

Elder Staples and I went home and read our scriptures. Then I took a few minutes to go over my lines. I couldn't believe that they were making me do this. But it looked as if the only way I was going to get out of it was to die. Maybe I'd die of embarrassment.

I had only one more day to live.

34

TAKE A SEAT

I had called President Clasp, and he seemed to think the idea of me acting in a pageant for nonmembers was a splendid one. In fact, he promised that he'd try to be there. We did a quick dress rehearsal the next day. It went pretty well.

Toby and Pete spent the day making sure that the big stage was in working order and adjusting the lighting. Leo and CleeDee went into Virgil's Find to pass out even more invitations. I was starting to believe that every person in the state of Tennessee who could read or hear would know about the play. Knowing and doing, however, were two very different things. I still couldn't imagine anyone who wasn't directly involved, taking the time to hike in.

After the dress rehearsal we set up all the rented chairs. It seemed as if there were thousands of them. If we filled one-fourth of them the following day, I would consider the pageant a smashing success. We wheeled the piano from out of the boardinghouse over to the stage.

Sister Heck brought out the curtain that she had made

and Digby and Sybil Porter worked well into the night hanging it up. When all was said and done, things looked pretty good.

"This is going to be huge," President Heck said almost to himself, bustling with pride.

"Yeah, huge," I repeated less enthusiastically.

"Do you think it will bring people back to church?" President Heck asked almost reverently.

"Hey, anything's possible," I said, wanting to encourage him. Then I thought of Feeble and his vision, Roswell's translation, Paul's holy finger and the huge bread loaf.

"Anything's possible," I repeated with more conviction, "anything at all."

35

LIGHTS, CAMERA, TRACTION

The town was packed. I had never in my life seen more people gathered in one spot. Half an hour before the play, every chair was filled and people were spilling out onto blankets or lawn chairs they had brought themselves. There were at least seven different news teams, each with huge cameras waiting to catch this monstrous human interest story as it unfolded. A few extremely rugged look-ing trucks had even worked their way down the path and into our town. If I had been nervous before, I was now ready to choke up a lung. I had not signed on for this. I remembered quite clearly twenty months ago when I had shuffled into Thelma's Way. I remembered the small orange signs posted on the electric poles informing folks of the pre-planning meeting. I remembered thinking that it was absolutely none of my business, seeing how I would be so far away when the pageant was actually performed.

There were multiple tables set up with piles of food for

all those in attendance. People milled around eating and waiting for the big show. I couldn't believe that this was happening to me.

President Heck, Leo, Pete, CleeDee, Toby, Frank, Elder Staples, and I all huddled behind the closed curtain on stage. We were all dressed in our costumes and trying to contain our performance night jitters. (All of us but Elder Staples that is, who was calm as a summer's day and looking forward to some good laughs.)

Every couple of seconds Toby would crack open the curtain and peek out into the darkening sky at the huge crowd.

"There's got to be over a hundred people out there," Toby whispered in fear.

"A hundred," I replied. "There's at least five thousand, maybe more."

"Wooo," Frank blew.

"What time is it?" I asked to no one in particular.

"We've only got a few minutes 'til starting time," President Heck answered.

"Where's Sister Watson anyway?" Pete Kennedy shook. I saw him reach for the spot on his hip where his gun would have been. He did it without thinking about it. Maybe it gave him comfort. "I haven't seen her around all day," he added.

"Patty went to fetch her," President Heck replied. "I guess she's been really resting up all day in preparation for tonight."

No sooner had President Heck spoken when Sister Watson appeared. She was with Patty Heck, Teddy Yetch, and Grace. I tried not to look at Grace for fear of losing it. I was barely holding myself together as it was. Patty Heck was the first to speak.

"Sister Watson has lost her voice," she said quite dryly.

"You've got to be kidding," I said.

"It's no joke." Sister Heck was very serious. "She must have lost it yesterday during dress rehearsal. She can barely whisper. She's been icing her throat all day, hoping it would get better. It hasn't."

"What are we going to do?" Leo moaned.

Sister Watson shook her head and began to weep.

Toby pulled his Ace bandage out of his pocket and began to wrap Sister Watson's neck. It was almost sweet.

"Does anyone here know Sister Watson's lines?" Patty Heck begged. "You've all been practicing with her, someone's got to remember what she says?"

"I was too busy trying to learn my own lines," Toby apologized.

"I could give it a go," Leo said, wanting to help.

"Thanks Leo, Toby, but I meant any of the ladies. CleeDee, do you think you know Sister Watson's lines well enough to do them?" Sister Heck asked.

"I've been too busy dating Leo to really pay attention," CleeDee replied.

"What about Miss Flitrey?" I asked.

"The costume won't fit her," Patty Heck answered matter-of-factly.

This was just great. For twenty months they had been planning this pageant, and now five minutes from show-time, the whole thing was falling apart. Sister Watson was the leading lady. Drusa brings Parley back to health. She sings four of the eight songs by herself. Her character is on stage alone for a third of the play.

"Can't we just leave her part out?" Pete asked. "You know, work around it?"

Sister Watson shook her head firmly.

"This is the most important part in the whole play," I said. "There is no pageant without it. I can't believe this."

"Five minutes 'til showtime," President Heck announced mournfully.

We needed a miracle. There were five thousand spectators to feed and not a single slice of talent to divide up. We stood there in shock.

Then Grace said softly, "I know the lines."

Everyone turned to look.

"I've heard Sister Watson say them a hundred times," she explained. "I've also read over the script. I might not know them exactly, but I think I could get close."

It was a stunning moment. Grace was the town recluse. She hid herself up in the hills and avoided people like the plague. Was she really offering to walk out unrehearsed in front of thousands of people?

"Would you do it?" Patty Heck asked, disbelieving.

Grace nodded with confidence, even certainty.

"There's songs," President Heck informed his daughter.

Grace hadn't sung in public since she was eight years old. Toby told me she had sung at her own baptism and did such a terrible job that people actually covered their ears and hummed something else.

"She can't be worse than no singing at all." Leo tried to be practical.

"I don't know about that," Toby replied. "If you remember—"

"We have no choice," President Heck interrupted. "I'm certain Grace's voice has matured. Right, Grace?"

"We could just cancel the play," Grace offered, underwhelmed by everyone's confidence.

Sister Watson shook her head. "Places," she whispered.

We scurried off to our positions. My insides were beginning to knot up. I half-wished Pete had been allowed to bring his gun so he could put me out of my misery.

I was certain President Clasp would not have allowed me to be in this play if he knew it would be Grace that nursed my character back to health. The thought of being in Sister Watson's arms as she sang to sick Parley had seemed innocent enough before.

This was going to be some pageant.

The wind was beginning to pick up. I could hear the crowd growing restless and then Sister Heck started playing the introduction on the piano.

We were about to make history. One way or another.

I could barely see Digby up on the scaffolding above me. He pulled on the ropes and opened the curtain. Our narrator, President Heck, stepped to the middle of the stage where Pete flipped on a light and beamed it down at him.

The crowd was quiet.

Patty Heck tickled the ivories softly as President Heck

spoke into his hand-held microphone. He was only shaking slightly.

"On behalf of the Thelma's Way pageant committee, I—"

SRRRRRRREEEEEEEEEPPP!!!

Feedback ripped through the air. The audience jumped in their seats. A startled President Heck held the microphone away from his mouth and continued.

"I would like to welcome one and all to the sesquicentennial production of 'All Is Swell.' While it is based on a true story, we would like you to know that those historical figures being represented didn't actually sing."

The lights went off and Pete began to flick them on and around in dramatic sequence. It's hard to make a couple of colored yard lights look spectacular, but Pete was giving it his all. He swung the big swivel light through the air, finally resting it on President Heck, who was still standing in the middle of the stage.

"The history behind the land you're sitting on is not necessarily pretty," President Heck spoke. "In fact at moments it's been just plain ugly. As you will see tonight, it took much work and a handful of miracles to bring us to where we are. 'Where are we?' you ask. Well, this is Thelma's Way, Tennessee."

It was a big crescendo, but nobody clapped. President Heck coughed nervously.

"A hundred and fifty years ago," he hurried on, "on this exact day, a young, inspired girl named Thelma wandered into this valley with a host of worn-out travelers. Their only ambition in life was to be able to worship for free."

The lights slapped off for a second and then flipped back on. They were shining on Narlette, who was playing the part of Thelma, as she lead Leo, CleeDee, and Toby across the stage. Both Leo and Toby were pulling what looked to be two of the most modern-looking handcarts I had ever seen. In fact, if I didn't know any better, I would have sworn they were red metal wagons. Narlette stopped in the middle of the stage and spoke.

"I say this is a good place to stop," Narlette said haltingly. "The heavens have really, really, really, blessed us with blessings." Narlette stared at Leo, who was suddenly locked up with fear.

"I mean they have really blessed us," Narlette prodded. Toby elbowed Leo.

"They have," Leo finally said.

"Perhaps we should give thanks to our Creator in song," Toby clamored. "Hymns are a way of praising."

My heart raced. I knew we were just moments away from the first song. Once they heard us sing, I expected half the crowd would pick up their things and try to sneak off.

"We shall call this place home," Narlette said, warming to the idea of performing in front of thousands.

Da, da, da, Sister Heck began on the piano. The cast on stage began to sing:

> *We've found a piece of heaven,*
> *tucked here in Tennessee.*
> *We're waiting for the blessings*
> *that we've been guaranteed.*

Ed stepped forward with flair,

The Girth will give us water,

CleeDee belted out,

The land will be our friend,

Narlette shouted,

We'll worship here in Thelma's Way
until the bitter end.

They all then danced and marched in a circle around the wagons. I counted sixteen circles before I gave up and said a prayer asking for mercy. The lights flicked off and everyone shuffled off stage. President Heck took front and center again. Pete lit him up.

"Two years after they entered this valley an apostle for the Mormon church paid a visit. His name was Parley P. Pratt. He taught the locals many wonderful things. As a way of showing their thanks the town had a big dinner celebration in his honor. The dish served up was ham, and the ham served up was infected."

The entire congregation *Ewwwed*.

"Parley P. Pratt became very ill," President Heck finished.

The light flashed off of President Heck.

I was on.

I walked to the center of the stage. I could hear my heart beating. I could see Sister Watson off to the side praying for me. Pete shined the light on me. For an instant, I wished I were dead and heading towards it. All the extras gathered around as I stood on a small wooden box and pretended to preach.

"I bring you news from Zion," I began. "The work is moving forth."

"Let's have a dinner to celebrate," Toby recited.

"Why not," Leo boomed. "We have earned this cele-bration. I'm certain that the heavens will not punish us for being too smug."

This play contained some really powerful dialogue.

"Let the celebration begin," CleeDee announced.

This was the moment I think I was most dreading. The play was bad enough, but this dancing ham scene was going to kill me. Tables were pulled out from the corners of the stage and all of us actors began to act as if we were enjoying a great meal. Sister Heck played the piano softly as some of the young local kids danced around us dressed as food. Lupert was potato salad, someone was gravy, and another kid was a bag of jelly beans. We had discussed the fact that the pioneers probably didn't have jelly beans, but Sister Watson had seen the idea of wearing a big clear sack and stuffing it with blown up balloons in a *Woman's World* magazine and just couldn't resist making the clever costume.

After the kids had danced around for a few minutes, Frank Porter emerged from stage right disguised as the giant ham hock. Sister Heck began to pound on the piano, the music growing louder and more sinister. Frank crept up on me. I pretended not to see him until he leaped, throwing his arms around me. The rest of the cast began to sing as I wrestled with the wicked ham.

> *What is this meat that's got the man?*
> *It looks like Satan's loose again.*
> *How can we stand for what is true*
> *When Satan tampers with our food?*

Frank stopped squeezing just enough for me to sing my solo.

> *I've got a burning deep inside,*
> *but not from honor, truth, or pride.*
> *This current burning isn't great*
> *because it came from what I ate.*

Everyone sang in chorus:

> *Because it came from what he aaaaaaaate.*

Frank Porter squeezed me even harder. He picked me up, shook me around, and flung me to the ground. I could hear my insides bruising.

The lights snapped off, and the curtains began to close. I caught a fleeting glimpse of the audience as I was lying there before the curtain shut. They looked moved, or stunned. I couldn't tell which. With us all behind the curtain, Sister Heck began to play the interlude. I picked myself up and helped change the scenery. In a moment the place was transformed into what looked to be an old log cabin. Grace came onto the stage. Everyone moved off leaving her and me standing behind the closed curtain. Sister Heck was playing something soft and sweet.

"Are you ready," I asked Grace.

"I think so."

"How was it so far?" I asked. Grace had been watching from the side.

"It's a moving script," she joked.

"That bad, huh?"

I sat down on the edge of the bed now placed in the middle of the stage.

"When I practiced this scene with Sister Watson, she sort of brushed my forehead and pretended to comfort me," I explained. "But it might be best if you just kind of sat there near me."

Grace smiled as President Heck stepped out in front of the curtain and began introducing the next scene.

"Sadly, Parley P. Pratt was extremely sick because of the ham," President Heck recited. "He didn't move for a week. He just laid in bed moaning. The town began to lose hope. Until one day out of nowhere a woman wandered into town. Her name was Drusa. No one had seen her before, and no one knew where she had come from. But she was here, and she took it upon herself to nurse Parley back to health."

I laid down on the bed, and Grace took a seat in the chair next to it. The curtain opened, and the light shined down on her. I was pretty impressed. Grace's red hair was tied back behind her head, her green eyes so strong that I'm certain those in the back row knew just what color they were.

"Parley," she lamented. "If only there was something I could do."

It was time for Grace to sing.

The cast held their breath, except for Toby, who held his ears. I watched Grace as she opened her mouth. It was soft at first. In fact, I could see the entire five thousand lean in closer to get a better listen. But gradually it became strong and sure. Okay, so she was singing some of the dumbest lyrics I had ever heard, but with her voice she seemed to change the words into text worth tasting. It was beautiful, at least to me.

> I'm here to see your load is light
> To see you through this longest night.
> Through thick and thin, through poor or wealth,
> I bid you Parley go to health.

When she finished her song, everyone just stared at her. There was a kind of hush all over the meadow. Finally, Pete turned off the lights and the curtains closed. Sister Heck began to play the between scenes music. The scenery started to move about. I stood up from the bed and looked at Grace. Toby took his hands off of his ears.

"How was it?" he asked.

"It was . . ." I began to say in amazement.

"Places," Elder Staples whispered. "Places."

Suddenly Elder Staples was pushing me around, and Toby grabbed Grace and started hooking her up to a wire harness. I wanted to brag about Grace's singing a bit, but there was no time—this next scene was pretty crucial. It was to be the most visually spectacular scene of the entire production. It was where Parley gets better and Drusa is hoisted up like an angel on wires and appears to float while she sings. They had practiced it fifty times with Sister Watson. But it was all new to Grace.

I could hear President Heck in front of the curtains.

"Drusa saved Parley P. Pratt's life. Her kindness and caring helped bring him back to full health. Thelma's Way was blessed. Everyone thought that they had truly been visited by an angel. Heaven had opened its windows and dumped out Drusa. Sure, it turned out that she was actually just a midwife from one town over who had come here to get away from her unruly kids for a few days. Even so, her efforts were miraculous."

The curtains opened to expose Grace and me.

"How can I ever thank you?" I said while staring intently at her eyes.

Da, da, da, da, Sister Heck played loudly as the rest of the cast strode on stage singing and waving small sticks with tinsel glued to the ends of them.

> *How can he ever thank you?*
> *What could he ever say?*
> *Where are the words to show you*
> *You really saved the day.*

Grace sang her lines as she began to be lifted up.

> *We must be ever willing*
> *To help out our fellow man.*
> *We must replace, "I will not,"*
> *With the simple words, "I can."*

244

I looked up at Grace as she began to ascend above us all. I could see Digby up on the platform trying to wind her up. As soon as she was midway she stopped. I looked at Digby, who was desperately trying to get her moving again. The wire had looped and knotted, leaving her stranded in the air. Those in the audience couldn't tell that anything was wrong. People just figured this was part of the play. But all of us on stage knew full well that this was not what we had rehearsed. Grace was supposed to be lifted up, ending the scene. Digby tried to close the curtains but the knotted wire was binding the curtain pulley as well. All of us were stuck below Grace, faced with the fact that we were going to have to improvise.

I was worried. This cast didn't exactly break records for spontaneous thought—unless there was a record for least amount. It was too much for Frank; he just took off running. Those of us left began to sweat and wing it.

"Parley, we thank you again for visiting," Toby said nervously. "It's not often we get someone like you that comes to visit us. It's really neighborly of you to visit us all."

"And I thank you all for sharing your town with me," I acted. "You have been the most sharing of towns. The Prophet would be happy with what you have done."

"What have we done?" Toby asked, confused.

"You have helped me get better, and stuff," I ad-libbed.

"I hope we didn't treat you too rough," Toby said, feeling that our conversation was supposed to rhyme.

We continued to act out pointless dialogue below the now-swinging Grace. The wind was beginning to really move her. I watched as she tried to remain composed up on the wire.

I saw President Heck climb up the scaffolding to help Digby. Once up there, he began to yank and pound on the wire. Leo, realizing that our improv was going badly, decided to break out in song. He marched around us singing words even more nonsensical than the ones Sister Watson had written. CleeDee became embarrassed by what Leo was doing and tried to slip off stage unnoticed. Her slinking away finally let the audience know that something was wrong. For a minute they laughed, and then they seemed to remember that they were supposed to be entertained. A couple of hecklers began to holler out.

Sybil Porter, who had been playing one of the extras on stage, raised her fist to the audience and taught them a couple of new words. The crowd began to boo. President Heck was still banging like crazy on the wire. I looked up and over at Pete sitting behind the light. I would have looked away, but I couldn't help noticing him pull a small gun out from a tiny holster on his ankle.

Pete aimed the gun at the wire.

Before I could scream anything he fired, snapping the wire and grazing Digby's left arm. Grace yelled as she fell on top of me. We both slammed down onto the stage and through the unnecessary trap door that Toby had insisted on building. Digby lost his balance and began to fall from the scaffolding. President Heck reached out to grab him but had to quickly steady himself by clinging onto the lights. Digby caught hold of the large net that was hidden above the stage and full of balloons for the finale. He ripped the net and swung down to the ground. Balloons whipped everywhere in the wind. President Heck followed after Digby, pulling the lights down and into the curtains. The lights exploded, and the curtains shot up in flames. The balloons caught on fire, flashing in the dark wind.

The audience went crazy. I couldn't see too much from beneath the stage, but I could hear sounds that both humans and chairs didn't usually make. I could also tell that the entire stage was falling apart, cracking, and breaking all over as fire consumed the entire thing. Grace and I crawled out from under just seconds before. Pete jumped off his perch and into the meadow. People were running everywhere.

It seemed as if everyone was heading for the path out of Thelma's Way. The few trucks that had made it into town were tearing away. I lost Grace in the mess of it all. I spotted Sister Watson, who was shuffling around looking dazed and confused. Her wig was hanging to the side, covering her right ear. Her pageant had gone haywire. We had not even made it to the fifth act.

President Heck grabbed me by the arm.

"Are you okay?" he hollered.

I looked around at the wild riot, not knowing if I could honestly answer *yes*.

"We've got to get this fire out!" I yelled.

Lit balloons were dropping all over. The crowd covered their heads in fear.

Elder Staples came running up and into me. He had a couple of trash cans that had been over by the once-erect food tables. He dumped the trash out of them. We started a chain from the river to the stage, passing the trash cans back and fourth until the fire was finally out.

By the time it had died down, the place was relatively deserted; not a single outsider had stayed around to help. Yes, a couple of the TV crews had remained to document the fire, but we sort of wished they hadn't. The meadow was a complete disaster. Chairs were everywhere, as well as food and paper. The stage was burned to the ground. Sister Heck picked up a charred piece of the curtain and shook her head.

"I don't think this night will gain us any respect," she hoarsely whispered.

"I don't know," President Heck replied. "I think it depends on how the papers handle it."

"We're ruined," Sister Watson coughed. She handed back the now slightly singed Ace bandage to Toby.

"I thought the small part of the play that actually got played was right neat," Toby offered.

"Yeah," Leo agreed. "Real fancy."

Sister Watson just sat there crying as we all tried to tell her it would be okay. Of course, I don't know that any of us actually believed it.

36

SMEARED

The papers murdered us. There was not a single kind thing said about the pageant or the tragedy. Words like *pathetic, backwards, ridiculous,* and *incompetent* were peppered throughout every report of the play. Sister Watson had wanted the world to attend; well the world had been there all right, and apparently they were sickened. I felt horrible. It was as if the entire planet was now in the business of putting down our town.

The meadow was a pit. It took us a couple of days to get things picked up. Even then it still looked awful. We tried to clear away the remains of the stage, but the kids seemed to enjoy playing in the big pile of ashes, so we decided to leave it and let Mother Nature take her couse.

The disaster had worked out well for Paul. According to him, he had been at home reading scriptures and praying that we all might be forgiven for not joining his religion and preventing him from being in the play when the tragedy struck. He went on and on about how sad it was that it took these acts of heaven to show us all how wrong we were.

Sister Watson was probably the worst off. She felt personally responsible for it all. She seemed destined to live in an eternal funk until President Heck asked her if she would begin planning a Christmas play for the following year, stressing only that it be a little less elaborate than the last one. She went right to work setting up an agenda for the pre-planning meeting.

I hadn't seen Grace since she had fallen on me. My neck was still sore from the encounter. I actually wanted to thank Grace for putting the play out of its misery. The way I saw it, we were lucky the stage caught fire before the crowd lit it themselves.

President Clasp had not made it to the play and, consequently, had missed out on all the fun. When I called him to tell him what happened, he told me quite clearly that he would be to Thelma's Way in a few weeks to deliver the transfer news. It looked as if my days in Thelma's Way were numbered at last. I couldn't believe it. I only wished I wasn't deserting these people at such a painful time.

I tried to push the feelings aside. I tried to act as if it was really none of my business. I tried in vain.

37

A BURNING IN THE BOSOM

MONTH TWENTY-TWO

A few weeks later, right before sacrament meeting, Elder Staples received a transfer out of Thelma's Way. He was out, I was still in. I was going to be serving the twenty-second month of my mission in the same place. President Clasp had come to town to speak at our ward and deliver the transfer news. He met with Elder Staples and me before church.

"But President," I had questioned after getting the news.

"You're not finished here," he smiled, his crooked teeth straightening as he tilted his head.

President Clasp had brought my new companion with him. Actual transfers were not for a couple of days, but my new companion, Elder Herney, had caused a few problems in his last area, and they had to get him out of there fast. He was an emergency transfer. Mission rumor was that he had been sneaking out to watch Star Trek movies at the midnight theater by himself. President Clasp thought Thelma's Way would be the perfect place for him to straighten out.

Elder Herney was not exactly a people person. In fact, he was one troubled individual. His parents had pushed him onto his mission hoping he would come back looking like some of the clean-cut elders they had seen in Church videos. It seemed to me he was moving in the opposite direction. He talked as if all wind entered and exited his nostrils. He had dark eyes that looked ringed, and thin skin that appeared blue under natural light. He was about six inches shorter than I and liked to pinch his lips as he spoke endlessly about science fiction movies and how they correlated with gospel principles. We had talked maybe fifteen minutes so far, and the entire conversation had been about the gospel accuracy of the Star Wars saga.

"The force is actually the priesthood," he explained. "And Yoda is the prophet."

I sat down glumly next to Elder Herney in the chapel. Elder Staples was still here, all smiles to be leaving. President Clasp sat up in front by the podium. Usually I blessed or passed the sacrament due to so few priesthood holders being in attendance. But today Toby Carver was blessing with Digby Heck, and Leo Tip was passing. I sat in my pew and sulked silently. I was hoping that to the naked eye sulking would look like reverence.

I didn't know what it was with me. Why was I still in Thelma's Way? I liked to pretend that there was some great cosmic reason for my being kept in one place. But the truth was probably something closer to the idea that President Clasp simply had it out for me. His smiling presence was just a funny front for a rather conniving nature. I had learned a lot in Thelma's Way. I really felt as if I had grown from my experiences, but I also felt I could use some rounding out. Couldn't I? I loved these people, but didn't a real mission require broadening? Shouldn't I be shifted around?

It had been a few weeks since the pageant, and things were still in confusion. Paul was claiming the failure of the pageant as proof that we all had been living in sin. He was currently promising people thicker hair, more energy, and three years longer life if they joined up with the People of Paul. So far Frank Porter was the only one to take him up on the offer. Frank figured if he had been desperate enough to smear Sister Lando's spotted frog larvae on his bald head in an attempt to overcome his baldness, then what could it hurt to take up a new religion as a potential cure? It seemed so much cleaner.

Paul wanted people to know that his being accused of stealing the Book of Mormon, and then being banned from the disastrous play, was the pattern God used to pull prophets out from among the rank and file. For the last two days, he had been over at the boardinghouse giving free workshops on how to recognize truth.

It was funny to think that a man who once claimed he had invented chicken cordon bleu and helped work out the bugs on the paper clip, could go into great depths about the importance of honesty. Paul wasn't keeping himself in check any longer. He had been falsely accused, we knew it, and we were going to pay.

The table next to the podium sat empty as usual. The Book of Mormon still had not been found. I focused on the empty table while listening to Elder Herney whistle through his nose as he breathed. I was tempted to reach over and pinch the thing closed. Sister Watson took a seat right in front of us. Patty Heck was sitting with Narlette across the aisle. By the time the meeting started we had about twenty-five members there. All told, our attendance was up by about fifteen people since the time I had arrived almost two years ago. Two years. Fifteen people. It was not an impressive record. I would read and reread the scriptures about the worth of one soul, and the importance of bringing just one person unto Him. But these were Thelma's Way souls we were talking about. It probably took about five of them to equal one ordinary spirit, right?

Possibly it was the other way around.

And where was Grace in all of this? Ever since the pageant, I had been overly hopeful that she would start coming back to church again. Not yet. I had ordered myself to stop thinking about her so many times that I was now having to tell myself to stop thinking about not thinking about her. She weighed more on my mind than my brain had strength to heft. I had told President Clasp after he decided to not transfer me that I was thinking way too much of her. He didn't fall for it. He simply told me I would be done with my mission in a couple of months and that I was welcome to come back and visit her then.

Some advice.

Sacrament meeting moved along slowly. And halfway through President Clasp's talk, I began to feel ill. It wasn't the normal queasy feeling that I sometimes got at church. It was something different altogether. I tried to brush it off.

I squirmed in my seat. I could feel beads of sweat running down my face. I loosened my tie just a bit and fanned myself with the hymnbook. The back of Sister Watson's head began to sway and contract. I needed some fresh air.

I looked over at Elder Herney.

"You don't look right," he droned.

I needed to get to the bathroom. I stood up to go, and Elder Herney and Elder Staples followed. It looked like I was taking half the congregation with me as I left. I went into the tiny church bathroom and splashed water on my face.

"I don't feel well," I said.

"You look awful," Elder Herney assisted.

I leaned against the wall and held my stomach.

"You were fine before you found out you were staying," Elder Staples accused. Then he threw a couple of pretend punches at me, wounding the air immediately in front of my stomach.

There was no way I could go back into the chapel. The wood walls of the building seemed to puff up, and the windows sort of slid down to the floor. I desperately pulled at my tie. I could feel my wrists turn slippery.

"I was fine just a . . ." I suddenly didn't know if I could stand for much longer. I stumbled.

"What do we do?" Elder Herney breathed at Elder Staples.

"He's your companion," Elder Staples said, no longer willing to take responsibility for me.

"I'll give you five bucks if you carry him home," Elder Herney bartered.

Elder Staples picked up my six-foot-two frame as my knees buckled and tossed me over his shoulder. My head knocked the door frame as he stepped outside.

"Owww!" I moaned.

"Easy, Sport," Elder Staples said.

He carried me back to our place and put me in bed. It would be quite some time before I got out again.

38

ANGEL OF HERESY

MONTH TWENTY-THREE

There are varying degrees of sickness. Forget them all. I had gone well beyond any known mark of discomfort. I lay in bed for weeks doing nothing but moan—slipping in and out of a vegetative state. At first folks thought I was faking it for attention. But after watching me struggle to keep my food down, they began to realize there were better ways to get noticed.

Toby Carver had attempted to heal me with his Ace bandage, but somehow a mere spandex wrap wasn't enough to lower my body temperature or calm my nausea. A real doctor (although we couldn't call him that to Toby's face) was called in from Virgil's Find to look me over. He diagnosed me with a rare strain of flu called Wilbur's Affliction.

Wilbur had been a woodsman who resided below Hallow Falls about a hundred years ago. He had lived out his days in obscurity until someone named an epidemic after him. He was a simple man who raised chickens and sold eggs. Every spring, in an effort to boost sales, he would take a bunch of his eggs and make a homemade spicy spread like a mayonnaise but with more kick. He bottled it and sold it to his neighbors from out of his wood shack.

One year the economy of the area went sour and in an effort to single-handedly restore regional prosperity, Wilbur whipped up an extra big batch of his concoction. But hard times equaled low sales, and he only sold half the goods.

Ever the savvy businessman, he packed away the excess supply in his warm attic and sold it at fire sale prices the following spring. The town never recovered.

Apparently, my doctor's great grandfather had almost died of the dreaded affliction. That's how come he knew so much. Now anytime anyone came down with complications of mayonnaise, the diagnosis could only be Wilbur's Affliction (not to be confused, he said, with Briant's Curse, which was a whole different story.)

The doctor handed me some medicine for the pain and prescribed three weeks without eggs. The pills helped a little, but I spent my days in relative misery, tossing between the sheets. The one time I actually felt a little better, Elder Herney and I tried to go visit Judy Bickerstaff. I got twenty steps out the door before I knew I wasn't going to make it. I crawled back to my bed feeling worse than ever.

Thanks to the kindness of the townspeople, I always had visitors. Leo and CleeDee came by almost every day to show me neat-looking sticks or leaves they had found. Wad had been over a few times to sit by me and read me some of his old magazines. Teddy Yetch and Sister Lando brought food that I couldn't even look at, and Sister Watson came over twice to scrub our place sterile with her homemade bar soap. Even Paul came by to say he had foreseen my doom and wondered when I was planning to die.

Elder Herney had just about had enough of my being sick. He had not spent a single day with me outside the cabin. Occasionally he went on splits with Digby while President Heck stayed with me. He attended church thanks to Pete Kennedy sitting in. But when we were together, all we did was fight. We tried to have companionship studies, and we prayed a lot that we would get along, but it didn't seem to help. Both of us were at our wits' end.

It was Thursday afternoon, I think. I was feeling stronger physically, but mentally I was still fogged under. I was so stir crazy I thought I would rather die than stay inside. But the doctor had told me to stay in bed for at least a few more days before attempting to go anywhere. I was wearing a long red nightshirt that my mother had just sent. She had made it for me in homemaking. It was about three sizes too big and had a rather silly-looking neck ruffle, but considering the trouble she had gone to, I felt dutybound to wear it at least once.

"You look stupid," Elder Herney commented.

"My mother made this," I argued as I shuffled across the room to get some water.

I had taken some cold medicine a few minutes earlier, and it was beginning to play on my brain. I had downed a double dose in the hopes of knocking myself out for the night.

"This isn't a mission," Elder Herney whined, "this is a baby-sitting job."

"Hey, I'm s-s-sorry I'm sick," I slurred, getting back into bed.

"This—"

Elder Herney was interrupted by a knock on the door. He jumped up, happy to have something to do. He answered the door, and President Heck came in.

"Could I borrow your companion?" President Heck asked me as I lay in bed. "I just need to talk to him outside." He was nervous about something.

"Sure," I said, beginning to really feel the effects of the medication.

"We'll just be out here," President Heck said, walking out the door with Elder Herney.

They left the door open so that I could see outside, but they had moved towards the cemetery and out of my view. I stared at the open door for a while, watching birds make tracers across the late afternoon sky. Wow. I began to hallucinate. From out of thin air, my mind conjured up Grace. I had seen a lot of weird things while I had been sick. My eyes had played so many tricks on me that I was beginning to doubt everything I saw. This vision of Grace slipped in the door and stood against the wall.

I sort of bobbed my head, squinting at the illusion.

The mirage smiled back.

"Nice pajamas," it said.

I patted my red nightgown. "Thanks," I replied, my voice echoing in the empty room.

"I just wanted to say good-bye," she fluttered, "before you go home and I . . . *we* never see you again."

"Grace?" I said, fathoming for the first time that it was really her.

She was still against the far wall.

"I'd better go," she said. "My father can only cover me for so long."

"Don't go," I begged, sluggishly.

She turned and paused.

"Do you remember last Halloween?" she asked with some hesitation.

In my present condition I couldn't accurately remember ten minutes ago. Last Halloween seemed like another life. I sort of nodded, toppled, and shook my head. I felt like a wino with bad rhythm.

"I heard what you said as you and your companion sat on the porch," Grace whispered, her soft voice barely carrying across the room. "Was it true?"

I had no idea what she was talking about. In my medicated state it sounded like a riddle. What had I said last Halloween? And was she happy or sad about it?

I just stared at her. She was beautiful then. Her red hair against the wood wall was poetic, moving.

"I've got to go," Grace said again nervously.

"What about . . ." I tried to ask.

But she was already gone. She slipped away like soap on glass. My heart peeled like an immodest orange, and for some reason my eyes were wet. Grace had come to say good-bye.

261

"Lutumt," I mumbled, my tongue feeling thick in my mouth.

Elder Herney came back inside complaining.

"I still don't know what President Heck needed to talk to me for. He just went on and on about how he thinks missionaries are good. There's a news flash for you—this just in, missionaries are good."

I looked up. The room was spinning.

"Why are you crying?" he snapped. "You're not that sick. Get a grip, Elder. My football coach used to always say, 'feeble of mind, feeble of body.'"

"Feeble," I giggled, the word sounding funny. "Feeble Weeble."

"President Clasp has got to get me out of here," Elder Herney continued. "I can't take being cooped up in this hole with you any longer. I feel like a lame horse."

The horse remark did it. It was like a revelation, except, of course, that it was drug-induced.

Feeble Weeble . . . lame horse . . . It all came back to me. That Halloween night, on the porch, Elder Weeble had called Grace a horse, and I had let it slide, not wanting to be confrontational. That's what Grace had been asking about. She probably thought I was a real idiot. She must have the completely wrong impression of me. I didn't think she was a horse. What I thought was that I might be in love with Grace Heck.

I had to talk to her—that couldn't be the end. My head pounded as sweat pushed up through my skin. My illness was toying with me again. I could feel the red nightgown my mother had made me sticking to my skin.

I watched Elder Herney pace back and forth across the floor, complaining about everything. I saw the walls move in, and felt the pressure of being cooped up come to a boil. The ceiling began to jiggle. I couldn't take it any longer.

I don't know what happened next, or what pushed me over the edge, but I jumped up and ran out. I had to get out of there. I couldn't take lying in that bed for one more minute. And since I was running, I decided that I might as well be running for Grace. I couldn't let those words she had whispered be our last good-bye. I had to find her and tell her that I remembered the porch conversation, and that I was sorry for not standing up for her. I had thought that Elder Herney would have the sense to run along after me as I took off. Nope.

I ran across the field, my red nightgown blowing in the wind. The sun was low in the cloudy sky as I scanned the horizon for Grace. But there was no one in the meadow, no one to witness the sick missionary who was running foolishly by himself. My head thumped as the exhilaration of being alone and out of our cabin made my heart swell. My sick limbs flew through the air, pulling my body behind. I knew that I had to catch up with Grace before she got too deep into the forest. My medicated mind and my poor sense of direction could be a deadly combination.

I reached the edge of the meadow and pushed on into the trees. The hill became steep as I scrambled through the foliage. The medicine in my blood kept signaling my brain to lock up. I had no idea where I was going. I just kept running, counting on fate to turn me in the right direction.

My lungs filled with cool air as my legs found the strength to keep me going.

"Grace!" I slurred loudly. "Grace!"

Eventually I came to the spot where I thought the Heck house should be. It was gone. Either they had moved and taken their whole house with them or I was lost. I stopped to catch my breath.

"Grrraccce," I mumbled. My stomach was beginning to act up.

I turned around a few more times to see where I had come from. But each direction looked identical. The beautiful forest of Thelma's Way had become a mirrored fun house—I could almost see myself in the endless maze of trees. The low clouds seemed to rumble even lower, bringing Mother Nature's ceiling down. The sun was beginning to sink behind it, coloring the sky purple.

I was really lost.

I decided to climb to the top of a nearby hill and see if I could spot any houses or help. My mind was so goofy by now that I could barely put one foot in front of the other. I began to see things, and hear things. Trees shifted on me, and the ground bristled like a shivering dog. I tried to pray, but my mind was too muddled. I should never have left my companion. I tried to pray out loud, hoping that vocally I could pull it together. I reached the top of the hill and looked down. There were no houses in sight, but I could see someone walking. It took me a few moments to figure out who it was. It was Paul, striding across the landscape. He was the answer to my prayers.

He could help me back. We didn't get along, but

certainly he wouldn't leave a sick man out to die. I stood at the top of the hill and waved my arms. The sun was setting behind me.

"Pauuuullll," I tried to say. "Pauuuuull."

Paul stopped and looked around. He put his hand to his eyes and gazed up at me. Then his face filled with fear. I probably looked ridiculous in my mother's nightgown, but he didn't need to be rude about it.

"Palif eig eiitdkfeeeeffL," I tried to say, no longer able to construct words within my sick head.

Paul dropped the walking stick he was carrying and fell to his knees.

"Who are you?" he yelled back.

"Elllfienfld wilfjiggged," I answered.

He was trembling like crazy. His tiny, poorly arranged features ticked and popped. I could feel the sun setting behind me, and I looked down to see my oversized nightshirt rippling in the wind. The thin material my mother had used to construct it was glowing in the sunset, the fancy neck ruffle dancing about my head.

"Pawwl," I tried to explain.

"What have I done, great messenger," he yelled in fear.

"Paul I swump wa deee lop don." My tired tongue mangled the words as they came out.

"What do you wish of me?" he screamed.

"What?" I yelled.

"What do you wish of me?"

It suddenly hit me like a cannonball to the temple— the setting sun, my glowing nightgown, Paul shaking like watery Jell-o during an 8.8 earthquake. Paul thought I was something other than I was. It was too much. I couldn't resist egging him on.

"R-r-repent!" I managed yell, amazed that I could get the word out clearly.

Paul held his skinny hand to his heart and let his big mouth gape. His chest was heaving.

"Repentafgr," I yelled again, feeling dizzy and rather full of myself.

I could see Paul begin to sob, his thick hair bouncing as he trembled. He really believed I was some sort of messenger. As much as I was enjoying myself, I couldn't keep up the charade.

"Paul, it's muflelf," I said, my tongue tangling again. I waved my hands and began to approach him.

Paul wasn't about to let a heavenly visitor get hold of him. He stood up and took off running.

"Paul!" I yelled, running after him.

I couldn't let him get away. I would never find my way back on my own.

"Pawwwul."

Paul ran like crazy, looking over his shoulder every few seconds. I tried hard not to think of anything but catching him. If I started focusing on how tired I was, or how sick I felt, I knew I would fall to the ground in exhaustion. We ran around through a stream, and then back up another hill and down into the meadow. I knew right where I was. I should have just stopped and waited for somebody else to come along. But I kept running. I think I was too sick to rationally realize that I could give up. I wanted to let him know it was just me.

266

He crossed the meadow, jumped down onto the bank of the Girth, and pushed out across it on a raft. I too crossed the meadow, still yelling after him. I jumped down onto the bank of the Girth and hopped onto a small raft that was lying on the shore. I pushed off and into the current. I knew in an instant that it was a mistake.

The Girth was moving swiftly this time of year. I paddled as well as a sick man could.

"Paul!" I tried again, realizing now more than ever that I needed his help. "Paul!"

I was running out of time. The river had pushed me past the meadow and beyond our place, water lapping up over the lip of my raft. I watched Paul make it to the distant shore. He didn't even waste a second to look back; he just kept on running. I paddled like crazy, but I was weak and my paddling was wimpy. In a few seconds Thelma's Way was behind me, the Girth having carried me past its border. The water became more and more rapid, rocky growths sticking up from the river's floor and teasing the water into a fury. My hand slipped, and my paddle dropped away. I was smack dab in the middle of the river.

Desperate and foolish, I jumped off my raft and tried to swim to shore. It was no use. The rapids had become higher and the water swifter. My tired legs and arms turned to mush. My body froze in the cold whipping water. The river dipped a few more times and then leveled out. For a moment it was flat and slick, dragging me along smoothly with speed. I watched the shoreline.

A horrible noise entered my head—a low roar that

gradually began to get louder, piercing my heart and shaking my sick head sober.

Hallow Falls.

The roar increased. I struggled frantically to swim, my long wet nightgown feeling heavy and restrictive. I pulled it off over my head and pushed it away. I thrashed at the river. It was no use; I was going to go over the falls. I couldn't see it up ahead, but I knew it was there.

Hallow Falls was an eighty-foot drop. The previous summer, Elder Jorgensen and I had hiked down to it on one of our P-days. I remember being in awe of its massive weight. Looking up from below, the mist seemed to drift for miles. I had taken some pictures and sent them home to my family. How ironic that they would already have seen the scene of my violent death.

The roar became so loud that I felt my heart would stop. I made a couple more futile attempts to swim away from what was coming. I prayed like I had never prayed before. If God could part the seas, surely he could push a missionary upstream. I thought about all the things I had done wrong, and all the many legitimate reasons God had to not help me. I kept praying.

It was no use.

The Girth River pushed me along, impatient for my demise. The fear in my gut permeated my bones and seeped out of my mouth as I screamed. Then, with one giant push, I was thrust over the falls and into the air—flying through the sky, my arms flailing, the river below racing up to smack me.

I blacked out before I ever hit bottom.

39

PULLED AND PRODDED

I opened my eyes to see the back of Roswell's head.

He was pulling me through thick trees. I was in a red wagon, dressed in some tattered jeans and a plaid shirt.

Suddenly I remembered the falls. I grabbed my head to make sure it was still there. I wiggled my arms and legs to test them out. Everything seemed to work.

Roswell looked older than when I had last seen him almost two years ago, before his supposed translation. If he was what a resurrected body looked like, I wanted no part. His head was puckered. His skin was gray.

I had to be dead, because I no longer felt sick. In fact, I felt pretty good. My head was clear, and my body felt healthy. I figured one of two things must have happened. Either the falls had killed me and I had made it to heaven, where a translated Roswell was the only friend or family member who had come to meet me at the veil; or the falls had killed me but I hadn't deserved heaven, so it was me and Roswell in outer darkness forever. Either way, things didn't look good.

"Where are we?" I asked Roswell.

I startled him. He jumped, dropping the wagon handle and cursing.

"You ain't supposed to get conscious yet," he informed me, holding his wrinkled hand to his skinny chest.

"Sorry," I replied.

"Just great," he ranted. "Now what the heck am I supposed to do with you?"

"Do with me?" I asked. "What do you mean?"

"You seen me," he ranted. "You know I ain't been translated."

"Oh, that," I said coming to the realization that I was still alive. "I knew that weeks ago."

"You thought you knew that," Roswell corrected.

"I knew I knew it," I said, still sprawled out in the wagon. "Your cousin Stubby told me. He also told me you stole the Book of Mormon."

Roswell muttered something about his cousin under his breath. It didn't sound complimentary.

"What happened?" I asked, rubbing my head.

"To what?" Roswell questioned.

"To me."

Roswell took out his pipe and stuffed it.

"Found you in the river," Roswell puffed. "You're lucky them falls didn't kill ya. I seen 'em do worse. I dressed you up with some of my better threads. I'll need 'em back," Roswell insisted.

"So you saved me?" I asked, bewildered at the thought.

"Well, I couldn't just leave you there. Took you to my private fishing shack and tried to wake you up. I got tired of staring at your quiet face. So I decided I'd better take you home."

"How long was I out?" I asked.

"Three days," he snickered.

"You're kidding," I said, jumping out of the wagon. "Three days?"

Roswell grunted.

"My companion's probably going ballistic," I moaned.

"Look, kid," Roswell retorted, "we all got problems."

"I've got to get back," I insisted. "Right away."

"I was taking you back," Roswell pointed out. "But now that you're alive I think I'll let you find your own way."

"You can't," I snapped. "I don't know where I am."

"The forest is tricky," Roswell lamented.

"Take me back and I promise I won't tell anyone I saw you." I was prepared to barter.

Roswell thought about this for a minute.

"How 'bout we make a deal?"

"What kind of deal?" I asked.

Roswell sat down on an old tree stump. I sat back in the wagon.

"I'm tired of living all hidden up," he said. "Sick of having to keep myself tucked away. I'm a person's person. Like my neighbors to be curious about my doings. Found out I don't make myself very good company. I'm stubborn. Can't talk myself out of anything."

Roswell paused to puff.

"I'm a simple man—no skeletons in the closet, no

271

demons to conquer," he continued. "Makes for lousy conversation."

"What about your brother?" I asked, begging to differ about the skeletons.

"I didn't kill Feeble," Roswell insisted. "My dear brother found out from Stubby that I'd taken the Book of Mormon and started having a fit. He began saying silly things like how honesty and integrity were more 'portant than money. Feeble found me out just two days before he passed on. He teased me with that dumb little statue. Kept saying I was an embarrassment to the family. He even said he was going to turn me in. I couldn't take it." Roswell paused to rub his eye. "I told him I was leaving and he chased after me."

We were both quiet for a moment.

"It wasn't much of a chase," Roswell finally said. "Feeble had a heart attack about ten steps into it. Figured I'd better hightail it out of there if I didn't want any questions asked. So I hid up in my fish shack. I was eventually going to show my face, but I overheard Sister Watson talking about me being translated and all. Me, translated," he laughed. "It sounded so regal, I decided to stay hid. I'm a proud man," Roswell admitted.

"So why'd you steal the Book of Mormon?" I asked, staring at him and wondering how a proud man could wear two different pieces of plaid clothing.

"Had to steal it," Roswell replied. "I'd made a bet with Clove Timpleton in Virgil's Find that his newborn red cow was the heifer of prophecy. Turns out she was just dirty from birth. Washed up to be almost white."

I tried not to look dumbfounded.

"Take me back," I said, suddenly wary of Roswell's company.

Roswell made an offer. "You tell folks that I descended in a cloud from heaven to save your life, and I'll take you back."

"No way," I protested. That was too much to ask.

"You gotta give me something," he whined.

"Okay," I reasoned. "You come into town with me and I'll tell them you saved my life."

"And . . ." Roswell prodded.

"And," I continued, "you make up the rest."

That seemed to satisfy him, at least for the time being. We hiked for about an hour before I could tell where we were. I got back into the wagon, and Roswell wheeled me into town.

"Elder Williams, Elder Williams!" Sister Watson had spotted us. She was sitting on the porch of the boarding-house. The meadow exploded with folks popping like popcorn. My buttery family. Roswell pulled me right up to the porch, a small cloud of dust puffing up as the wagon came to an abrupt stop. Sister Watson threw herself down by me, kissing my forehead.

"Crazy boy. Foolish kid."

President Heck was the next to maul me.

"Where? How? I can't believe it!"

Teddy practically cut off my circulation as she hugged me tightly, and Nippy nodded so violently that I became concerned about her head remaining attached to her body.

"We thought you was dead," they all said. Everyone was so happy to see me that they hardly even noticed Roswell.

273

He just sort of stood there looking like he always had, content not to be the center of attention for the moment.

President Clasp came out of our cabin and ran up to greet me. I could tell he wasn't sure if he should hit or hug me, not that he would have really done either. He and Elder Herney had been in the process of packing up my stuff. I guess they and about forty law officers from all over the state had spent the last three days combing the forest of Thelma's Way. They had almost given up.

I called my family from the boardinghouse to tell them I was okay. My mom cried with joy. My father guardedly gushed. As soon as I hung up, President Clasp informed me we were leaving. This was it. He wanted both me and Elder Herney out of Thelma's Way. In a whirlwind we collected all of our stuff and briskly hiked out of town towards Virgil's Find. It happened so fast I barely had time to register what was going on.

My transfer had arrived, and the timing couldn't be worse.

I didn't want to leave. It was too sudden. I didn't even get a chance to properly say good-bye. I was just whisked away. Folks lined the path as we made our grand exit. These people were my family. I had endured and endeared them for the past two years. I scanned the crowd for a glimpse of Grace.

Salvation was out of sight.

Everyone stood there staring at me as if I were their son going off to war.

"God bless," Toby Carver said aloud, his Ace bandage waving in the air.

People followed us for a few steps, and then they slowly turned back. They would cope without me. I hoped the same of myself. I scanned the trees the rest of the way, hoping to see Grace.

From Virgil's Find we took a big van back to Knoxville. President Clasp tried to lecture and love me into understanding. I understood all too well. I spent the night in a real bed, in a real house, in a real town.

I couldn't ever remember being more uncomfortable.

40

KNOCKS-VILLE

THE LAST DAY

I spent the final month of my mission in Knoxville, serving with an Elder Jones. We had a baptism, and I learned what it was like to spend six hours a day tracting in a suburban neighborhood. Elder Jones was probably the best elder I ever served with. He had a better sense of the gospel and a real sense of purpose. He lacked some of Elder Jorgensen's raw enthusiasm and wasn't quite as endearing, but he was solid.

This last month in Knoxville, I had been amazingly homesick for Thelma's Way, and Grace. My time had seemed too short there. I kept telling myself that I was just overly emotional because of how I had been ripped away. I knew, however, that my attachment to Thelma's Way was due to far more than a bad sendoff.

As I packed my bags to leave the mission field, I thought long and hard about all that I had been through. This was it. I had made it the entire two years. I was considerably more melancholy than I had anticipated I would be.

At the beginning of my mission, I had thought constantly of how great it would be when I was finally able to fly home. To be done. I had imagined myself on the plane smiling over how fulfilling my time had been and how wonderful it would be to see Lucy and my family again. Now, as I packed to go home, the approaching plane ride seemed frightening. Every mile I soon flew, I knew, I would feel more and more distanced from the people I loved in Thelma's Way.

I met a lot of great people during my last month in Knoxville, but it wasn't the same. These people used Saran Wrap only to cover food, and Ace bandages were applied no more than once. Gatherings were civil and predictable, stripped of soul and commotion.

I closed my suitcase, looked around the room, and walked out to the van. We would be at the airport in no time.

My mission was over.

41

JUSTIFICATION

Southdale in late October is a funny thing. People are so busy prepping themselves for the upcoming holidays that they fail to have any fall fun. The wide streets are cluttered with cars driving back and forth to this and that, for which and whatever. Things are busy but as empty as the once-bushy trees.

I missed Thelma's Way. I had gotten lost there and in the process been found. I tried not to be one of those ex-missionaries who spends all his time yearning for the past. I tried to distance myself from the people of Thelma's Way. I tried to find the positives in Southdale. Paved streets, large stores, cable TV—big deal. Where were the heart and purpose of it all?

College had been going well, but I was keeping to myself more than I probably should have. Often I would sit out on the benches watching the beautiful sun-kissed coeds and missing my Grace. Their tans would fade long before I was fully over her.

I had tried to talk about it with my father. He told me

to forget about Thelma's Way. "Life is business, my boy, business," he had said. "You're polished past the point of worrying about those people."

I talked to my mother, hoping she would be kinder than my father. She too had little good to say. "Part of a mission is forgetting about those you served."

I wondered what manual Mom had been reading.

As October came to a close, I could feel my memories of Thelma's Way slipping. I had gotten a letter from President Heck about a month back. It was a long one explaining how CleeDee and Leo had gotten married in the Atlanta Temple on August eleventh. I had not been notified because Leo had wanted to test the branch's spirituality by not telling them about the wedding. He wanted to see if the Spirit would invite folks for him, prompting people to just show up. It was a lot cheaper than announcements, and it seemed to Leo to be a great barometer of local righteousness. Consequently, Leo and CleeDee got married without a single friend on hand.

Since Leo was now married, and had no need for his bachelor-mobile, he gave the car to Digby, who in turn gave his old motorcycle to Ed Washington. Ed was using it to commute back and forth to Virgil's Find, where he was taking a couple of college courses in business management. Ed had become a new man since he had moved out of his mother's place. And so had his mother. Apparently, she was using her newfound free time to make eyes at Briant Willpts. Who knew that all these years Ed had been cramping her style?

Sister Lando was coming out to church every week now

with Teddy Yetch. President Heck had helped solve Sister Lando's desire to wear her witch hat by assigning his wife, Patty Heck, to be her visiting teacher. Patty Heck had tactfully offered to make Sister Lando a dress incorporating the hat material in it. Since then, Sister Lando showed up every week in her black and white dress, smiling as if she had fooled the system.

The town had no problem forgiving Roswell. These people were pros at forgetting. Roswell had even come out to church a few times in honor of his departed brother. Yes, instead of people being mad about what he had done, most folks viewed it as a miracle that he had returned. President Heck said it was kind of nice to spot him sitting on the porch like old times. Besides, he was old and wouldn't be around forever. Why argue his presence when time was not on his side?

The Book of Mormon still had not turned up. Folks were waiting for someone to start purchasing a lot of nice things—increased spending power would be a surefire giveaway if someone had hocked it for cash. As of yet, no one had purchased anything out of the ordinary.

While shopping for an engagement ring, Miss Flitrey and Wad had found an old-fashioned hearing aid at one of the Virgil's Find garage sales. It was an awkward thing that had an antenna and a thick head strap. It wasn't modern, but it worked, and it was too big for Nippy to swallow. She wore it everywhere now, walking around the meadow looking like a wrinkled space alien.

Since there were no longer any full-time missionaries in Thelma's Way, President Heck and Toby Carver were teaching the lessons to Judy Bickerstaff. She had been out to church once, and was willing to come again as long as it didn't interfere with any of her possible acting auditions.

Sybil Porter, Frank Porter's strong daughter, had moved in with Sister Watson. Sybil had wanted to get out on her own for a while. Sister Watson was presently teaching Sybil grooming and how to act like a lady. Sybil gave Sister Watson something to focus on besides the upcoming Christmas play.

It had been over six months since our exclusive one-night engagement of "All Is Swell." The fallout had subsided—President Heck had even received a few letters from people around the state wanting to know about Mormonism. They figured any group of people who would go through so much trouble for nothing were worthy of investigation. President Heck sent them out what he called a "Thelma's Way care package," containing a Book of Mormon, a Church magazine, a complimentary bar of Sister Watson's soap, and a picture of the ward members at the Labor Day breakfast. I figured anyone who joined after seeing that picture would have to have been converted by the Spirit.

Amazingly, Paul had come around. According to President Heck's letter, Paul had had a vision of a red avenging angel who had scared him into coming back to church. He was so unnerved by the incident that true humility had finally gotten a chance to work him over. President Heck used words like *kind, submissive,* and *willing.* Paul was begging for forgiveness. It looked like the town would hold no grudge. President Heck also mentioned that once when Sister Watson showed up to church wearing a red dress, Paul had almost passed out.

President Heck had high hopes for the branch. He felt that Paul's new activity could help the meadow to mellow spiritually. Perhaps the numbers would begin to come back to where they were before Paul had pulled things apart.

Perhaps.

President Heck's letter had been great. Still, as I folded it and put it away for safekeeping, I knew he had failed to tell me what I most wanted to know. Forget all the other outrageous and quirky doctrines of Thelma's Way, I wanted to hear something about Grace.

He had written not a word.

I had tried writing to Grace once. I spilled out my heart. I told her everything. I tried to explain my feelings and my confusion. Did we have a future? I asked. Then I tore it up into little pieces and threw it away.

I had gotten a letter from Elder Jorgensen. He was still serving in Tennessee. His leg had healed, and he was currently companions with Elder Herney. He went on and on about how fantastic he and Elder Herney were doing. Elder Jorgensen's amazing attitude was just what Elder Herney needed. He had also included a picture. It was a snapshot of him and me at Leo's baptism. I got homesick every time I looked at it.

It was early afternoon. I had spent the day raking up leaves in our front yard. The big trees had shivered themselves bare, their naked branches ripping across the sky. I had raked the leaves into piles, tiny communities organized beneath the barky overlord. Leaves that had traversed the space from limb to soil, willing to rot and nourish the very trees that had let them go.

I cleaned up and drove to the local super-sized, bigger-than-necessary grocery store where, for your convenience, you could pick out new car tires while pinching tomatoes for freshness. When I finally found an employee to help me, he couldn't tell me anything except where the bathroom was and that the registers were up front.

I was perusing the more than one hundred brands of pancake syrup when I heard a recognizable voice one aisle over. Because of sky-high shelving I couldn't see who it was. I tried to place the voice, but I drew a blank. I walked around the aisle ready to say hi and saw them there. It was Lucy and Lance. Larger and glossier than life. They were trying to decide which self-tanning lotion to buy. I couldn't believe it.

I had wanted to see Lucy, thinking it would be such a big deal when I did. I had wanted her to know that I had grown up. I had turned out, despite her lack of confidence. I thought we would see each other and be blown away by all the sweet memories, the could-have-beens and should-have-beens.

That didn't happen.

They didn't notice me until I had *ahemed* a few times.

"Trust?" Lucy finally clued in.

Her skin was too dark for late October. Her hair was too shiny, and her lips were too thin.

"Hey, Lucy," I replied.

Lance sort of smiled, his big, perfect head tilting in condescension.

"So this is Trust," he *ho-ho-hoed*, his hands on his hips, looking like a poster boy for imitation humans.

Lucy struck a pose. I had caught her condescending to shop in a common supermarket, and that made her uncomfortable. She placed the tanning lotion back on the shelf like a hostess on a game show.

I wanted to say something to her but I couldn't. I couldn't find a single word worth wasting on her. I couldn't believe I had ever wanted what now stood before me. Lucy was a nice person, but she lacked soul.

"How was your mission?" she finally asked, needing to break the uncomfortable silence that had developed.

This was a great moment. True, I was no Lance, but I had never felt better about my appearance than now. Yes, here I was, looking better than Lucy had ever seen me look, and she looking like less than I had preceived she could possibly be. Most people would probably think she was perfect, not me. She was everything I no longer watned. She was salvation by works.

"My mission was great," I replied.

"Did you ever get out of that weird town?" she asked, gazing at me curiously, as if I were behind glass.

I didn't answer. I just stood there thinking until she and Lance became self-conscious and walked off.

"Weird guy," I heard Lance say, as they carted themselves away.

I put my tomatoes and pancake syrup back, went outside, got into my car, and drove to the airport.

I had some unfinished business to take care of.

42

RESTORATION

The path to Thelma's Way had never seemed so long.
It had taken me just over a day to get to Virgil's Find. It
was about two o'clock in the afternoon. I had made decent
time, but couldn't help feeling I was months behind schedule. I picked up my feet and ran. The late October air filled
my lungs.

When Thelma's Way finally came into view, my heart
just sort of liquefied. It pushed through my veins and up
into my throat. Still, I managed to stroll into town looking nonchalant.

There were kids in the meadow and folks hanging out
on the boardinghouse porch despite the cold. I could see
Leo walking hand in hand with CleeDee, and Digby in
Leo's old car. As much as I loved each and every one of
these people, they weren't the ones I had come to see. I
walked with purpose to the old wagons and turned, heading towards the woods. For a few moments folks ignored
me, not realizing who I was. But the second Narlette
climbed up on one of the covered wagons, she recognized

me. She then made the announcement I was longing to holler.

"Elder Williams is back!"

Folks froze. They put their hands to their hearts and mouths. I wanted to stop, to clap backs and give hugs, but I couldn't let them slow me down.

I was on a mission.

I watched people dive off the boardinghouse porch and chase after me. I'd never seen old Roswell move so quickly. Wad, who was giving Miss Flitrey a haircut, put down his scissors and rolled over to greet me. Kids clustered about me like bees on a hive. Narlette grabbed my hand as I walked.

"Elder Williams," she cried happily. "What are you doing here?"

Four words.

"I'm going for Grace."

The crowd burst into cheers and guffaws.

"He's going for Grace," they told each other, beginning to understand as they said it.

I walked quickly. The crowd fell in behind me. I had kind of hoped to do this on my own, but as I reached the edge of the forest no one turned back.

"What's going on?" people would ask as we passed them on our way. "He's going for Grace," someone would yell and they would join in, cheering and whooping.

When we got to the Heck house, everyone grew quiet to see what would happen next. I pushed back my longer-than-missionary hair and tried to calm down. I knocked on the door and waited. Practically the whole town was circled around me. My nerves were shorting out, and my fingers and arms felt loose and rubbery.

President Heck answered the door.

"Elder Williams," he said in amazement, his gray hair shorter than I remembered it, and his eyes more alive.

I spoke before I chickened out. "Is Grace here?" I asked.

"No," he answered, surprised.

The crowd behind me "ohhhhed" in disappointment.

"Do you know where she is?" I asked desperately.

Patty Heck came up beside him to see what was going on.

"I haven't seen her for a couple days," Brother Heck replied, acting like he was thinking extra hard for my sake.

Before he said another word, I stepped off the porch and marched further into the forest. I knew where I had to go. I had to find that cabin. Grace would be there. I just hoped I could remember the way.

President and Sister Heck joined our merry band. I heard Pete Kennedy fill them in behind me.

"He's going for Grace."

"Our Grace?" Patty Heck questioned.

My Grace.

We hiked over a couple of hills and down a ravine. More and more people gathered, all of them staying in my wake. As we passed Toby Carver's place I ran smack dab into Toby and Paul standing outside. They were arguing over the price of firewood, or some such thing. Toby, I was thrilled to see. Paul, on the other hand, still looked to me like the self-righteous apostate I had known so well. His face puckered when he realized it was me.

We stared at one another. Everyone hushed. I thought of a million things I could say to make him see the damage he'd done, and to check if he really had changed. But all that would take time, and I had an appointment to keep.

So I stuck out my hand, and he stuck out his. We shook and everyone cheered. I began hiking again. Paul patted me on the back, falling into step directly behind me, acting like we had been best friends for years. I was more than willing to let him feel that way. This, after all, was my town, and these were my people.

This was a big day.

Finally I spotted the rock chimney above the trees. Smoke curled from the top.

She was home. She was in there.

I thought I was going to pass out.

Softly, I pushed Narlette aside. Everyone stayed just where they were. The forest crunched beneath my feet. My blood turned from whole milk to skim.

I stepped up to the door and knocked.

No one answered, but I thought I heard movement inside. I knocked again and then tried the knob. It was locked. I felt the crowd step closer behind me.

"Grace," I hollered. "It's me, Elder Williams. Trust."

No answer. Pete Kennedy coughed.

"Grace, if you're in there, open up," I said.

Closed door. Miss Flitrey sneezed.

"Gesundheit," Wad whispered.

I wanted to see Grace now more than ever. I wanted to look into her face like only a returned missionary could. I wanted to tell her the things that my mission had prevented me from saying. I wanted to say I remembered what I had said on the boardinghouse porch almost exactly a year ago. I wanted to say I was I was wrong. I thought about breaking down the door. I thought about climbing down the chimney.

I turned to face the crowd and shrugged.

These were the people I had come to love. These were the ones who had watched me become the man I now was. God had given me the patience to discover their secrets and their accomplishments. Like a pop top, He had twisted my life and revealed my purpose—I could feel the guiding pressure of His palm. Now here He was pouring me back into the half-full glass of Thelma's Way.

Feeble had been right all those years ago. His prophecy had come to pass. Things had changed. The person I was today would hardly have recognized the reluctant boy who once wandered into this valley.

How could I have ever doubted a Creator who saw it all? He had changed me. I had been too busy trying to figure it out to notice. He had planted me here, provided the sun and water, and let me push my own way out of the seed. So often on my mission I had thought that I was doing God some great favor by serving. Now I knew that He had given me more in those two years than I could ever account for. He didn't mold me into some suave business-man. He carefully shaped me into a true son of God. He had sent me home safely and pushed me back here to see what the future could bring. I stood in front of that door smiling as the cosmos whispered its secrets into my ear.

I knocked again. I would knock all day if I had to. I

would stand in front of that door forever, if there were the slightest possibility that someday Grace would open up and let me in.

I've heard it said that when God closes a door, He splits a crowd, or something to that effect. God was working His wonders. As I stood there staring through the window, I could hear the townsfolk begin to whisper.

"There she is."

"Move over."

"Here she comes."

I looked around and saw the ring of spectators shift, opening up for Grace to walk through. Grace had not been in the cabin, she had been about the forest as usual. She had small branches in her hands and wind in her hair. She looked at me as if *I* were a mirage—I drank her in as if she were an oasis. She was wearing jeans and a white shirt. Her red hair looked dark against the contrast of white, her deep eyes made the evergreens look dull. I watched her pink lips as they tried not to smile. I could see she was thinking. She was calculating me in. My feet turned to clay, my toes chipping off and rattling around in my shoes. I could feel the back of my neck fizzle, like cold water running over a hot pan.

She was calculating me in!

She walked through the crowd and right up to me. Afternoon light surrounded her like a heavenly aura. She stopped and looked into my eyes.

"You came back," she said softly.

"I love you," I answered.

"I thought you might," she replied, believing the words as she spoke them.

"I wanted to give us a try."

Grace smiled, giving bliss a whole new definition. "It might take a bit," she reasoned.

"I've got forever."

The entire town *Ahhhed*.

The low clouds dispersed with a burst, bits and pieces of them shooting off throughout the universe. The wind started to whisper, blowing beautiful thoughts around in a billion languages. Trees and bushes shook their limbs in jubilation, the rich ground singing the bass. Hats were thrown into the air and hugs were passed around like baby photos at a family reunion.

I looked at Grace and stuck out my hand as if to reach for her. She dropped her branches, breathing softly. I pulled her to me and held on for dear life. I could feel her shake.

"Are you okay?" I whispered.

I felt her hair in my face and her back beneath my hands. Gratitude streamed down my face.

From the corner of my eye I watched the crowd wipe their eyes. Toby's bandage would go home wet today.

Grace loved me.

All was well.

ABOUT THE AUTHOR

Robert Farrell Smith lives in Albuquerque, New Mexico, with his wife, Krista, and his daughters, Kindred and Phoebe. He is the owner of Sunrise Bookstore in Albuquerque. Inspired by the saying: "Given enough time, a thousand monkeys banging on a thousand typewriters could eventually write a book," Robert picked up a pen and began writing early in life. As a result, Robert is already the author of two hilarious LDS novels. This is his first Deseret Book publication.